D0871339

cloth 7

CLASSICS
OF
RUSSIAN
LITERATURE

НИКОЛАЙ ЛЕСКОВ

ОЧАРОВАННЫЙ СТРАННИК

и ДРУГИЕ РАССКАЗЫ

ИЗДАТЕЛЬСТВО ЛИТЕРАТУРЫ
НА ИНОСТРАННЫХ ЯЗЫКАХ
Москва

NIKOLAI LESKOV

THE ENCHANTED WANDERER

AND OTHER STORIES

FOREIGN LANGUAGES
PUBLISHING HOUSE
Moscow

TRANSLATED FROM THE RUSSIAN BY GEORGE H. HANNA

EDITED BY J. KATZER

DESIGNED BY M. TARANOV

CONTENTS

The first song is sung with a timid blush.

Old Saw

LADY MACBETH OF MTSENSK

(A SKETCH)

CHAPTER THE FIRST

IN OUR PART of the world one sometimes comes across people of such character that one cannot recall them without a shudder even when many years have elapsed since the last encounter. To this type belonged Katerina Lvovna Izmailova, a merchant's wife, who at one time treated us to such a terrible drama that some wit dubbed her *Lady Macbeth of Mtsensk*, and it was by that name that she was afterwards known amongst the local gentry.

Katerina Lvovna was not inherently beautiful although she was a woman of very pleasing appearance. At the time our story begins she was in her twenty-fourth year; although not tall, she was graceful, her neck was like white marble, her shoulders well-rounded, her bosom firm, her nose fine and straight, her eyes black and vivacious, her white forehead high and her hair of that dense blackness that seems almost blue. She was given in marriage to our merchant Izmailov of Tuskar, in Kursk Gubernia, not for love or even infatuation but because he asked for her hand and she, a girl of poor family, could not afford to pick and choose. The house of Izmailov was not the least in our town; they dealt in flour, rented a big mill in the district, owned a big orchard just outside the town and kept a good town establishment. In general they were merchants of affluence. Their family, moreover, was quite small: the father-in-law, Boris Timofeyich Izmailov, already close on eighty and long a widower, his son Zinovy Borisich, Katerina Lvovna's husband, a man well over fifty, and, lastly, Katerina Lvovna herself. Although she had been married to Zinovy Borisich nearly five years there were no children. Nor had Zinovy Borisich any children from his first wife with whom he had lived twenty years before her death and his marriage to Katerina Lvovna. He thought and hoped that in his second marriage God would grant him an heir to his merchant's name and capital; but he had no better luck with his second wife than with his first.

This childless state was a source of great grief to Zinovy Borisich, and not to him alone, but to old Boris Timofeyich as well; even Katerina Lvovna sorrowed over it. The boredom of the merchant's cloister-like house with its high wall and savage dogs running loose in the yard was at times so oppressive that the young woman was a prey to a melancholy that dulled her brain; how glad she would have been—God knows how glad she would have been—to have a babe to fondle; she was, moreover, tired to death of the reproaches—"Why did you marry, what did you want to marry for, what did you want to foist yourself on a man for, if you're barren"— just as though she had committed some crime against her husband, against her father-in-law and against the whole of their honest merchant tribe.

For all its sufficiency and comfort, Katerina Lvovna's life in her father-in-law's house was of the dreariest. She rarely went out anywhere and even when she went with her husband to visit his fellow merchants there was but little pleasure in it. They were all of them so strict, they would watch to see how she sat down, how she walked and how she got up; and Katerina had such a lively nature and, coming as she did from a poor family, she had been used to simplicity and freedom; she would gladly have run down to the river with her buckets, bathing in her shift under the landing stage, or throw sunflower seed husks at any young fellow who passed her gate; but here everything was different. Her father-in-law and husband were early risers; at six o'clock they would drink tea and then go about their business while she was left to lounge about the rooms doing nothing. The whole place was clean, the house silent and empty, the lamps burning brightly in front of the icons, but nowhere was there a sound of any living thing or of a human voice.

Katerina Lvovna would wander from one empty room to another, would begin to yawn from boredom and then climb the ladder to their conjugal bedchamber in a high but small attic room. Here she would sit and watch the people weighing hemp or pouring flour at the sheds down below—again she would yawn and be glad of it; she would doze for an hour or two, but would awake again to that Russian ennui, the boredom of a merchant's home, to escape which, it is said, even to hang oneself is a pleasure. Katerina Lvovna was no lover of reading and, anyway, there were no books in the house apart from the Kiev *Lives of the Christian Fathers.*

It was a monotonous life that had been her lot in her father-in-law's house for those five long years of her marriage with an unloving husband; but nobody paid the slightest attention to this boredom of hers, everybody treated it as a matter of course.

CHAPTER THE SECOND

In the sixth spring of Katerina Lvovna's married life the Izmailovs' mill-dam burst and at a time, too, when there was an abundance of work at the mill. The breach was a big one, the lower beams of the dam impounding the mill-pond were torn away and the water escaped at such a rate that it could not be quickly stopped. Zinovy Borisich took people from all over the district and sent them to the mill and he himself spent all his time there; the old man was able to manage their town affairs and for days on end Katerina Lvovna was left all alone in the house. At first she was even more bored without her husband but then it began to seem better without him; she had more liberty when she was alone. She had never been particularly fond of him and without him, at any rate, there was one person less to order her about.

One day Katerina Lvovna was sitting at the window in her high room, yawning and thinking of nothing in particular until at last she grew ashamed of her yawning. The weather was wonderful: warm, bright and jolly and through the green garden fence she could see perky birds jumping from branch to branch on the trees.

"What's the matter with me, yawning so much?" she asked herself. "I might at least get up and take a walk in the yard and through the garden."

She threw an old brocade coat over her shoulders and went out.

It was light outside and so easy to breathe; roars of merry laughter came from the gallery around the store-houses.

"What are you all so happy about?" Katerina Lvovna asked her father-in-law's warehousemen.

"Oh, Katerina Lvovna, madame, they're weighing a live pig," answered the senior.

"What pig?"

"That pig Aksinya, what had a son, Vasily, and didn't ask us to the christening." The bold answer came promptly; the speaker was a young fellow with a cheeky, handsome face framed in curls as black as pitch and a newly sprouting beard.

At that moment the flushed, fat face of Aksinya the cook peeped out of a flour tub hanging from the scale beam.

"Devils, imps of Satan," cursed the cook, struggling to get hold of the iron beam and climb out of the swinging tub.

"Eight poods she weighs, before dinner. Give her a measure of hay for supper and you won't find weights enough for her," said the handsome young man, and, tipping over the tub, threw the cook on to a heap of sacks lying in the corner.

The woman, swearing drolly, started putting her dress in order.

"See how much I weigh," joked Katerina Lvovna and, catching hold of the rope, jumped on to the scale board.

"Three poods seven pound," answered that same handsome young man, Sergei, throwing weights into the scale pan. "It's a miracle!"

"What's miraculous about it?"

"That you should weigh three poods, Katerina Lvovna. As I see it, a fellow could carry you in his arms all day. He wouldn't get tired, but it would make him feel good!"

"Do you think I'm not human, or what? You'd probably get tired all right," answered Katerina Lvovna, blushing slightly, being unaccustomed to such speeches and feeling a sudden urge to chatter away, to have her fill of jokes and merriment.

"Good Lord, I'd carry you all the way to happy Araby," said Sergei in answer to her comment.

"Your thinking is all wrong, young man," said an elderly peasant who was pouring flour into a bin. "What is it gives you weight? Your body, young man, is nothing on the scale: it is your strength, your strength that counts and not the body!"

"Yes, I was awfully strong when I was a girl," put in Katerina Lvovna again, unable to contain herself. "Not every man, even, could get the better of me."

"Then let me try your grip if it's true, what you say," asked the handsome young man.

This confused Katerina Lvovna but still she held out her hand.

"Oh, let go, the ring hurts!" she cried when Sergei squeezed her hand, and with her free hand she gave him a push in the chest.

The young man let go of the mistress's hand and staggered a couple of paces back from the force of her push.

"Well, there's a woman for you," said the elderly peasant.

"Will you please let me test your strength like this, like we was wrestling," said Sergei, turning to her and tossing his curly head.

"All right, then," answered the now happy Katerina Lvovna and lifted her elbows.

Sergei put his arms round the young mistress and pressed her firm bosom to his red shirt. She only had time to jerk her shoulders before Sergei had lifted her off the floor and seated her gently on an upturned flour measure.

She did not have a chance to make use of her boasted strength. Flushing a deep red, she sat on the measure and adjusted the coat on her shoulders, then went quietly out of the storeroom while Sergei coughed pertly and shouted:

"Come on, you sainted blockheads! Pour it in an' tip the measure. All you scrape off you keep."

He pretended to be paying no heed to what had just happened.

"That damned Sergei is a rare 'un for the skirts," Aksinya the cook was saying as she plodded along behind her mistress. "He gets 'em all ways—he's tall an' handsome an' he has the sort of face they like. Take any woman—why that devil flatters an' flatters her till he gets what he wants. But he doesn't stick to one for long; he's as fickle as they make 'em."

"And you, Aksinya.... That ... boy of yours," said the young mistress as she walked ahead, "is he still alive?"

"Of course, he's alive, ma'am, why shouldn't he be? Them as aren't wanted always go on living."

"Where did you get him from?"

"Hm-m. Just like that, I live amongst people, don't I—they all want their bit of fun."

"And that young fellow, has he been with us long?"

"Who d'you mean? Sergei?"

"Yes."

"About a month. He used to work for the Konchonovs but the old man kicked him out." Aksinya lowered her voice and continued: "They do say he had an affair with the mistress.... He's got guts, all right, damn his soul!"

CHAPTER THE THIRD

Warm, hazy twilight settled on the town. Zinovy Borisich had not yet returned from the mill-dam. Boris Timofeyich, the father-in-law, was also away: he was visiting an old friend on the occasion of a name-day celebration and had ordered Katerina Lvovna to take supper without him. Having nothing better to do, Katerina Lvovna supped early, opened the window of her attic and sat there nibbling sunflower seeds. The house servants had their meal in the kitchen and then went away to sleep—some in the shed, some in the store-houses and others to the high, fragrant haylofts. The last to leave the kitchen was Sergei. He went about the yard, unleashed the watch-dogs and, whistling as he went, walked past Katerina Lvovna's window, looked up at her, and bowed low.

"Good evening," she said softly from her attic window, but the yard remained as quiet as a cloister.

"Madame!" somebody breathed outside her locked door some two minutes later.

"Who's that?" she asked in frightened tones.

"You don't have to be afraid, madame: it's me, Sergei," answered the clerk.

"What do you want, Sergei?"

"There's a little bit of business I want to talk over, madame: just a small matter for which I crave your kindness: allow me to come in for a moment."

Katerina Lvovna turned the key and let Sergei in.

"What do you want?" she asked, backing towards the window.

"I've come to ask you whether you haven't got a book for me to read, Katerina Lvovna. I'm bored to tears here."

"I haven't got any books, Sergei, I don't read them," she answered.

"It's so dull here, I'm sick of it," complained Sergei.

"You're a fine one to say it's dull!"

"God bless me, of course it's miserable here: I'm young and this here place is no better than a monastery. It looks as how there's nothing coming but lonesomeness to the very grave. Sometimes I do get desperate."

"Why don't you marry?"

"That's easier said than done, madame. Who can I marry? I'm not a man of importance: a rich girl won't have me and the poor 'uns, you know yourself, Katerina Lvovna, haven't got no manners because of their poverty. What do they know about real love? And what do rich people think about this business, anyway? You, for instance, would be a comfort to any other man, to one with feelings, and they keep you locked up like a canary in a cage."

"Yes, it's so wearisome."

The admission burst from her lips.

"You must have had enough of such a life! If you had someone on the side like all the others have—but you don't even get a chance to see anyone."

"Now you're going a bit too far. It's this way: if I had a baby I think I might be happy with him."

"But let me tell you, madame, there's a reason, too, for babies coming, they don't just arrive. Living all these years with different masters and seeing how the merchants' wives all lead miserable lives, I also, you understand, know a thing or two. There's a song that says: 'Life is dull when the sweetheart's gone. . . .' and that's why, believe me, Katerina Lvovna, my heart's heavy, it's on account of it feeling for you in your boredom—I could take a knife and cut it out and throw it at your feet. It would be easier, a hundred times easier, for me if I did. . . ."

There was a quiver in Sergei's voice.

"What are you telling me all this about your heart for? That's got nothing to do with me. Go away. . . ."

"Forgive me, madame," whispered Sergei, taking a step towards Katerina Lvovna, his whole body trembling. "I see and I feel for you and I understand; you don't lead any better life than I do; only now," here his voice sank so low that he scarcely breathed the last words, "now, at this very moment, everything's in your hands, it's in your power. . . ."

"What are you saying? Why did you come to me? I'll throw myself out of the window," said Katerina Lvovna, feeling herself seized by an indescribable terror and clutching the window-sill.

"You are all my life to me. Why do such a silly thing?" whispered Sergei boldly, and pulling the young mistress away from the window took her in his strong arms.

"Oh, oh, let me go," she groaned softly, weakening under Sergei's burning kisses and pressing herself involuntarily to his powerful body.

Sergei lifted the mistress like a child and carried her in his arms to a dark corner.

The silence that fell on the room was disturbed only by the rhythmic ticking of her husband's watch that hung at the head of her bed: but that did not make any difference.

"Go away," said Katerina Lvovna half an hour later without looking at Sergei and straightening her dishevelled hair before a small mirror.

"Why should I go away now?" asked Sergei in a happy voice.

"My father-in-law will lock all the doors."

"Oh, my darling, what sort of people have you lived amongst if they only know how to get to a woman through doors? To get to you I come and go as I please, there are doors everywhere," answered the young man pointing to the posts that supported the gallery.

CHAPTER THE FOURTH

Another week passed and still Zinovy Borisich did not return home and all that week, night after night until dawn broke, his wife enjoyed the company of Sergei.

And on those nights in Zinovy Borisich's bedroom much wine from the father-in-law's cellar was drunk, many were the titbits eaten, and the kisses implanted on the mistress's sweet lips, her hands playing long and lovingly with black curls on a soft pillow. Not always is love's path smooth, however, sometimes there are potholes in the way.

On one of those nights Boris Timofeyich could not sleep: in his cotton shirt of many colours the old man roamed about the silent house and, lo and behold, what did he see but merry Sergei in his red shirt sliding down the post under his daughter-in-law's window. Here was a fine to do for you! Boris Timofeyich rushed out at the young fellow and grabbed him by the legs. Sergei turned to give his master one of the best in the ear but stopped as he remembered that he might cause a commotion.

"And where," said Boris Timofeyich, "have you been, scoundrel that you are?"

"Where I've been, Boris Timofeyich, there, sir, I no longer am," answered Sergei.

"Did you spend the night with my daughter-in-law?"

"There again, sir. I know where I spent the night; but you, Boris Timofeyich, you, sir, mark my words— what has been done can't be undone. At any rate, don't you bring shame on a good merchant's house. Now tell me what you want from me? What do you expect to get out of me?"

"I want to give you five hundred lashes, you viper," answered Boris Timofeyich.

"I'm in the wrong, so do what you like," agreed the young fellow. "Tell we where to go so you can have a good time drinking my blood."

Boris Timofeyich led the way to his brick-built storehouse and thrashed Sergei with a horsewhip until his own arms ached. Not a groan escaped Sergei's lips but his teeth gnawed away half his shirt-sleeve.

Boris Timofeyich left Sergei for his flayed back to heal; he gave him an earthenware jug of water, hung a huge padlock on the door and sent for his son.

Even today a journey of a hundred versts over Russia's country roads is no light undertaking and Katerina Lvovna felt she would not be able to live another hour without her Sergei. Suddenly her expansive nature made itself fully apparent and she became so determined there was no holding her back. She found out where Sergei was and talked to him through the iron door and then started looking for the keys. "Let him out, let Sergei out," she said to her father-in-law.

The old man turned green. He had never expected such impertinence from a daughter-in-law who, even if she had sinned, had always, until now, been submissive.

"What are you talking about, you so-and-so?" he began calling Katerina Lvovna shameful names.

"Let him out," she said. "I tell you honestly there has been nothing bad between us."

"Nothing bad," he said, gritting his teeth. "And what were you doing with him all those nights? Beating up your husband's pillows?"

But she wanted to have her own way: let him out, that's all.

"If that's the way it is," said Boris Timofeyich, "I'll tell you something: when your husband comes we'll take you, you faithful wife, to the stables and flay you with our own hands and that blackguard I'll have sent to prison tomorrow."

That was what Boris Timofeyich had decided: but that, however, was not to be.

CHAPTER THE FIFTH

At supper Boris Timofeyich ate salted mushrooms and gruel which gave him heartburn; then came a sudden pain in the pit of his stomach; he vomited terribly and by morning he died in the same way as those rats in his storehouses for which Katerina Lvovna with her own hands prepared special food with a dangerous white powder that had been entrusted to her care.

Katerina Lvovna released her Sergei from the old man's storeroom and, never worrying about what people might say, let him recover from her father-in-law's blows in her husband's bed; and those who buried her father-in-law, Boris Timofeyich, suspected nothing. There was nothing unusual about the matter, and nobody gave it a second thought. Boris Timofeyich had died after eating salted mushrooms, as many others who had eaten them had died before him. They buried Boris Timofeyich hurriedly without even waiting for his son, for the weather was warm and the messenger had not found Zinovy Borisich at the mill. He had happened to hear of some timber going cheap another hundred versts or so away and had gone to take a look at it without telling anybody exactly where he had gone.

Once she had got this business off her hands Katerina Lvovna let herself go. She was no timid woman and there was no knowing what to expect from her; she paraded about the house giving orders right and left and would not let Sergei leave her side for a moment. This caused surprise in the household but Katerina Lvovna's full hand soon settled that. "The mistress is sweet on Sergei," they said, understandingly, "that's all. It's her own look-out," they said, "she's the one who'll have to pay for it."

In the meantime Sergei got better, was soon in his old form and was again strutting around Katerina Lvovna for all the world like a turkey-cock, and again their life of love began. Not for them alone, however, did time roll on: after a long absence, Zinovy Borisich, the cuckold husband, was hurrying home.

CHAPTER THE SIXTH

It grew terribly hot after dinner and the frisky flies were a perfect torment. Katerina Lvovna closed the shutters of her bedroom window, hung a woollen shawl on the inside and then lay down beside Sergei to rest on her husband's high bed. She was asleep and at the same time not quite asleep, she was simply exhausted; the perspiration streamed down her face and it cost her an effort to breathe. She felt it was time to rouse herself; it was time to go into the garden for tea but still she could not get up. At last the cook came and knocked at the door: "The samovar's under the apple-tree and it's getting cold." Katerina Lvovna forced herself to roll over and began stroking the cat. And that cat was rubbing itself against them, between her and Sergei, such a wonderful, big grey cat, as fat as fat can be, with gorgeous whiskers. Katerina Lvovna ran her fingers through its thick coat and it came closer and rubbed its head against her; it pushed its snub nose against her firm bosom and was all the time softly purring as though it were telling her a tale of love.

"How did that great cat get in here," wondered Katerina Lvovna. "I put the cream on the window-sill in here: sure enough he'll guzzle it all up. I'll chase him out," she decided and tried to get hold of the cat to throw it out but it slipped through her fingers like mist.

"But where could that cat have come from?" wondered Katerina Lvovna in the middle of her nightmare. "We never had any cat in the bedroom and see what a big brute has got in here now."

Again she tried to get hold of the cat but once more it was not there to take hold of.

"Now whatever can it be? Is it really a cat or what?" Katerina Lvovna asked herself. Fright drove the dream and the sleepiness away. She looked round the room— there was no cat anywhere, only handsome Sergei was lying there, his strong arm pressing her breast to his hot face.

Katerina Lvovna got up and sat on the bed. She kissed and fondled Sergei time and again, then straightened the crumpled quilt on the bed and went into the garden for tea; the sun had gone down and a cool and wonderful evening breeze wafted over the heated earth.

"I overslept," Katerina Lvovna told Aksinya as she sat down to tea on a carpet spread under an apple-tree in blossom.

"And what does it all mean, Aksinya?" she began questioning the cook and at the same time wiped a saucer on the tea-cloth.

"What does what mean?"

"It wasn't like a dream, it was just real, a cat came rubbing against me. What could it be?"

"What are you talking about?"

"I mean it, a cat came."

Katerina Lvovna told her about the cat.

"Why did you want to stroke it?"

"Don't be silly. I don't know why I stroked it."

"It's strange enough, I'm sure."

"It's something I can't make out."

"It sure enough means someone's going to be close to you or something else, maybe, something else will come of it."

"But what?"

"Exactly *what* nobody can tell you, madame, but something's sure enough going to happen."

"I keep seeing the moon in my dreams, and now there's that cat," she continued.

"The moon means a baby."

Katerina Lvovna blushed.

"Should I send Sergei here to you, madame?" asked Aksinya who hoped to become her mistress's confidante.

"I don't know," answered Katerina Lvovna, "all right, go and get him; I'll give him tea here."

"That's what I think, I'd better send him here," decided Aksinya and waddled away towards the garden gate.

Katerina Lvovna also told Sergei about the cat.

"Idle dreams, that's all," was Sergei's verdict.

"Then why is it I never had any idle dreams about a cat before, Sergei?"

"Lots of things we didn't have before! I used to get all moony when I saw you out of the corner of my eye, and now what? All your pretty body belongs to me."

Sergei put his arms round her, turned her head over heels in the air and jokingly threw her on to the soft carpet.

"Oh, you make me dizzy," exclaimed Katerina Lvovna. "Sergei, come and sit here close to me," she called him lazily, stretching herself in a voluptuous pose.

The young man bent down to get under the low branches of the apple-tree, which was in full bloom, and sat down on the carpet at Katerina Lvovna's feet.

"Did you always long for me, Sergei?"

"Of course I did...."

"But how did it feel? Tell me all about it."

"What is there to tell? How can I explain what longing is? I was sad...."

"Then why didn't I feel it, Sergei, why didn't I get to know you were moony about me? They say you can feel that sort of thing."

Sergei gave no answer.

"If you were yearning for me so much why were you always singing songs? Eh? You know, I heard you singing on the gallery," she continued and all the while fondled him.

"What if I did sing? D'you think mosquitoes hum all their lives because they're happy?" answered Sergei drily.

A short pause followed. Katerina Lvovna was filled with ecstasy on hearing Sergei's admissions.

She wanted to talk on in the same vein but Sergei only frowned and sat silent.

"Look, Sergei, it's paradise, just heaven!" she exclaimed, looking through the flower-laden branches of the apple-tree that completely covered her; she looked straight up to the deep blue sky in which hung a full, bright moon.

The moonlight slanted down through the leaves and blossoms making whimsical coloured patterns that flickered over the face and body of Katerina Lvovna as she lay there on her back; there was silence in the air; a faint, warm breeze stirred the sleepy leaves, bringing with it the fragrance of flowering grasses and trees and a breath of something languid, inducing idleness, voluptuousness and dark desires.

As Katerina Lvovna was not answered, she lay back in silence, gazing through the pale-rose of the apple blossoms at the sky above. Sergei did not speak either, although he was not interested in the sky; with his arms clasped round his knees he stared at his boots.

A golden night! Silence, moonlight, fragrance and a precious life-giving warmth! Away beyond the gully, on the far side of the orchard, somebody began singing a sweet melody, in the bird-cherry thicket by the fence a nightingale called and then burst into loud song, a quail in a cage on a high pole murmured in its sleep, a well-fed horse in the stable sighed deeply and some dogs raced noiselessly across the common by the orchard fence and disappeared into the ugly black shadows of the old half-ruined salt warehouses.

Katerina Lvovna raised herself on one elbow and gazed at the high grass in the orchard; the grass seemed to be playing in moonlight, broken into checkered patches by the leaves and flowers of the trees. The grass was all turned to gold by those dainty patches of light that flickered and quivered as though they were living, fire-coloured butterflies or as though all the grass under the trees had been caught up in a net of moonlight and was swaying from side to side.

"Oh, Sergei, it's gorgeous!" exclaimed Katerina Lvovna as she looked round.

Sergei glanced round indifferently.

"Why are you so miserable, Sergei? Perhaps you've had enough of my love?"

"Why talk so silly?" Sergei answered drily, stooped down, and lazily kissed her cheek.

"You're not true to me," said Katerina Lvovna, jealously, "you're fickle."

"I can't get angry, even at them words," answered Sergei in calm tones.

"Then why did you kiss me like that?"

Segrei did not say another word.

"That's the way husbands kiss their wives," she continued, playing with his curls, "that's how they blow the dust off each other's lips. You ought to kiss me so that the young flowers fall off this tree we're sitting under."

"Like this, like this," she whispered winding her arms round her lover and kissing him with passionate tenderness.

"Listen, Sergei," said Katerina Lvovna a little while later, "why do they all call you fickle, why do they all say the same thing?"

"Who's been telling lies about me?"

"That's what people say."

"May be I did throw over them as weren't worth keeping."

"Why were you fool enough to get mixed up with them if they weren't worth it? You didn't ought to make love to them that aren't worth while."

"It's all right for you to talk. Is it something you do in your right mind? You get tempted, that's all. Sinning with a wench comes quite simple, and then she goes and hangs herself round your neck. That's all there is to it!"

"You listen to me, Sergei! I don't know and don't want to know how it was with the others, but you yourself led me on to this love of ours and you know just how much I started of my own free will and how much was temptation on your part, so if you, Sergei, throw me over, if you think you can jilt me for anybody else, whoever she may be, then remember, Sergei, my friend, I shan't be alive when we part."

Sergei gave a start.

"How can you, Katerina Lvovna!" began Sergei. "You are everything to me. And just you look how things stand with us. You say you can see I'm sulky today but you don't try to think what the reason is. For all you know my heart may be bleeding."

"Tell me, Sergei, tell me your troubles."

"What is there to tell? The first thing that's going to happen, the Lord be praised, is your husband will be back and then it's all up with Sergei Filippich. He'll have to go back to the yard with the musicians and sit under the shed and watch the candle burning in Katerina Lvovna's bedroom while she shakes up the feather bed and gets into it with her lawful spouse, Zinovy Borisich."

"That will never be!" drawled Katerina Lvovna merrily and waved her hand.

"How can it not be? As far as I can see you can't do anything to stop it happening. But, Katerina Lvovna, I've got a heart, too, and I can see I'm going to have a bad time soon."

"All right, let's not talk about it."

Katerina Lvovna liked to feel that Sergei was jealous and with a laugh again gave herself up to kissing him.

"And then, again," continued Sergei, quietly freeing his head from her arms, which were bare to the shoulders, "again I must say that I've got such a modest position that I think ten times, one way or another, and not just once. If I were, so to say, your equal, if I were some gentleman or merchant, then, Katerina Lvovna, never in my life would I part with you. But you must know how it is, what it's like for me to be with you.

When I see that old man of yours take you by your lily-white hands and lead you into the bedroom, my heart will have to bear it all and maybe, even, all my life I shall be a man to despise on account of it. Katerina Lvovna! After all, I'm not like other men, who are satisfied enough to get their fill of a woman. I know what real love is, I feel it eating into my heart like a black serpent...."

"What are you telling me all this for?" Katerina Lvovna interrupted him.

She was getting very sorry for Sergei.

"Katerina Lvovna! What else can I do but tell you? How can I keep silent? Perhaps everything has been told to your old man with all the details; perhaps it won't be some time in the future but even tomorrow that Sergei will have to clear out and there won't be a sign of him left in the house."

"No, no, don't say that, Sergei! Never, never, not for anything will I part from you!" exclaimed Katerina Lvovna, soothing him with more of her blandishments. "If it comes to that pass... either he won't live or I won't, but I intend to have you."

"That can't be, not by no means, Katerina Lvovna," answered Sergei, shaking his head sadly and sorrowfully. "It's a dog's life for me, too, on account of this love. If I hadn't loved somebody above my station I'd have been satisfied. D'you think you can always have me to make love to? Is it an honour for you to be my mistress? I'd like to be your husband and marry you before the altar and then, even though I'll always consider myself beneath you, I can at least tell the world how much I respect my wife...."

These words of Sergei's, his jealousy, his anxiety to wed her, put Katerina Lvovna in a daze; it is always pleasant for a woman to have somebody want to marry her, even if her connections with the man before marriage were of the shortest. For Sergei's sake she was now prepared to go through fire and water, into prison or on the cross. He had made her so much in love with himself that there was no limit to her loyalty to him. She was beside herself from happiness. Her blood was overheated and she would hear nothing more. With a swift movement she placed her hand over Sergei's lips, pressed his head to her bosom and said:

"And I know now how I'll make a merchant of you and live with you in the proper way. Only don't make me sad about nothing before the proper time."

Again the kissing and fondling began.

An old clerk who slept in the shed heard through his sound sleep how the silence of the night was broken by whispering and soft laughter, as though mischievous children were conferring together how best to make fun of an old man; then came roars of laughter and merriment as though saucy mermaids were tickling somebody. All this came from where Katerina Lvovna, bathed in moonlight and rolling on the soft carpet, played and frolicked with her husband's young clerk. And the white flowers kept falling, falling, from the old apple-tree until at last they ceased to fall. In the meantime the short summer night had passed, the moon hid itself behind the steep, high roofs of the warehouses and stared more and more wanly at the earth; from the kitchen roof came a piercing feline duet; this was followed by spitting and angry snorts after which two or three tom-cats crashed noisily from the roof on to a heap of boards nearby.

"Let's go to bed," said Katerina Lvovna slowly, as though she were worn out; she got up from the carpet and just as she had lain there, in her shift and petticoat, walked across the silent, deathly silent merchant yard and Sergei followed her carrying the carpet and the blouse she had thrown off during their play.

Katerina Lvovna had only just blown out the candle and, fully undressed, lain down on her feather bed, when sleep overtook her. After playing and amusing herself to her heart's content she slept so soundly that her legs were asleep and so were her arms; and again through her sleep she seemed to hear the door open and the cat that had recently visited her fall on the bed in a heavy heap.

"Now what sort of a pest is that cat?" she wondered wearily. "This time I made sure the door was locked, I locked it myself, and the window's closed tight but it's there again. I'll throw it out right now," and Katerina Lvovna wanted to get up but her sleeping arms and legs would not obey her; and the cat walked up and down her whole body purring strangely, as though it were saying human words. And shivers ran over her, ran over her whole body.

"No," she thought, "there's nothing else for it but to get holy water tomorrow and sprinkle the bed because it's a queer old cat that's in the habit of coming to me."

And the purring was right under her ear and a nose pushed against her and the cat said, "What sort of a cat am I? Why d'you call me a cat? That's smart of you, Katerina Lvovna, calling me a cat when you know I'm Boris Timofeyich, a merchant of standing. Only I'm feeling bad now because all my insides are cracking up from what my kind daughter-in-law has treated me to. That's why I got small," he purred, "and look like a cat to those who know little about me, about who I really am. How are you getting on nowadays, Katerina Lvovna? How are you faithfully observing the law? I came from the graveyard specially to see how you and Sergei Filippich are keeping your husband's bed warm.

Purr, purr, purr.... I don't see anything. Don't you be afraid of me: you see my eyes have fallen out from your food. Look me straight in the eyes, girlie, don't be afraid!"

Katerina Lvovna looked and screamed at the top of her voice. The cat was again lying between her and Sergei but this cat had the head of Boris Timofeyich, full size, and instead of eyes there were two circles of fire that kept turning and turning in different directions.

Sergei woke up. He soothed Katerina Lvovna, but all sleep had left her and it was as well for her that it had.

As she lay wide-eyed, she suddenly heard what she thought was somebody climbing over the gate. The dogs started dashing about but soon fell silent. They must have been fondling up to somebody. Another minute passed and the iron latch on the door below rattled and the door opened. "Either I'm dreaming all this or it's my Zinovy Borisich come back, because that door was opened with his spare key," thought Katerina Lvovna and hurriedly shook Sergei.

"Listen, Sergei," she said, propping herself up on one elbow and listening intently.

Somebody was coming carefully up the staircase, treading warily, one foot at a time, and approaching the locked bedroom door.

Katerina Lvovna jumped from the bed in her shift and opened the window. That same moment Sergei jumped barefoot out of the window on to the gallery and wound his legs round the post that he had used so often as the way out of the mistress's bedroom.

"No, don't, don't. You lie down here and don't go too far away," whispered Katerina Lvovna; she threw Sergei's clothes and boots out of the window and herself darted back under the covers to wait.

Sergei obeyed her: instead of sliding down the post he found a place for himself under a basket on the gallery.

Meanwhile Katerina Lvovna heard her husband approach the door and stand listening, holding his breath. She could even sense the rapid beating of his jealous heart; it was not, however, pity that Katerina Lvovna felt, but an evil joy.

"Go and look for yesterday," she thought, smiling and breathing as gently as an innocent babe.

This lasted for about ten minutes: at last Zinovy Borisich grew tired of waiting and listening to his wife's slumber, and tapped at the door.

"Who's that?" called Katerina Lvovna in a sleepy voice after a while.

"Me," answered Zinovy Borisich.

"Is it you, Zinovy Borisich?"

"Yes, me, can't you hear it is!"

Katerina Lvovna jumped out of bed just as she had been lying, in her shift, let her husband in and dived back under the covers.

"It's chilly before dawn," she said, wrapping herself up in the blanket.

Zinovy Borisich entered, looked round, prayed at the icons, lit a candle and again looked round the room.

"How are you getting along?" he asked his wife.

"All right," she answered; sitting up in bed she began to put on a wide cotton wrap.

"Shall I go and get the samovar started?" she asked her husband.

"No, you can call Aksinya, let her light it."

She slipped her bare feet into her shoes, ran out and did not return for half an hour. In that time she had lit the samovar herself and had gone quietly out on to the gallery to talk to Sergei.

"Stay where you are," she whispered.

"How long?" asked Sergei, also in a whisper.

"You've got no sense. Stay here till I call you." And Katerina Lvovna pushed him back into his old place.

Sitting on the gallery, Sergei could hear all that was happening in the bedroom. He heard the door bang as Katerina Lvovna came back to her husband and could hear every word they said.

"What have you been doing so long?" Zinovy Borisich asked his wife.

"I've been putting up the samovar," she answered calmly.

A pause followed. Sergei heard Zinovy Borisich hang his coat on the hook. Now he was washing himself, snorting and splashing the water all round him; then he asked for a towel; the conversation began again.

"How did you bury Father?" inquired the husband.

"Well, he died and so we buried him."

"Isn't that strange?"

"Maybe it is," answered Katerina Lvovna, rattling the cups.

Zinovy Borisich walked sadly up and down the room.

"What have you been doing to pass the time here?" he again inquired of his wife.

"Everybody knows what pleasures we have: we never go to a ball at all and to theatres just as often."

"You don't seem to be very pleased to welcome your husband," began Zinovy Borisich, giving her a side glance.

"We're not so young, you and I, to go crazy on meeting each other. What else do you want? I'm running about, doing things for you."

Katerina Lvovna again ran out of the room to fetch the samovar and again she visited Sergei, shook him and said, "Keep your eyes open, Sergei!"

Sergei had no very clear idea of what all this was going to lead to, but nevertheless he held himself in readiness.

When Katerina Lvovna returned Zinovy Borisich was kneeling on the bed hanging a silver watch with a bead chain on a nail over the head of the bed.

"Why is it, Katerina Lvovna, that when you are alone you make a bed for two?" he asked his wife slily.

"I was expecting you all the time," answered Katerina Lvovna looking calmly at him.

"For which we humbly thank you. . . . And how did this thing come to be lying on the bed?"

Zinovy Borisich picked up Sergei's thin woollen belt from the bedsheet and held it by one end in front of his wife's eyes.

Katerina Lvovna was not in the least put out.

"I picked it up in the garden," she said, "and used it to hold up my skirt."

"Yes," said Zinovy Borisich with emphasis. "I've also heard a few things about your skirts."

"What have you heard?"

"About all your goings on."

"There haven't been any goings on."

"I'll find out all about that, I'll find out all right," answered Zinovy Borisich, pushing his empty cup to his wife.

She did not answer him.

"All those goings on of yours, Katerina Lvovna, we'll bring out into the light of day," he continued after a long pause, frowning at his wife.

"Your Katerina Lvovna isn't so terribly scared. She's not awfully afraid of that," she answered.

"What? What?" shouted Zinovy Borisich, raising his voice.

"Nothing much, get on with it," answered his wife.

"Here, you, look out. You've got too talkative while I've been away!"

"And why shouldn't I be talkative?" asked Katerina Lvovna.

"You ought to look after yourself better."

"I've no need to look after myself. It's not enough for long tongues to talk scandal to you, on top of it all I have to put up with insults!"

"It's got nothing to do with long tongues, I know the truth about your love affair."

"About what love affair?" shouted Katerina Lvovna, flashing up, this time without any pretence.

"I know all about it."

"If you know, then tell me straight out!"

Zinovy Borisich sat silent for a while and again pushed his empty cup towards his wife.

"I can see there's nothing to talk about," snapped Katerina Lvovna contemptuously, throwing a spoon excitedly into her husband's saucer. "Come on, tell me what the informers have told you about. Who's this lover of mine you know about?"

"You'll know in time, don't be in too much of a hurry."

"They've told you some lies about Sergei, haven't they?"

"I'll find out, I'll find out, Katerina Lvovna. Nobody has taken away my power over you and nobody can . . . I'll make you tell me yourself. . . ."

"Ee-ee! I've had enough of this," screamed Katerina Lvovna, grinding her teeth; white as a sheet she suddenly jumped up and disappeared through the door.

"Here he is," she said a few seconds later, returning and leading Sergei by the sleeve. "Ask him and me together about what you know. Maybe you'll learn something more, something you didn't bargain for."

Zinovy Borisich was bewildered. He looked first at Sergei who was standing in the doorway, then at his wife who sat calmly on the edge of the bed with her arms folded, and didn't know what was going to happen next.

"What are you doing, you viper," he managed to blurt out, still sitting in his chair.

"Ask us about what you say you know so well," said Katerina Lvovna, insolently. "You thought you were going to scare me with threats of a club," she continued, winking significantly, "but there won't ever be anything of the sort: maybe I knew what to do with you before I heard those promises of yours, and, anyway, I'll do it."

"What's that? Get out!" roared Zinovy Borisich at Sergei.

"How so?'" Katerina Lvovna mocked him.

Adroitly she locked the door, put the key in her pocket and again flopped on the bed in her wrap.

"Come along, Sergei, come here, to me, dearest," she called the clerk to her side.

Sergei shook his curls and boldly sat down beside the mistress.

"Oh, Lord! Good God! What are you doing? What are you up to, you savages?!'" screamed Zinovy Borisich, his face red with anger as he got up from his chair.

"Say now, isn't it wonderful! Look, look my pretty boy, how wonderful it is!"

Katerina Lvovna laughed and kissed Sergei passionately right in front of her husband.

At that very moment a stinging slap resounded on her cheek and Zinovy Borisich made for the open window.

CHAPTER THE EIGHTH

"Ah ... ah ... so!... All right, old friend, many thanks. That's all I was waiting for!" shrieked Katerina Lvovna. "Now I see all right ... it won't be as you want but as I want. ..."

With a single movement she pushed Sergei away

from her and sprang swiftly at her husband so that before Zinovy Borisich had time to reach the window she had seized him from behind, grasping his throat in her slim fingers, and threw him to the floor like a sheaf of damp hemp.

As Zinovy Borisich went down he banged the back of his head on the floor and fell into a panic. He had not expected such a sudden climax. His wife's first attack showed him that she was determined to go to any length to get rid of him and that his present position was one of extreme danger. Zinovy Borisich realized all this in a flash, at the very moment when he fell, and, therefore, did not cry out, knowing that his voice would not reach anybody's ear but would only speed matters up. In silence he looked round and brought his eyes, filled with rage, reproach and suffering, to rest on his wife whose slim fingers were firmly gripping his throat.

Zinovy Borisich did not defend himself; his arms with their tightly clenched fists were stretched full length and jerked spasmodically. One of them was quite free but the other Katerina Lvovna held pressed to the floor with her knee.

"Hold him," she said indifferently to Sergei and turned towards her husband.

Sergei sat on his master, pressed both his arms down with his knees and was going to put his hands under Katerina Lvovna's on Zinovy Borisich's throat but instead he suddenly let out a scream. At the sight of the man who had wronged him the idea of vengeance aroused in Zinovy Borisich a last effort: fiercely he tore himself away, pulled his arms from under Sergei's knees, seized Sergei's curls in his liberated hands, and, like a wild animal, bit him in the throat. It was over in a moment, however, for Zinovy Borisich immediately dropped his head with a heavy groan.

Katerina Lvovna, pale and hardly breathing at all, stood over her husband and her lover; in her right hand was a heavy metal candlestick which she held by the upper end, the heavy base downwards. A thin stream of crimson blood flowed down Zinovy Borisich's cheek.

"Get a priest ..." groaned Zinovy Borisich, dully, in disgust throwing his head as far back as possible from Sergei who was sitting on him. "Confession ..." he muttered still less audibly, shuddering, his eyes fixed sideways on the blood that was clotting under his hair.

"You'll be all right as you are," whispered Katerina Lvovna.

"We've wasted enough time on him already," she said to Sergei, "take a good hold of his throat."

Zinovy Borisich croaked.

Katerina Lvovna bent down and pressed her hands on Sergei's as they lay on her husband's throat and pressed one ear to his chest. Five silent minutes later she got up and said:

"That's the end of him."

Sergei also stood up to get his breath. Zinovy Borisich lay strangled, his head cut open. At the back of his head, on the left side, there was a small patch of blood which had stopped flowing since it had coagulated under the matted hair.

Sergei carried the body to a cellar in that same stone-built warehouse where he had recently been locked up by the late Boris Timofeyich and then returned to the attic room. In the meantime Katerina Lvovna had rolled up her sleeves, tucked her petticoats up high and was carefully washing away, with soap and a bast scrubber, the pool of Zinovy Borisich's blood on the floor of his bedroom. The water was still warm in the samovar from which Zinovy Borisich had soothed his masterful spirit with poisoned tea and so the blood was washed away without leaving any trace.

Katerina Lvovna took up the copper washbowl and bast scrubber.

"Show me a light," she said to Sergei, as she walked towards the door, "lower, lower down," she said, carefully examining the floor-boards over which Sergei had dragged the body all the way to the cellar.

In two places only there were specks no bigger than cherries on the painted floor. Katerina Lvovna wiped them with her scrubber and they vanished.

"That's what you get for creeping up on your wife like a thief," said Katerina Lvovna, straightening up and looking towards the warehouse.

"Now it's all over," said Sergei, shuddering at the sound of his own voice.

When they returned to the bedroom a faint rosy streak of dawn had appeared in the east, turning the light blossoms of the apple-tree golden and peeping through the green stakes of the garden fence into Katerina Lvovna's room.

The old clerk was plodding slowly across the yard from the shed to the kitchen, a sheepskin coat thrown over his shoulders.

Katerina Lvovna carefully pulled the cord opening the shutters, and examined Sergei attentively as though trying to peer into his soul.

"Now you're the merchant," she said, placing her white hands on his shoulders.

Sergei did not answer her.

Sergei's lips trembled, and he was in a fever. Katerina Lvovna's lips were cold, and that was all.

Two days later big calluses appeared on Sergei's hands from the crowbar and spade he had been using; they had helped to pack away Zinovy Borisich so well in his cellar that without the aid of his widow or her lover nobody could have found him until Judgement Day.

Sergei went about with a red handkerchief round his neck, complaining of a sore throat. But before the toothmarks implanted by Zinovy Borisich on Sergei's throat had time to heal, people began to ask after Katerina Lvovna's husband. Sergei himself began to talk about him more than anybody else. In the evening he would sit with the other young men on the garden seat near the gate and would start the talk going: "What can have happened to the old man? Why hasn't he got back yet?"

The other young people also wondered why.

Then came the news from the mill that the merchant had hired horses and had set out for home long ago. The driver who had brought him said that Zinovy Borisich had seemed to be upset about something and paid him off in a strange fashion: he had stopped the cart near the monastery, about three versts from the town, taken his bag and walked off. The story only made people wonder all the more.

Zinovy Borisich had disappeared and that was the end of it.

A search was made but nothing was discovered: the merchant might have vanished into thin air. The deposition made by the arrested driver stated that the merchant had got out of the cart above the river near the monastery and had walked off. No explanation was forthcoming and the widow lived openly with Sergei. Conjectures were made that Zinovy Borisich was in one place or another, but he did not return, and Katerina Lvovna knew better than anybody else that he never would.

A month passed, then a second and a third and Katerina Lvovna felt herself heavy with child.

"We'll get all the money, Sergei: I have an heir," she

42

said and then went to the municipality to complain: things are so and so, she was pregnant, and business was at a standstill: they should let her take control of everything.

A commercial undertaking could not be allowed to run to ruin. Katerina Lvovna was her husband's lawful wife, there were no debts and so there was no reason why she should not take over. She did.

Katerina Lvovna ruled the place with a firm hand and Sergei was called Sergei Filippich on account of her. Then, suddenly, like a bolt from the blue, came more trouble. The mayor received a letter from Livni to the effect that Boris Timofeyich had been using not only his own capital to trade with, but money belonging to a young nephew, a minor, Fyodor Zakharov Lyamin, and that the matter should be investigated and control not given to Katerina Lvovna alone. First this news came, the mayor spoke to Katerina Lvovna about it, and then, about a week later, an old woman arrived from Livni with a little boy.

"I'm the late Boris Timofeyich's cousin," she said, "and this is my nephew, Fyodor Lyamin."

Katerina Lvovna received them herself.

Sergei, who saw the arrival and Katerina Lvovna's reception, went as white as a sheet.

"What's wrong with you?" asked the mistress, seeing his deadly pallor when he entered the house immediately after the newcomers, then stared at them and remained in the hall.

"Nothing," said the clerk, turning from the hall into the outer room. "I was just thinking how fine it all is," he added with a sigh, closing the door behind him.

"What are we going to do now?" Sergei asked Katerina Lvovna that evening as they sat at the samovar. "That's put paid to us as far as the business is concerned."

"Why do you think that, Sergei?"

"Because everything will have to be shared now. What are we going to get out of it, for ourselves?"

"Surely there'll be enough for you, Sergei?"

"I'm not thinking about myself; only I don't think there'll be any happiness for us."

"Why not? Why shouldn't we be happy?"

"Because, Katerina Lvovna, I love you so much I want to see you a real lady, and not living like you've been doing till now," answered Sergei Filippich. "And now it seems there'll be less capital and we'll have to put up with being worse off than we were before."

"But surely you don't think it's money I need, Sergei?"

"That's right, maybe you're not exactly interested but I am, because I respect you and in the eyes of the common, envious people it'll be painful. You can have your own way, of course, but I can never be happy with things as they are. I have my own ideas on the subject."

And so Sergei went on and on, harping on the theme, that he had become the most unfortunate man on account of this Fyodor Lyamin, that he had been deprived of future opportunities to raise her high above the level of the common run of the merchant class. Each time Sergei led up to the same subject: were it not for this Fyodor, Katerina Lvovna, who would bear a son before her husband had been missing nine months, would get all the capital and their happiness would know no bounds.

CHAPTER THE TENTH

Sergei soon stopped talking about the heir, but not before the boy had become fixed in Katerina Lvovna's mind and heart. She even became moody and ungracious to Sergei. Whether she was sleeping or busy in the household or saying her prayers, she always had the same thing on her mind: "How can such things be? Why should I lose capital on account of him? How much I have suffered, how many sins I have to answer for, and here he comes along and takes it away from me without any trouble.... It wasn't as if it was a grown-up man, he's only a boy, a little babe...."

The early frosts had set in. It goes without saying that no word of Zinovy Borisich had been heard from anywhere. Katerina Lvovna grew stouter and walked about deep in thought; there was a lot of talk about her in the town—how came it that this young Izmailova, who till then had been childless and pining away, had suddenly started to swell in front. Meanwhile the co-heir, the minor, Fyodor Lyamin, played about the yard in his little squirrel coat, breaking the thin ice that had formed on the puddles.

"Now then, Fyodor," Aksinya the cook would shout at him as she ran across the yard, "is that the way for a merchant's son to behave, stamping in puddles?"

And the co-heir, who bothered Katerina Lvovna and her lover, romped about as carefree as a young kid, and slept just as carefree opposite the old woman who had charge of his upbringing, never dreaming that he had crossed anybody's path or cut short anybody's happiness.

At last Fyodor caught chicken pox, which was made worse by a cold on the chest, so the boy was put to bed. At first they treated him with herbs and things, but later sent for a doctor.

The doctor began to call regularly, prescribed some medicine which was given to the boy hourly by his aunt or by Katerina Lvovna when she was asked to.

"Be so kind," the old woman would say, "Katerina, you are in the family way yourself and are awaiting God's judgement: be so kind."

Katerina Lvovna did not refuse the old woman. When the latter went to evening mass to pray for "the youth Fyodor lying on his bed of sickness" or to early mass again to pray for him, Katerina Lvovna would sit with the sick child, would give him a drink when he needed it and his medicine at the proper time.

Once, the old woman, who was going to evening and late service on the occasion of the Presentation of the Blessed Virgin Mary, asked Katerina Lvovna to look after Fyodor who was getting better.

Katerina Lvovna went into Fyodor's room and he was sitting up in bed in his little squirrel coat, reading the *Lives of the Christian Fathers.*

"What are you reading, Fyodor?" she asked as she sat down in a chair.

"*Lives*, auntie, I'm reading the *Lives.*"

"Are they interesting?"

"Very interesting, auntie."

Katerina Lvovna rested her chin on her hand and began to watch his whispering lips and suddenly it seemed as though demons had broken loose from their chains and she fell prey to her former thoughts of the wrong this boy was doing her and how good it would be if he did not exist.

"And what's more," thought Katerina Lvovna, "he's sick; they give him medicine ... anything might happen to a sick person.... The doctor didn't make the right medicine, that's all."

"Isn't it time for your medicine, Fyodor?"

"If you please, auntie," answered the boy and after sipping the medicine from the spoon, added, "it's very interesting, auntie, the way the saints are described."

"All right, go on reading," said Katerina Lvovna and casting a cold glance over the room stopped at the frost-covered windows.

"I must tell them to close the shutters," she said and went into the drawing-room, from there to the hall and then to her own room upstairs where she sat down.

Five minutes later Sergei in a sheepskin coat trimmed with seal came up to her room and entered without saying a word.

"Have they closed the shutters?" Katerina Lvovna asked him.

"Yes, they have," answered Sergei, brusquely, snuffing the candle with the scissors.

A silence followed.

"Will late mass last long tonight?" asked Katerina Lvovna.

"Yes, it's a big holiday tomorrow: it'll be a long service," answered Sergei.

Another pause.

"I'll go to Fyodor. He's alone in there," muttered Katerina Lvovna, getting up.

"Alone?" he asked her, frowning.

"Alone," she answered in a whisper, "what about it?"

Something like a lightning flash passed from her eyes to his but not another word was spoken.

Katerina Lvovna went downstairs and walked through the empty rooms; it was silent everywhere; the icon-lamps burnt peacefully; her own shadow flittered across the walls; now that the windows were covered by shutters, the frost on them began to thaw and water was dripping from them. Fyodor was sitting up and reading. When he saw Katerina Lvovna he only said to her:

"Auntie, please take this book and give me the one that's on the icon cabinet."

Katerina Lvovna acceded to his request and gave him the book.

"Wouldn't you like to sleep, Fyodor?"

"No, I'll wait for auntie."

"Why wait for her?"

"She promised to bring me some holy bread from church."

Katerina Lvovna suddenly turned pale; for the first time her own child had turned below her heart, and she felt cold in her bosom. She stood for a while in the middle of the room and then went out rubbing her chilly hands.

"Well?" she whispered as she silently entered her bedroom and found Sergei still in the same position beside the stove.

"What?" asked Sergei in a scarcely audible voice and choked.

"He's alone."

Sergei raised his brows and began to breathe heavily.

"Come on," said Katerina Lvovna and turned sharply to the door.

Sergei quickly pulled off his boots and asked:

"What shall I take?"

"Nothing," breathed Katerina Lvovna and led him quietly after her by the hand.

CHAPTER THE ELEVENTH

The sick boy shuddered and dropped the book on to his knees when Katerina Lvovna came into the room for the third time.

"What's the matter, Fyodor?"

"Oh, something frightened me, auntie," he answered smiling fearfully and cringing into one corner of the bed.

"What frightened you?"

"Who was that with you, auntie?"

"Where? Nobody came with me, dearest."

"Nobody?"

48

The boy stretched toward the foot of the bed, screwed up his eyes, looked towards the door through which his aunt had come, and grew calmer.

"I suppose I must have imagined it," he said.

Katerina Lvovna stood still, leaning on the rail at the head of her nephew's bed.

Fyodor looked at his aunt and remarked that for some reason or other she was very pale.

In answer to that remark Katerina Lvovna forced a cough and looked in expectation towards the door of the drawing-room. In there only a floor-board creaked.

"I'm reading the life of my patron saint, Theodore, the Soldier of God, auntie. He served God well."

Katerina Lvovna stood there in silence.

"If you like, auntie, sit down here and I'll read it again for you," said the nephew, fondly.

"Wait a minute while I trim the icon-lamp in the drawing-room," answered Katerina Lvovna and hurried out of the room.

There came a very faint whisper from the drawing-room: but in the dead silence of the house it reached the boy's sharp ears.

"Auntie! What are you doing? Who are you whispering to?" he screamed in a tearful voice. "Come back here, auntie: I'm afraid," he called still more tearfully a second later and heard Katerina Lvovna say, "All right" in the drawing-room and thought it was said to him.

"What are you afraid of?" Katerina Lvovna asked him in a somewhat hoarse voice as she walked into the room with bold, determined steps and stood beside his bed so that the drawing-room door was hidden from the sick boy by her body. "Lie down," she said immediately afterwards.

"I don't want to, auntie."

"Now then, Fyodor, do as I tell you, lie down, it's late ..." repeated Katerina Lvovna.

"But why, auntie? I'm not at all sleepy."

"No, you lie down, lie down," said Katerina Lvovna, her voice changing again, so that it was no longer firm; she took the boy under the arms and laid him down at the head of the bed.

At that moment Fyodor let out a frantic scream: he had seen the pale, barefooted Sergei entering the room.

With her hand Katerina Lvovna covered the mouth the frightened boy opened in his terror and shouted:

"Come on, hurry up, hold him out straight so that he can't struggle!"

Sergei seized Fyodor by the arms and legs and Katerina Lvovna, with a single movement, covered the babyish face of the sufferer with a big down pillow and pressed her strong, firm bosom on top of it.

Some four minutes the room was as silent as the grave.

"He's dead," whispered Katerina Lvovna and had only just stood up to put everything in order when the walls of that old house that had seen so many crimes trembled under deafening blows: the windows rattled, the floors shook, the vibrating chains of the hanging icon-lamps cast fantastic shadows on the walls.

Sergei shuddered and ran away as fast as his legs would carry him; Katerina Lvovna went after him and the noise and uproar followed them. It seemed as though some unearthly forces were shaking the sinful house to the foundations.

Katerina Lvovna was afraid that, in his terror, Sergei would run out into the yard and betray himself by his fright; but he made his way to the attic bedroom.

Sergei ran full pelt up the stairs and in the darkness banged his head on the half-open door; with a groan he rolled down the stairs, completely out of his mind from superstitious terror.

"Zinovy Borisich, Zinovy Borisich!" he muttered,

flying headlong downstairs, knocking Katerin
off her feet and dragging her with him.

"Where?" she asked.

"He flew over us on an iron sheet. There, there
again! Ai, ai ..." screamed Sergei. "Listen to him
tling, he's rattling again."

It was now quite clear that many hands were banging at the windows from the outside and that somebody
was trying to break open the door.

"You fool! Get up, you fool!" screamed Katerina
Lvovna, and with those words darted back to Fyodor,
laid his dead head on the pillows in the most natural
pose as though he were asleep and then with a firm
hand opened the door which the crowd was trying to
break down.

A terrible scene met her eyes. Katerina Lvovna looked
out over the crowd that was besieging the porch and
saw row after row of unfamiliar people climbing over
the fence into the yard while in the street there was a
hum of human speech.

Before Katerina Lvovna realized what had happened,
the crowd on the porch forced her back and threw her
into the room.

CHAPTER THE TWELFTH

And this is how the alarm was raised: on the eve of
the festival of the Presentation people crowded all the
churches of the town Katerina Lvovna lived in, which,
although it was only a district town, was quite big and
had some factories; the church that was to celebrate its
saint's day on the morrow was not only full of people,
but even the churchyard was packed for midnight mass.
The church boasted a choir of merchants' apprentices
led by a choir master who was also an amateur in the
vocal art.

4* 51

ple are pious and assiduous churchgoers. In
, they have an artistic temperament; the gran-
, the solemn church chorals is one of the loftiest
purest forms of enjoyment known to our people.
erever a choir is singing almost a half of the town is
ertain to gather, especially the younger men from the
trading establishments: shop assistants, shop boys,
clerks, factory hands as well as the master men and
their wives—they all crush into one church; everybody
wants at least to stand on the porch, at least to stand
under a window in the fierce heat or biting frost to hear
how the octaves are rolled out or how an arrogant tenor
handles the most capricious fugues.

The Izmailovs' parish church was dedicated to the
Presentation of the Blessed Virgin Mary and on the eve
of that festival, therefore, at the time of the incident with
Fyodor described above, the youth of the whole town
had been in that church; leaving church in a noisy crowd,
they discussed the merits of a well-known tenor and the
accidental flukes of an equally well-known bass.

Not all of them, however, were interested in matters
musical: there were those in the crowd who were interested in other problems.

"You know, you chaps, they're saying funny things
about that young Izmailova woman," said, as they ap-
proached the house, a young mechanic brought from St.
Petersburg by a merchant to run his steam mill; "they
say she's at her pranks with their clerk Sergei every
minute of the day...."

"Everybody knows it," answered another in a sheepskin, cloth-covered coat. "She wasn't in church today,
either."

"Church! She's such a dirty bitch and she doesn't
fear God, or her conscience or the public eye."

"Look, they've got a light up there," said the mechanic, pointing to a crack between the shutters.

"Let's have a look through the crack and see what they're up to," muttered a number of voices.

The mechanic climbed on to the shoulders of two of his associates and had no sooner applied his eye to the crack than he screamed at the top of his voice:

"Oh, look what they're doing. They're smothering somebody in there, smothering him!" And the man battered desperately at the shutter with his fists. A dozen other men followed his example, climbed up to the windows and began banging at the shutters.

Every second the crowd grew and the siege of the Izmailov house, which we already know of, began.

"I saw it myself, I saw it with my own eyes," testified the mechanic standing over Fyodor's dead body. "The boy was stretched out on the bed and those two were smothering him."

Sergei was taken to the police station that same night, while Katerina Lvovna was removed to her upper room and two guards were placed there to watch her.

The cold in the Izmailov house was unbearable for the doors were open most of the time. One dense crowd of curious sightseers followed another. They all came to see the body of Fyodor lying in his coffin and to view another big coffin covered with a heavy pall. On Fyodor's forehead lay a strip of white satin covering the red scar left by the postmortem examination of the skull. The examination by the police doctor showed that Fyodor had died of asphyxiation and when Sergei was confronted with the body, at the priest's first words about the last judgement and the awful punishment awaiting unrepentant sinners, he wept and not only frankly confessed to the murder of Fyodor but also asked that the body of Zinovy Borisich that he had buried without a proper funeral service, be dug up. The body of Katerina Lvovna's husband, which had been buried in dry sand, was not fully decomposed: it was disinterred and placed in a big coffin. To the horror of all, Sergei named the young mistress as his accomplice in both these crimes. To all questions Katerina Lvovna answered, "I know nothing about anything like that." Sergei was confronted with her and forced to expose her. Katerina Lvovna listened to his confession, stared at him in dumb amazement but without anger, and then said indifferently, "If he's so anxious to say all that, there's no reason for me to be stubborn: I killed them."

"What for?" she was asked.

"For him," she answered pointing to Sergei who sat with his head hanging.

The criminals were kept in prison and the case that had aroused public attention and indignation was dealt with very quickly. At the end of February the court announced to Sergei and to widow Katerina Lvovna, of the Third Guild of Merchants, that the sentence was punishment by public flogging on the market square and exile to penal servitude. At the beginning of March, on a cold frosty morning, the executioner raised the allotted number of reddish-blue weals on Katerina Lvovna's naked white back, then administered Sergei's portion on his shoulders and branded his handsome face with three criminal brands.

All this time Sergei, for some reason or another, aroused more popular sympathy than Katerina Lvovna. Covered in blood and dirt he staggered as he descended the black scaffold but Katerina Lvovna walked away quietly, striving only to prevent the thick shift and coarse prison coat from touching her lacerated back.

Even when her baby was brought to her in the prison hospital she only said, 'Don't bother me with it!" and turning towards the wall, without groan or complaint, lay face downwards on the hard bed.

The convict party to which Sergei and Katerina Lvovna were detailed set out when spring had just begun by the calendar but when the sun, as the saying goes, "shines brightly but gives no warmth."

Katerina Lvovna's child was given to be brought up by the old woman, Boris Timofeyich's sister, and as he was regarded as the legitimate son of the murderess's dead husband he now remained the sole heir to the entire Izmailov property. Katerina Lvovna was very satisfied with this arrangement and gave up the child with complete indifference. Her love for the child's father, like that of many excessively passionate women, did not by one particle pass over to the child.

Incidentally, light and darkness, good and evil, joy and boredom did not exist for her; she did not understand anything, or love anybody, not even herself. She only waited impatiently for the party to set out on the road, when she hoped to see her Sergei again, and she even forgot to think of the child.

Katerina Lvovna's hopes were not in vain: fettered with heavy chains, the branded Sergei passed through the prison gates in the same group.

Man gets used to any situation, even the most abominable, in any situation he retains, as far as possible, his ability to pursue his own few joys; Katerina Lvovna did not have to adapt herself in any way: she would see Sergei again and with him even the convict's road promised happiness.

Katerina Lvovna had not brought many things of value with her in her canvas bag and still less ready money. But long before they reached Nizhny-Novgorod all of it, however, had been distributed amongst the sergeants of the escort for an opportunity to walk beside Sergei on the road and to embrace him for an hour or so at night in the cold, dark, narrow corridors of the transit prisons.

Katerina Lvovna's branded friend, however, did not seem so very amiable towards her: he did not greatly value these secret meetings with her, meetings for which she, foregoing food and drink, paid 25 kopeks from her scanty purse, and he often said, "Instead of coming to hide in corners with me it would be better to give the money to me and not the sergeant."

"I only gave him 25 kopeks, Sergei, dear," said Katerina Lvovna in justification.

"Isn't that money? D'you find 'em lying about in the road, those 25 kopeks, and you've paid a lot of 'em already, anyway."

"But still, we've been able to meet."

"And d'you think it's so wonderful to meet after all this suffering? I'm ready to curse my very life, not only these meetings."

"But I don't care, Sergei, as long as I can see you."

"That's all nonsense," answered Sergei.

At times Katerina Lvovna bit her lips till they bled when she heard such answers and in eyes unused to weeping there appeared tears of rage and chagrin during those meetings in the dark of night; still she put up with it all, kept her silence and tried to deceive herself.

In this way, with their relations on this new footing, they went as far as Nizhny-Novgorod. Here they were joined by a party on its way to Siberia along the Moscow highway.

In this big party, containing many people of all sorts, there were two interesting characters in the women's section: one of them, Fiona, a soldier's wife from Yaroslavl, was a fine, luscious woman, tall, with a thick braid of black hair and languid hazel eyes veiled by heavy lashes; the other was a 17-year-old, thin-faced blonde with dainty, pink skin, a tiny mouth, dimples on her fresh cheeks and light golden curls that escaped capriciously from under her coarse convict's kerchief. This girl was known as little Sonya in the party.

The beautiful Fiona was gentle and morally lazy. In their party everybody knew her well and none of the men were particularly glad when they had success with her just as none of them were very much upset when they saw that she bestowed those same favours on others who sought them.

"Our Aunt Fiona is a kindly woman, generous to all," the convicts agreed jokingly.

Little Sonya, however, had a different character.

"She's slippery, she's always close by but you can't get your hands on her," was what they said of her.

Little Sonya had taste, she liked to pick and choose and was, in fact, very finical. She did not want passion dished up to her uncooked; she wanted it served with a piquant sauce, with suffering and sacrifice; while Fiona had a Russian simplicity too lazy even to say, "Go away" to anybody and knew only one thing—that she was a woman. Such women are highly valued in gangs of thieves, in convict parties and St. Petersburg Social-Democratic Communes.

The appearance of these two women in a combined party together with Sergei and Katerina Lvovna had tragic consequences for the latter.

CHAPTER THE FOURTEENTH

From the first days of the journey from Nizhny-Novgorod to Kazan, Sergei began very obviously seeking favours of Fiona, and not without success. The languid, beautiful Fiona did not repulse Sergei any more than she, in her kindness of heart, rejected anybody else. On the third or fourth stage Katerina Lvovna had, by bribery, arranged a meeting with Sergei at early dusk and was lying awake, waiting all the time for the sergeant on duty to come into the room, nudge her and whisper, "Run quick!" The door opened once and a woman darted out into the corridor; the door opened a second time and another woman slipped down from the bed of boards and ran into the corridor after her escort; at last somebody tugged at the coat that covered Katerina Lvovna. The young woman rose quickly from the shelf bed polished by the sides of countless convicts, threw the coat over her shoulders and pushed the escort standing in front of her.

When Katerina Lvovna went down the corridor, which was feebly lit at one place only by a wick in a saucer of oil, she came across two or three couples that were scarcely discernible from any distance. As she passed the men's room she could hear subdued laughter coming through the observation hole cut in the door.

"Ugh, playing the fool," mumbled Katerina Lvovna's escort and, holding her by the shoulders, pushed her into a corner and went away.

With one hand Katerina Lvovna felt a coat and a beard; her other hand touched a woman's hot face.

"Who's that?" asked Sergei in a low voice.

"What are you doing here? Who's that with you?"

In the darkness Katerina Lvovna pulled the kerchief off her rival's head. The woman slipped away to one side and, stumbling over somebody, ran off down the corridor.

Hearty laughter came from the men's cell.

"You swine," whispered Katerina Lvovna and struck Sergei across the face with the ends of the kerchief she had torn off the head of his new friend.

Sergei would have raised his hand but Katerina Lvovna ran lightly down the corridor and entered her own door. The laughter from the men's cell was repeated as she ran, and so loudly that the sentry standing stolidly in front of the dim lamp and spitting at the toe of his boot, raised his head and growled, "Quiet, there!"

Katerina Lvovna lay down without a word and remained prone until morning. She wanted to tell herself, "I don't love him," but felt that she loved him more ardently than ever. And before her eyes she kept seeing his hand trembling under *that woman*'s head and his other arm embracing her warm shoulders.

The poor woman wept and involuntarily yearned for that same hand to place itself under her head, for that same arm to embrace her hysterically trembling shoulders.

"Well, anyway, are you going to give me my kerchief back?" asked the soldier's wife Fiona, waking her next morning.

"And so that was you, was it?"

"Give it back to me, please."

"Why did you separate us?"

"How did I separate you? Surely you don't think I'm so much in love or need him so badly that you should get angry about it."

Katerina Lvovna thought for a second and then pulled from under her pillow the kerchief she had captured the night before, threw it to Fiona and turned to the wall. She felt easier at heart.

"Phew," she said to herself, "surely I'm not going to get jealous of that painted swill-tub? May she rot in hell. It's horrible even to compare myself with her."

"And you, Katerina Lvovna, just listen here," said Sergei when they were on the road next day, "please get it into your head once and for all that I'm not Zinovy Borisich, and secondly that you're no high and mighty merchant any more; so don't get huffy, I ask you. This isn't the place for making a fuss."

Katerina Lvovna made no reply and for a week walked beside Sergei without exchanging a word or a glance. As the offended party she stood on her dignity and did not want to make the first step towards reconciliation after her first quarrel with Sergei.

While Katerina Lvovna was still angry with Sergei, the latter began trying to preen himself and make up to little Sonya. He would bow to her "with our best respects," smile at her and when they met would try to get his arms round her and squeeze her. Katerina Lvovna saw it all and it only made her blood boil all the more.

"Perhaps I ought to make it up with him?" she wondered stumbling along as though she did not see the ground before her.

But now, more than ever before, her pride would not allow her to be the first to go to him to make up. In the meantime Sergei was getting more and more entangled with little Sonya and the general opinion was that the unapproachable blonde, who was so elusive and never gave herself into anybody's hands, was suddenly being tamed.

"You shed tears about me," said Fiona one day to Katerina Lvovna, "and what did I do to you? I took the chance when I had it and now it's gone, but you keep your eye on that Sonya."

"My pride has gone. I simply must make up with him today," decided Katerina Lvovna at last and her only thought was of how to effect the reconciliation in the best possible manner.

Sergei himself got her out of this difficult situation.

"Lvovna," called Sergei to her during a halt. "Come out to me tonight. There's something I want to talk about."

At first Katerina Lvovna did not answer.

"Are you still angry? Won't you come?"

Again Katerina Lvovna did not answer.

But Sergei and everybody else who watched Katerina

Lvovna saw her edge her way towards the senior sergeant as they neared the transit prison and push into his hand seventeen kopeks that she had saved from money given as alms on the way.

"As soon as I can, I'll give you another ten," Katerina Lvovna promised.

"All right," said the sergeant and hid the money in his coat cuff.

When these negotiations had been completed Sergei gave a short cough and winked to Sonya.

"Oh, Katerina Lvovna," he said, taking her in his arms on the steps at the entrance to the prison, "there's no one in the whole world to compare with you."

Katerina Lvovna blushed and almost choked with joy.

As soon as night fell, the door opened slightly and she immediately slipped out; she trembled as she felt with her hands for Sergei in the dark corridor.

"Katya, darling," whispered Sergei, embracing her.

"My own bad boy!" answered Katerina Lvovna through her tears and pressed her lips against his.

The sentry passed down the corridor, halted, spat on his boots and walked on; worn-out convicts snored in their cells, a mouse gnawed at a quill pen, crickets under the stove tried to outchirp each other, and Katerina Lvovna was in the seventh heaven.

But the raptures came to an end, only to be followed by the inevitable prose.

"It hurts so much: from my ankles right up to the very knees, the bones are aching," complained Sergei sitting beside Katerina Lvovna on the floor in the corridor.

"What can I do about it, Sergei?" asked Katerina Lvovna, making herself comfortable under his coat.

"Should I ask to be sent to hospital in Kazan?"

"Don't say that, Sergei."

"They hurt so much, I'll die, then."

"How can you remain behind while they drive me on?"

"What else can I do? They keep rubbing and rubbing and soon the chains will cut me to the bone. If only I had woollen stockings to put on, maybe...." continued Sergei a moment later.

"Stockings? I've got some new stockings, Sergei."

"But no, I can't," answered Sergei.

Without a further word, Katerina Lvovna darted back into her cell, emptied her bag out on the shelf bed, then hurried back to Sergei in the corridor with a pair of thick blue woollen stockings with brightly coloured clocks on the sides.

"Now everything will be all right," whispered Sergei, saying good-bye to Katerina Lvovna and taking her last pair of stockings.

The happy Katerina Lvovna went back to her place and fell sound asleep.

She did not hear Sonya leave the room after she returned, nor did she see her return just before morning.

All this happened just two days before they were due to arrive at Kazan.

CHAPTER THE FIFTEENTH

A cold, gloomy day with gusts of wind and sleet greeted the convict party as they left the gates of the stuffy transit prison. Katerina Lvovna left smartly enough but she had no sooner taken her place in the ranks than she began to tremble and turned pale. Everything went dark before her eyes: she felt a pain in all her joints and they refused to support her. In front of Katerina Lvovna stood Sonya in the well-known blue stockings with the bright clocks up the sides.

Katerina Lvovna moved off more than half dead: only her eyes stared terrifyingly at Sergei and never once left him.

At the first halt Katerina Lvovna walked calmly up to Sergei, whispered, "You swine" and unexpectedly spat straight into his eyes.

Sergei wanted to spring at her, but he was held back.

"Just you wait," he muttered as he wiped his face.

"She's got guts enough to tackle you, all right," the other convicts mocked at Sergei, and Sonya's laughter was the merriest of all.

The love affair she had got mixed up in was exactly to Sonya's taste.

"You won't get away with that," Sergei threatened Katerina Lvovna.

Exhausted by the march and the bad weather and broken in spirit, Katerina Lvovna fell into a troubled sleep at the next transit prison and did not hear two men come into the women's cell in the dark.

When they entered, Sonya sat up, pointed Katerina Lvovna out to them, lay down again and covered herself with her coat.

The next moment Katerina Lvovna's coat was pulled over her head and the heavy end of a doubled rope wielded by a man's heavy hand lashed across her back, covered only by the coarse cotton shift.

Katerina Lvovna screamed out but her voice could not be heard under the coat that had been thrown over her head. She struggled but also without avail; a burly convict was sitting on her shoulders and holding her arms in a firm grip.

"Fifty," counted a voice at last, a voice which nobody would have had difficulty in recognizing as Sergei's, and the night visitors disappeared through the door.

Katerina Lvovna freed her head and jumped up; there was nobody there, only not far away somebody giggled maliciously under cover of a coat. Katerina Lvovna recognized Sonya's laugh.

Never had she felt so mortified; there was no limit to the malice that boiled at that moment in Katerina Lvovna's soul. She fell forward and dropped unconscious on to the breast of Fiona who caught her up.

On a full bosom that had but recently comforted Katerina Lvovna's faithless lover with the pleasures of lust, she wept out her unbearable sorrow and snuggled up to her foolish and flabby rival like a child snuggling up to its mother. Now they were equals: they had been reduced to the same value and both had been thrown over.

They were equals!... Fiona, who accepted any opportunity that came along, and Katerina Lvovna, who had played out the drama of love!

There was now nothing that could give offence to Katerina Lvovna. When she had exhausted her tears she seemed turned to stone and with an immobile countenance got ready for the roll-call.

The drum was beating: rub-a-dub-dub—convicts, fettered and unfettered, poured out into the yard: Sergei and Fiona, Sonya and Katerina Lvovna, an Old Believer shackled to a Jew, a Pole shackled to a Tatar....

At first they massed together in a crowd, then got into some sort of order and marched off.

It was the most sorrowful of sights: a handful of people, removed from the world and deprived of any hope of a better future, plodded their way through the thick, black mud of the dirt road. Their whole surroundings were horrible in their ugliness: the endless mud, the grey sky, the wet, leafless willows and the tousled crows that sat on their gaunt branches. The wind groaned and in its fury roared and howled.

The hellish, soul-rending sounds that completed the horror of the picture seemed to recall the words of Job's wife: "Curse the day thou wast born, and die."

Whoever does not want to listen to these words,

whoever is afraid of death, must, in this difficult situation, strive to drown out the howling voices with something still more ugly. The common man knows this very well: on such occasions he gives free play to all his simple bestiality and begins to mock himself, other people and their feelings. Under ordinary circumstances he is not particularly gentle, but in conditions such as these he becomes the very essence of evil.

* * *

"Hullo, Mrs. Merchant, do I find your honour in good health?" asked Sergei impertinently of Katerina Lvovna as soon as the party was out of sight of the village in which they had spent the night.

With these words he turned round to Sonya, covered her with the skirts of his coat and sang in a high falsetto:

I see through the window your sweet golden head,
I see that you sleep not, my darling,
I'll throw my cloak o'er you to hide your sweet
head...

At this point Sergei put his arms round Sonya and kissed her loudly in full view of the whole party....

Katerina Lvovna saw it all and yet saw nothing: she walked like one no longer alive. People began to nudge her, call her attention to the way Sergei was carrying on so disgustingly with Sonya, and make her the butt of their coarse jokes.

"Leave her alone," said Fiona, taking her part when somebody in the party tried to poke fun at Katerina Lvovna as she stumbled along. "Can't you see the woman's very ill?"

"She must have got her poor little tootsies wet," this from a young convict.

"Of course, she's from the merchant class, been brought up tenderly," responded Sergei.

"If she had warm stockings she'd be all right, of course," he continued.

Katerina Lvovna seemed suddenly to wake up.

"You dirty swine!" she hissed, "go on, laugh, you bastard, laugh!"

"Oh, no, Mrs. Merchant, I don't mean that as a joke at all: only Sonya here has some very fine stockings to sell and I just thought perhaps our merchant lady might buy them."

Many of them laughed. Katerina Lvovna marched on like an automaton.

The weather grew worse. Large flakes of wet snow began to fall from the grey clouds that covered the sky but they melted almost before they reached the ground and helped swell the sea of heavy mud. At last a dark, leaden strip appeared; the far side of it was out of sight. This was the Volga. A fairly strong wind was blowing across the river driving back and forth the broad, dark, slowly rising waves.

The party of wet and shivering convicts moved slowly towards the landing-stage and stood there awaiting the ferry.

When the dark ferry arrived, the crew began to accommodate the convicts.

"They say you can get vodka on this ferry," said one of the convicts when the ferry, covered with flakes of wet snow, put off from the shore and tossed on the waves of the raging river.

"Yes, it wouldn't be at all bad to have a small drop right now," answered Sergei and, continuing to bait Katerina Lvovna for Sonya's amusement, said, "Mrs. Merchant, for the sake of our old friendship, buy us a drop of vodka. Don't be stingy. Remember, my sweetheart, our former love, remember what good times we had together, my love, how we sat out the long autumn nights together, how we sent all your relatives to kingdom come without the benefit of book and clergy."

Katerina Lvovna was shivering with cold. Apart from the cold that penetrated to the very marrow under her wet clothes, other changes were taking place in Katerina Lvovna. Her heart was on fire; the pupils of her eyes were wildly distended, burning as they gazed intently at the passing waves.

"I'd like a drop of vodka, too," chirped little Sonya. "It's so cold I can't stand it any longer."

"Aren't you going to buy us a drop, Mrs. Merchant?" Sergei continued to pester her.

"Haven't you got any conscience?" said Fiona, shaking her head.

She was supported by the convict Gordyushka.

"Yes, it doesn't show you up at all well," he said. "Even if you aren't ashamed as far as she's concerned you ought to be in front of the others."

"Ugh, you anybody's woman," shouted Sergei to Fiona. "You're a fine one to talk about conscience. What's it got to do with my conscience? Maybe I never did love her at all and now ... Sonya's old shoe is prettier to me than her mug, the ugly old cat; what have you got to say about that? Let her make love to Gordyushka there with his twisted mouth; or to..." he looked towards a mounted officer in a long black cloak and military cap with cockade and added, "or still better make yourself nice to the officer: at any rate the rain doesn't get under his cloak."

"And everybody would call her Mrs. Officer," Sonya put in.

"I should say so! And she'd easily get what to buy stockings with, too!"

Katerina Lvovna did not attempt to defend herself: she continued to stare at the water and her lips seemed

to be mumbling something. She seemed to hear, between Sergei's foul remarks, howls and groans coming
from the waves as they gaped open and slapped to
again. Suddenly in one of the breaking waves she
seemed to see the blue head of Boris Timofeyich, out of
another appeared her husband embracing Fyodor whose
head was hanging down. Katerina Lvovna tried to remember a prayer and moved her lips to repeat it but
her lips kept saying, "How we had good times together, how we sat out the long autumn nights together
and sent people out of this world with violent death."

Katerina Lvovna shuddered. Her wandering eyes became fixed and wild. Her arms once or twice stretched
out nobody knew where into space and then dropped to
her sides again. Another minute and she swayed and,
without taking her eyes off the dark waters, bent down,
caught Sonya by the legs and with one single leap
went overboard with her.

Everybody was dumbfounded with amazement.

Katerina Lvovna appeared on the surface and then
disappeared again; another wave brought little Sonya
to the top.

"A boathook! Throw them a boathook!" shouted the
people on the ferry.

A heavy boathook with a long rope attached flew
through the air and splashed in the water. Sonya had
disappeared again. Two seconds later, carried swiftly
away from the ferry by the current, she again waved
her arms; at that very moment Katerina Lvovna appeared out of another wave, rose almost to her waist
above the water, hurled herself at Sonya like a big pike
at a soft little perch and both of them went under.

1865

THE ENCHANTED WANDERER

CHAPTER THE FIRST

CROSSING LAKE LADOGA, we left the island of Konevets bound for Valaam and on the way entered the harbour of Korela on ship's business. Most of us were glad to go ashore and we made a trip to that dreary township on sturdy Finnish ponies. By the time we returned the captain was ready to resume the voyage and we again set sail.

After our visit to Korela it was natural that we should get to talking about that poor though very ancient Russian settlement, than which nothing more desolate could possibly be imagined. Everybody on the boat seemed to be of the same opinion and one of the passengers, a man given to philosophical generalizations and political witticisms, observed that for the life of him, he could not understand why the authorities found it expedient to send people who were inconvenient to them in St. Petersburg to more or less remote places, thus entailing expense to the Exchequer for their transport, when there was such a wonderful place as Korela within easy reach of the capital, a place where no free-thinking or any sort of independence of mind could possibly stand up against the apathy of the population and the terrible boredom of such bleak and depressing surroundings.

"I'm quite sure," said the passenger, "that if it is not red tape that is responsible for this state of affairs it must be simply lack of proper information."

Another passenger who was familiar with those parts said that he knew that some exiles had lived there from time to time but, it seemed, they had not lasted long.

"One young student from a religious seminary was sent here as a junior deacon on account of his insolence (and that is an exile which I cannot understand). On his arrival he did his best to keep cheerful, hoping for

71

a judgement in his favour, but he soon sought solace in drink and became such a regular toper that he went completely off his head and sent a petition asking 'to be shot, enlisted in the army or hanged as one completely incapable of doing anything useful.'"

"What decision was made?"

"That I can't say because he didn't wait for any decision; he went and hanged himself."

"He did right," said the philosopher.

"Do you think so?" exclaimed the narrator, who looked like a merchant of some substance and, furthermore, religious.

"Of course," answered the philosopher. "Once dead he wouldn't suffer any more, anyway."

"Not suffer any more! What about life in the next world? Don't you know that suicides are doomed to eternal damnation and that nobody may even pray for them?"

The philosopher smiled venomously but did not answer, and at this point a new opponent entered the lists against him and the merchant, a man who surprised us by taking the part of the unfortunate deacon who had executed his own death sentence without awaiting permission from the authorities.

This was a new passenger who had joined us at Konevets unobserved by anybody. Now that we turned our heads to him we were all at a loss: how on earth had we failed to notice him before? He was a man of giant stature, swarthy and open of countenance with a huge wavy mane the colour of lead—for such was the strange hue of his greying hair. He wore the short cassock of a monastery novice, a wide monastic leather belt and a high, black cloth cap. Whether he was only a novice or had already taken the vows, it was impossible to say: monks on the Ladoga islands do not always wear a high kamelaukion when travelling or when at home on the islands but in their rural simplicity prefer the headgear of a novice. Our new passenger, who later proved to be an extraordinarily fascinating man, looked somewhat over fifty; he was in every sense of the word a Titan, a typical, simple-minded and good-natured Russian Titan reminding one of the legendary figure of Ilya Muromets in Vereshchagin's magnificent painting and Count Alexei K. Tolstoi's poem. You could not help getting the impression that he ought not to be wearing a cassock but should mount a "dapple-grey steed" and ride through the forests in enormous bast shoes, lazily inhaling "the scents of resin and wild strawberry in the gloomy pine woods."

Despite his very obvious good nature it did not take much observation to see that he was a man who had seen a thing or two in the course of his life or, as the saying goes, a man who "had been about a bit." He bore himself boldly and confidently but without any objectionable bravado, and spoke in a slow and measured but pleasant bass voice.

"What you have said means nothing," he began, letting each word fall lazily and softly from beneath a thick, grey moustache curled upwards hussar fashion. "I don't agree with what you say about suicides in the next world, that they'll never be forgiven. And it isn't true there's no one to pray for them since there is a man who can easily put things right for them and without going to too much trouble."

In answer to inquiries concerning the man who has taken it upon himself to look after suicides and promote their interests after death, the giant monk answered:

"There's a hard-drinking village priest in the Moscow diocese who was very nearly unfrocked for his boozing—he's doing his best for suicides."

"How did you come to know about him?"

"Why, bless my soul, not only I but all the Moscow diocese know about it for no less a person than His Grace the Metropolitan Filaret was personally concerned with the business."

A short pause ensued, during which someone murmured that the whole affair seemed to be rather dubious.

The monk did not seem to take offence at this remark.

"It certainly does seem dubious at first sight," he continued. "It is no wonder that we have doubts about it when even His Grace himself for a long time would not believe it, but later, when he had reliable evidence, he found it was impossible not to believe, and believe it he did."

The other passengers importuned the monk to relate this strange story. Nothing loath he began thus:

"The story goes that a certain archdeacon wrote to His Grace the Metropolitan to say that the village priest, Your Grace, is an awful drunkard, drinks vodka and neglects his parish. And it, the report, I mean, had some truth in it. So His Grace ordered the priest to be summoned to him in Moscow. One look at him was enough to convince His Grace that he was a real boozer and that it was time he lost his job. The poor priest was sorely troubled, so much so that he even stopped drinking.

" 'What a sorry pass I have brought myself to,' he wailed, 'what is there left for me to do but take my own life. That's all that's left for me,' he said, 'and then His Grace will take pity on my family and find my daughter a husband to take my place as breadwinner and feed my family.' And so he made up his mind to end his wretched life without further ado and even appointed the day for it but being naturally a good man he began to think:

" 'Good; suppose I die, what will happen to my soul?

I'm not a beast of the field, I have a soul to take care of. What will happen to it afterwards?'

"Thereupon he was even more sorely distressed. And so he grieved and grieved. His Grace, who had decided to take away his job on account of his drunkenness, one day after a meal lay down on a couch with a book to rest and fell asleep. Maybe he had fallen asleep or was just dozing off when the door of his cell seemed to open. He quite naturally called out, 'Who's there?' thinking that it was his attendant coming to announce the arrival of some visitor. But, lo and behold, who should walk in but a venerable old man whose face showed infinite goodness and whom His Grace immediately recognized as the Holy Sergius himself.

"So His Grace asked:

" 'Is it thou, Holy Father Sergius?'

" 'Yes, Filaret, servant of the Lord, it is I.'

" 'What dost thou, the pure in heart, require of me, thy most unworthy servant?'

"And the saint replied:

" 'It is mercy I require of thee.'

" 'On whom dost thou require me to show mercy?'

"And the saint named the priest who had lost his job through drunkenness, and then went his way. But His Grace woke up and asked himself what it could all mean. Had he seen an ordinary dream, was it idle fancy or was it a vision sent to guide his footsteps? He began to think it over and, being a man famed throughout the world for his great intellect, decided it was just an ordinary dream; could it be that St. Sergius who had spent his mortal life in fasting and good deeds would appeal on behalf of a priest of weak character and unrighteous life? Good. Having come to this conclusion His Grace left things to go on the way they had begun and himself continued in the ordinary way and, at the usual hour, went to bed again. But no sooner did he fall asleep than he again saw a vision and the vision was such that his great spirit was sorely troubled. Can you imagine a thunderous rumble, a noise so frightful that it cannot be described?.... Galloping horses ... knights without number dressed in green with armour and plumes tearing along, and their horses like black lions, and at their head the Lord of the host, similarly attired; and this Lord carried a black banner and on the banner was a serpent; in whichever direction he waved the black banner, in that direction the host would gallop.... Now His Grace knew not what this host might be but he heard their captain roar out a command, 'Tear them asunder for they now have no one to pray for them.' Saying these words he galloped away and the host followed their captain; after them, like a flock of lean geese in springtime, came a long procession of dismal spirits, all of them nodded their heads to His Grace beseeching him with moans and tears, 'Suffer him to go, for he alone prays for us!' No sooner did he awake than His Grace sent for the drunken priest and asked him how he prayed and whom he prayed for. The poor, weak-spirited priest was greatly troubled in the presence of the Metropolitan and answered, 'I serve in conformity with the orders of the Church, Your Grace.' It was with great difficulty that His Grace at last succeeded in getting an admission out of him. 'I must confess to be guilty of one deviation,' he said. 'I am weak in spirit myself and once thought of taking my own life, therefore in the Liturgy I always include a special prayer for those who died without absolution or have laid violent hands upon themselves.'

"On hearing this His Grace knew what those shades were that had floated past him in the vision like lean geese and, not wishing to bring joy to the spawn of hell that had gone before bent on their destruction, he gave his blessing to the priest. 'Go thy ways and sin no more,' said His Grace, 'and continue to pray as you have done before.' And with that he sent the priest back to his parish. And so you see this lowly priest can always help those who find life too great a burden to bear for he isn't likely to prove unfaithful to his vocation but will go on importuning the Creator for them and the Lord *must* forgive them."

"Why must?"

"Did not He Himself say, 'Knock, and it shall be opened unto you' and His word changeth not."

"Tell us, please, is there anybody who prays for suicides besides this Moscow priest?"

"That I don't know: they do say you shouldn't pray for them because they've sinned against the law of God, but it wouldn't surprise me if there were people who don't know this and who pray for them. It seems to me that on Trinity Sunday—or is it Whit Monday?—anybody can pray for them. There are special prayers said on that day, such moving prayers that I could listen to them for ever."

"Can't those prayers be said on other days?"

"I don't know; you must ask somebody who is well read, he'll probably know more about it; you see this business doesn't concern me so I've never had reason to talk about it."

"Haven't you ever noticed whether these prayers are repeated at other church services?"

"I haven't noticed it but you mustn't take my word for it since I don't go to church very often."

"Why not?"

"I'm too busy."

"Are you a priest or a deacon?"

"Neither. So far I'm just wearing the robe."

"But doesn't that mean you're at least a novice?"

"Yes, I suppose it does. At least people think so."

"They may think so," the merchant remarked, "but I've known cases of men wearing the cloth being taken into the army."

This remark did not cause any offence to the giant monk, he just pondered awhile and then said:

"I dare say you're right, there have been such cases, but I'm a bit too old for soldiering, I'm in my fifty-third year, and besides that, I know something of army life."

"Have you really served in the army?"

"I have."

"Sergeant, I suppose?" Again it was the merchant who asked the question.

"No, I wasn't a sergeant."

"What were you then? Private or some sort of N.C.O. or what?"

"You're wrong all the time. Still, I was a real army man, in fact I've been mixed up in regimental affairs since childhood."

"So you must be the son of a soldier and liable to military service," said the merchant, who was losing his temper and seemed determined to know the truth.

"Wrong again."

"Then who the hell are you?"

"I'm a *connoisseur*."

"A wha-a-at?"

"A connoisseur, in other words a horse expert employed to advise army officers buying remounts."

"Oh, so that's it!"

"I've selected and trained thousands of horses in my time. I've broken in the wildest horses, like those, for instance, that rear and throw themselves backwards with all their might and, like as not, crush the rider's chest with the saddle-bow, although no horse could ever do that to me!"

"How did you tame them?"

"Oh, I'm gifted by nature with a special skill in such

things. When I jumped on the back of a wild horse I'd give him no time to collect his wits, with my left hand I'd grab an ear and pull his head to one side, with my right fist I'd give him a bang between the ears and then grind my teeth in such a terrifying way that the horse would sometimes start bleeding at the nostrils and it looked as if his brains were coming out with the blood. After that he would naturally be as meek as a lamb."

"What next?"

"After that I'd dismount, look it all over and give the animal a chance to have a good look at me, too, so as to get me fixed in its mind, then I'd mount again and ride off."

"And after that the horse would behave properly?"

"Oh, yes, it would behave itself all right. You see, the horse is a clever animal, it knows immediately the kind of man that's handling it and what he has in mind about the horse. As far as what horses thought about me, why, they even loved and respected me. In the Moscow Riding School there was once a horse that had got completely out of hand, nobody could do anything with it and the savage, moreover, had learned the trick of biting its rider's knee. The devil would seize the rider's leg with its huge teeth and nip the knee-cap right off. That horse killed quite a lot of men. There was an Englishman by the name of Raleigh in Moscow at the time, the 'mad tamer,' he was called, but this mean horse nearly ate him up too—put him to shame, anyway. I heard tell that he only saved himself by wearing a steel guard on his knee so that although the horse bit him it could not bite through the guard so it threw him instead. But for that it would have killed him, too. But I cured that animal."

"How did you do it?"

"With God's help I did it, for, as I've said, I'm gifted that way. Mr. Raleigh, the so-called 'mad tamer' and all the others who had tried to break that horse in, thought that the secret lay in the reins, you had to hold the animal so it couldn't move its head one way or the other. I thought of a different way of dealing with it. When the Englishman, Raleigh, refused to have anything more to do with the horse, I said, 'Nonsense,' I said. 'It's easy enough, the horse is possessed of a devil, that's all that's wrong with it. The Englishman doesn't know about such things, but I do and I'm willing to do something about it.' The authorities agreed. So I told them to take him out beyond the Drogomilov Toll Gate. They took him out there. Good. We led him on a halter to the hollow at Fili, where the gentry have their summer cottages. I saw that the place was what I needed, it was big enough for the job, so I got down to work. Stripped to the waist and barefoot, wearing only a pair of wide breeches and a cap, I jumped on the man-eater's back. The only thing I wore on my bare body was a braided belt from the saintly Prince Vsevolod-Gavriil of Novgorod whom I greatly admired for his deeds of valour and in whose protection I had great faith; and the belt had his motto woven into it, *My Honour I Yield to No Man.* The only implements I took were a heavy Tatar whip with a lead ball of no more than two pounds weight at the end of it in one hand, and an earthenware pot of thin dough in the other. So there I was, on the back of this wild beast with four men pulling the reins in different directions so he couldn't get his teeth into any of them. And that demon of a horse, seeing they were going to get tough with him, started to neigh and squeal, broke out into a sweat and trembled all over with rage; he was determined to eat me up as I could plainly see so I shouted to the men who were holding him, 'Hurry up,' I said, 'take the bridle off him, the rascal!' They couldn't believe they had heard me aright, for they never expected such an order, but just stood gaping at me with their eyes popping out of their heads. 'What are you standing there for?' I asked. 'Why don't you do as you're told? Do you hear me? When I give an order I want it obeyed immediately!' And they replied: 'Ivan Severyanich' (they used to call me Ivan Severyanich before I took the cloth: Flyagin was my surname), 'do you really want us to take the bridle off?' I began to lose my temper for I could see and I could feel with my legs that the horse was getting mad with rage so I squeezed it tighter between my knees and shouted at them, 'Take it off!' They were going to say something else but I began to grind my teeth at them so they at once slipped off the bridle and ran away in different directions as fast as their legs would carry them. No sooner had they pulled off the bridle than I did something that horse didn't expect—bang! with the pot of dough on his head. The pot broke and the thin dough ran down into his eyes and nostrils. The poor beast got really scared and seemed to be wondering what was happening. With my left hand I snatched off my cap and kept rubbing the dough into his eyes with it at the same time slashing his flanks with the whip in my right hand.... Off he went and I kept rubbing the dough into his eyes so he couldn't see, and giving it to him with the whip. I just trounced him mercilessly and didn't give him time to take breath, or look round, but rubbed the dough all over his face to blind him, ground my teeth to put the fear of God into him and slashed his flanks hard with the whip to let him know that it was no joking matter....

"He understood me all right, for he didn't try to be obstinate and stamp around on the spot but just kept going hell for leather. Well, and so that poor devil carried me along on his back while I kept trouncing him and the faster he galloped the more I gave it to him and in the end both of us began to get a bit tired; my shoulder was aching and my arm too tired to lift, while I could see that he was no longer looking askance at me and that his tongue was lolling out of his mouth. I was sure he was giving up the struggle so I got off him, wiped his eyes, took him by the forelock and said, 'Stand still, you cur, you hell-hound!' And I gave him such a fierce tug that he dropped to his knees and from that time was so soft and gentle you couldn't wish for anything better; he would let any man mount and ride him, the only thing was he soon croaked."

"So he died after all, did he?"

"Yes, he died; he was too proud, that animal, he behaved gentle enough but it seems he couldn't get over his own character. But Mr. Raleigh offered me a job when he heard all about it."

"Did you accept?"

"No, sir."

"Why not?"

"How should I put it? In the first place I was a connoisseur and was sort of used to my trade. My job was to select horses, not to break 'em and all he wanted me for was to tame the mad 'uns. And secondly I didn't think he was acting square."

"In what way?"

"He wanted my secret."

"Would you have sold it to him?"

"Yes, I should have sold it to him."

"Then what prevented you?"

"I don't know ... perhaps he got scared of me."

"Will you please tell us that story, too?"

"Well, it isn't much of a story; he just said to me, 'Tell me your secret, old chap, and I'll give you a lot of money and make you my connoisseur.' Now I'm not one for cheating anybody so I said to him, 'What secret— that's all nonsense.' But he didn't believe me because he looked at it the English way, learned like. 'All right,' he said, 'if you don't want to let on without it let's have a drop of rum.' After we had put down so much rum between us that he got all red in the face he said, in the way he had, 'Come on, out with it: what did you do to that horse?' And I replied, 'It's like this...' and I looked at him something fierce and ground my teeth and as I hadn't got a pot of dough with me I snatched up a glass from the table (just by way of demonstration, you understand) and made as if I was going to hit him with it and when he saw that he dived under the table and then ups and leaps through the door and just disappears. Since then we've never met again."

"So that's why you didn't take his job?"

"Yes, that's why. How could I take a job with a man who was scared of even meeting me? It wasn't as if I didn't want that job, I wanted it badly enough for I'd sort of taken a liking to him during that rum-guzzling bout, but a man can't get away from his fate and I was doomed to follow a different calling."

"And what do you consider your vocation to be?"

"Truth to say I don't quite know what.... I've wandered plenty, I've been on horses and under 'em, I've been in captivity and in battle, I've beaten people up and I've been so badly crippled myself that not every man could have stood it."

"When did you enter the monastery?"

"Not long ago, after all the adventures in my life were passed and gone...."

"And did you feel you had a calling for that, too?"

"I don't rightly know how to explain.... Well, yes, I suppose I must have had."

"Why do you put it that way ... as though you weren't certain?"

"Because.... Well, how can I be sure of it when

there's been so much in my past life that I just can't fathom?"

"How is that?"

"Because so many things that I've done haven't been done of my own free will."

"Whose will, then?"

"It was on account of my parents' vow."

"What has happened to you on account of your parents' vow?"

"All my life I've been near death, but perish I could not."

"Is that true?"

"Perfectly true."

"Won't you please tell us the story of your life?"

"Why not, but the only way I can tell it is straight through from the beginning."

"Please do, it should be more interesting that way."

"I don't know how interesting it'll be but please listen, if you want to."

CHAPTER THE SECOND

The former horse-expert, Ivan Severyanich Flyagin, began his story this way:

I was born a serf and my parents were personal servants to Count K. of Orel Gubernia. Since then the estates have been divided up and sold by the young masters, but when the old count was alive they were very large. In the village of G. where the count lived there was a big mansion with separate guest houses, a theatre, a special skittle-alley, kennels, bearpits, where bears were kept chained to poles, hothouses and gardens; our own choir gave concerts and our own actors presented all kinds of plays; there were weaving sheds and workshops, but the greatest interest was shown in the stud-farm. There were people appointed for all these things but most attention was paid to the stables and it was the same as in the army in the old days, when regular soldiers' sons had to be soldiers and fight—a coachman's son became a postillion, a groom's son a stable-boy and the sons of the serfs who looked after the fodder learned to bring oats from the granary to the stalls.

My father was the coachman Severyan and although he wasn't one of the first because there were so many of them, he drove a carriage and six and once, when the Tsar visited us, was seventh in the procession and was presented with an old-style blue banknote.

I don't remember my mother who died when I was a baby because I was her *prayed-for son*, which means she had been childless for many years and prayed long to the Lord for a child and when her prayer was granted she died for I came into the world with an unusually big head and for this reason people didn't call me Ivan Flyagin but just *Golovan*.*

As I lived with my father in the coach-house I spent all my time in the stables and there learned the great secret of understanding an animal, and, I might say, learned to love horses, for even as a baby I would crawl on all fours between their legs and they did me no harm and I grew up thoroughly familiar with them. The stud-farm and the stables were quite separate and we stable people had nothing to do with the stud-farm but got horses from them to break in and train. Every coachman and his postillion had a team of six and all of them different: there were Vyatka, Kazan, Kalmuk, Bityug and Don horses brought in from outside, acquired at horse fairs, that is, although it stands to reason most of our horses came from the stud-farm but it's hardly worth talking about them since farm-born

* From the Russian *golova*—head.—*Tr.*

horses are usually gentle and have neither strength of character nor a lively imagination; but the wild ones we got, they were real terrors. The count used to buy them wholesale, a herd at a time, bought them cheap, eight or ten rubles a head, and as soon as we brought them home we'd begin breaking them in. All of them put up a stiff fight and so we had the very devil of a time of it. It sometimes happened that as many as half of them would die rather than submit. They would stand in the yard wondering where they were and would even shy away from the walls; all the time they'd stare up at the sky, like birds do. Sometimes I couldn't help being sorry for a horse for I could see he would gladly have flown away if only he'd had wings.... At first this sort of horse wouldn't eat oats or drink water from the trough, he'd just waste away until he dropped dead. Quite often we lost more than a half of them, especially when they were Kirghiz horses, that are terribly fond of their free life in the open steppes. Then again, of those that were tamed and lived, many would be crippled while in training for the only way of getting the better of a wild horse is by severity and those that got through all their breaking and schooling would turn out such top-notchers that nothing from the stud-farm could compare with them as coach horses.

My father, Severyan Ivanich, drove a team of six Kirghiz horses and when I grew up they made me his postillion. They were ferocious brutes, nothing like the cavalry horses officers get nowadays. We used to call 'em "court chamberlains," those officers' chargers, since there was no pleasure to be got out of riding 'em—why, even officers could sit 'em. But my father's horses were real brutes—beast, serpent and basilisk all rolled into one; just to look at their ugly jowls, their grinning teeth, their hoofs and manes was enough—they were horrors. They didn't know what it meant to be tired;

not merely eighty versts, but even a hundred and a hundred and fifteen versts from the village to Orel and back at the same speed was nothing to them. Once they got going you had to look out or you'd overshoot the stopping place.

At the time I was first put into the postillion's saddle I was only eleven, but I had the right sort of voice for the job, just the voice a nobleman's postillion needed the way things were in those days, a loud and piercing voice that I could keep going for half an hour in a long drawn-out "ally, ally, ho-o-o-o" and keep it on a high note, too. But my body was as yet too weak for me to stay in the saddle unaided on long journeys so they used to tie me to the horse, that is, they'd strap me to the saddle and girth with leather thongs attached to everything that would hold, and did it so cleverly I couldn't possibly fall off. Every bone in my body used to ache and sometimes I'd get so faint that I really would go right unconscious but as I had to stay tied in the same position the jolting in the saddle would bring me to again. Believe me, it was no easy job. On a long journey this would happen several times, I'd faint and come to again. When we got home they'd hoist me out of the saddle like a corpse and hold grated horse-radish under my nose. In time I got used to it and took everything as it came, and as we drove along I'd even manage to give a passing peasant a good hefty one across the shoulders with my whip. That was the time-honoured game we postillions played.

Once we were driving the count on a visit. It was a fine summer day and he was sitting in an open carriage with his dog, my father driving four-in-hand and I on the leading pair. We turned off the highway into a lane that led to a monastery known as the P. Hermitage, some fifteen versts from there. The monks made this lane because they wanted to attract visitors by making the way to their place as pleasant as possible; the state highway, naturally, was covered in all kinds of filth and the willows along it stuck out of the ground like a lot of crooked sticks, but the lane leading to the hermitage was clean and well swept, with birch-trees planted along it, all green and smelling wonderful, while at the end there were the wide open fields.... In a word it was all so wonderful that I wanted to let out a loud whoop which I wasn't allowed to do without reason. So I checked myself and drove on at a gallop, but when we were some three or four versts from the monastery the road sloped down and I suddenly noticed a black speck on the road ahead of me ... something crawling along like a hedgehog. I was glad of the opportunity and let out a prolonged "ally, ally, ho-o-o-o" and kept it going with all my might for a whole verst; I was so excited with my yelling that when we overtook the farm cart—that was the hedgehog I had been shouting at—I rose in my stirrups and saw a man lying on top of the hay in the cart; the sun no doubt warmed him pleasantly in the gentle breeze for he was fast asleep, knowing no cares in all the world, his face buried in the hay and his arms thrown out as though he were embracing the cart. I saw that his cart could not move to the side to let us pass so I kept to the edge of the road and, as we drew alongside the cart, still standing in my stirrups, I ground my teeth for the first time in my life and slashed him with my whip right down his back. His horses bolted downhill and he gave a jump, a little wizened old man, he was, in a novice's hat like the one I'm wearing now and his face was so woe-begone, like an old peasant woman's; he was scared of his life and the tears were streaming down his cheeks and he wriggled on his cart of hay like a fish in a frying-pan; he was probably still half asleep and couldn't see the edge of the cart for he tumbled off and fell under the wheels; he rolled in the dust and his feet got tangled up in the reins.... At first, the way he tumbled head over heels seemed very funny to me and my father, and even to the count, but then I saw the cart-wheel catch on a post at the bottom of the hill by the bridge... and the horses stopped and he did not get up or make any move.... When we reached him I saw he was all grey from dust and there was no nose on his face, only a big gash with the blood pouring out of it.... The count ordered us to stop, got out, took a look at the monk and said, "You've killed him." He threatened to have me flogged when we got home, but told me to drive on quickly to the monastery. From there some people were sent to the bridge for the dead monk and the count himself had a long talk with the abbot and in the autumn that year a whole train of carts loaded with gifts of oats and flour and dried fish went from our estate to the monastery; behind a shed at the monastery my father gave me the whip across the seat of my trousers but it wasn't a real thrashing for I had my job to do and had to get straight back into the saddle.

That was the end of it except that the same night the monk I had killed came to me in a dream and started crying again like a silly old woman.

"What do you want from me?" I asked him. "Get out of here!"

"You took my life," he answered, "without giving me time to repent."

"Worse things have happened," I replied, "and what can I do about it now, anyway? I didn't do it on purpose," I said, "and besides are you any worse off? You're dead and that's the end of it."

"You're right and of course I'm grateful to you," he said, "but just now I've come from your dead mother to ask you whether you know you're her *prayed-for* son?"

"Of course I do," I said, "Granny Fedosya often told me all about it."

"But do you know you're a *promised* son as well?"

"What do you mean?"

"You were promised to God."

"Who promised me?"

"Your mother."

"Then let her come herself and tell me, how do I know you haven't made it all up?"

"No," he said, "I didn't make it up but she can't come herself."

"Why not?"

"Because things are different here from what they are on earth; not all the people here speak or walk about; everybody does what he is most gifted in. If you want me to, I'll give you a sign that I'm speaking the truth."

"Yes, I want a sign," I said, "what is it?"

"This is my sign," he said. "Many times will you be near unto death but you will not perish until the appointed hour and then you'll remember your mother's promise and become a monk."

"Very well," I said. "I give my consent and shall await the day."

At that he disappeared and when I woke up I forgot all about him and did not even suspect that the trials and tribulations were going to begin right away and continue one after the other. But soon after that we went with the count and countess to Voronezh (their little daughter had deformed feet and we were taking her to visit the relics of a saint that had been newly affecting cures) and we stopped on the way in the village of Krutoye, in Yelets District, to bait the horses; I fell asleep under the horse-trough and again dreamed that the monk I'd killed came to me and said:

"Look here, Golovan, I'm sorry for you, ask your

master to let you enter a monastery at once—he'll let you go."

"Whatever for?" I asked.

He did not answer but said:

"Then look out, for much evil will you suffer!"

"All right," I thought, "I suppose you have to croak at me seeing I killed you," and with that I got to my feet, helped my father harness up and we drove off to where the road out of the village was as steep as steep can be, and on one side was a sheer drop into a deep ravine where so many people had been killed that nobody knew how many. The count said to me, "Mind, Golovan, be careful!"

But I was a tricky hand at my job and although the coachman had the reins of the wheel horses that had to be held in check going downhill, I knew lots of ways of helping him. His horses were strong and reliable and kept a firm foothold of the road—going downhill they all but sat back on their tails as they held the carriage back, but one of them, the villain, was a stargazer and if my father reined him back he'd throw up his head and gaze straight into the sky, curse him. There's nothing worse than a stargazer as a wheel horse, he's a real danger, especially in the shafts and the postillion always has to watch a horse of that kind since he doesn't look where he's planting his feet and is likely to get them God knows where. Of course, I knew all this about my stargazer and always did help my father manage him—I would check my own saddle horse and the off-horse by holding the reins in the crook of my left elbow and rein them back until their tails pressed against the muzzles of the horses behind with the shaft passing between the croups of my pair; in my right hand I would hold my whip over the stargazer's eyes and as soon as I saw he was aiming to take a look at the sky I'd fetch him one across the nostrils and down

91

would go his head and so we'd drive on in fine style. This time, too, I kept my eye on the stargazer as we drove downhill; I turned in my saddle and steadied him with my whip but suddenly realized that he didn't answer my father's reins or my whip any more, his mouth was bleeding from the bit and he was rolling his wicked eyes; before I realized what was happening I heard something go cr-r-rack behind me and the whole carriage lurched forward.... The brake had snapped....
"Hold on, hold on," I yelled to my father. "Hold on, hold on," he bellowed back at me ... but there was nothing to hold on to any more for the whole team was racing downhill like mad, not looking where they were going. Something flashed past me and, looking up, I saw my father fly off the box; the rein he was tugging had broken! In front of me was that terrible ravine....
I don't know whether I was sorry for my masters or myself but when I saw certain death staring me in the face I jumped out of the saddle straight on to the shaft and hung on to the end of it.... I don't know how much I weighed at the time but the shaft was like a lever and that was the same as if I'd weighed more. I almost throttled the wheel horses so that they gasped for breath and when I looked up I saw the lead horses were gone as though the traces had been cut. I, myself, was hanging over the edge of the ravine and the carriage had stopped plumb up against the wheel horses that I'd almost strangled with the shaft.

Only then did I have time to think and get scared— I let go of the shaft and flew off into space and remembered nothing more. I don't know how long I was unconscious but the next thing I remember is a peasant's cottage and a big peasant standing over me.

"So you really are alive then, sonny?"

"I suppose I must be," I said.

"Do you know what happened?"

I began to recall how the horses ran away with us and how I jumped on to the shaft and hung over that deep ravine; I hadn't the faintest idea what happened after that.

The peasant smiled at me.

"I don't suppose you would remember much more seeing how those horses got all smashed up before they reached the bottom but it seemed as though some unseen power saved you; you hit a lump of clay as you fell and slid down on it as though you were on a toboggan. We thought you had croaked, all right, but as you were still breathing we reckoned it must have been the rush of air took the spirit out of you. And now," he said, "get up if you can and go and pray to the saint. The count left money to bury you if you died or send you to Voronezh if you didn't."

So off I went to Voronezh and didn't say a word all the time, I just listened to the peasant who drove me playing *Mistress Mine* on his accordion all the way to the town.

When I got to Voronezh the count called me to his rooms and said to the countess:

"Here he is, your ladyship," he said, "you know, we owe our lives to this boy."

The countess only nodded her head but the count said:

"Ask me anything you like, Golovan, and you can have it."

I said, "I don't know what to ask for."

And he said, "Well, what would you like?"

I thought and thought and said, "An accordion."

The count laughed and said, "Well, you really are a fool, but that goes without saying; when the time comes I'll keep you in mind," he said, "and buy him an accordion."

One of the footmen was sent to a shop and he brought me the accordion to the stables.

"Here it is," he said, "now play it."

I took it and tried to play but soon found I couldn't, dropped it at once and some women pilgrims stole it next day, from under the shed.

I should have done what the monk advised, I should have taken advantage of the count's offer and asked him to let me enter a monastery; I don't know why I asked for an accordion and renounced my true calling but as a result I had to suffer one calamity after another, each more intolerable than the last; I always escaped with my life although everything the monk had foretold came true in this earthly life and all through my lack of faith.

CHAPTER THE THIRD

Thus enjoying the good will of my masters I returned home with them and a team of six horses newly purchased in Voronezh; no sooner did we arrive than I took it into my head to get a pair of crested doves, a cock and a hen, that I kept on a shelf in the stable. The cock was the colour of clay, but the hen was white, with such pretty red feet, a real beauty! I was very fond of them, especially when the cock would start his cooing at night and I loved listening to it; in the daytime they would fly about amongst the horses, sit on a manger, peck grain and kiss each other.... It was real pleasure for a young boy to have them.

After all the billing and cooing the youngsters came, they hatched out one pair that grew up and then started billing and cooing all over again, sat on their eggs and hatched out some more ... tiny little chicks, they were, all covered in soft down, no feathers at all and as yellow as the seeds you find in the grass, the kind called mallows; but they had huge beaks, like the noses of Circassian princes. One day I wanted to get a good look at those chicks and took one of them by the beak and could not tear my eyes off the sweet little thing; all the while the cock bird was trying to get it away from me. So I played with him, teased him with his baby, but when I put the chick back in the nest he wasn't breathing any more. Oh, what a pity that was! I warmed him in my hands, breathed on him and for a long time tried to bring him back to life, but it was no good, he was dead and done for. I lost my temper and threw him out of the window. It didn't matter much, there was another one in the nest; but that one, the goner, a white cat got him—just appeared from nowhere and snapped him up as she ran past. I took good note of the cat, all white, she was, except for a black spot like a cap on her forehead. "Oh, to hell with her," I thought, "let her eat the dead chick, if she wants to." But that night, when I was asleep, I suddenly heard the cock bird on the shelf above my head fighting angrily with someone. I jumped up and looked—it was a moonlight night and I saw that same white cat carrying off my other chick, the live one.

"She's not going to get away with that," I thought and threw a boot at her and missed and so she carried off my poor chick and, I suppose, ate him somewhere. My doves grieved for a time but soon started their billing and cooing again and in no time another pair of chicks was ready but that damned cat was right there, too. The devil alone knows how she found out about it, but there she was, in broad daylight, dragging off another chick and all so quickly done I hadn't time even to throw a boot at her. I decided it was time she was taught a lesson and fixed a trap in the window that caught her tight as soon as she showed her face that night; she sat there looking sorry for herself and miaowing pitifully. I took her out of the trap, stuck her head and forelegs into the leg of a top boot so she couldn't scratch me, took her hind legs and tail in my gloved left hand, got down my whip from the wall with my right and gave her a good thrashing. I must have given her about a hundred and fifty of the best when she left off struggling. I took her out of the boot and wondered how I could find out whether she was dead or not. I laid her across the threshold and chopped off her tail with my axe. She squealed, shuddered, turned about a dozen somersaults and was off like a flash.

"I bet you won't come stealing pigeons again," I thought and next morning, to frighten her still more, I took the tail I'd cut off and nailed it over my window outside and felt very pleased with myself.

Maybe an hour later, or maybe two, who did I see rushing into the stables but the countess's maid who'd never been there before in her life. She waved a parasol at me and shouted:

"So that's who it was, so that's who it was!"

"What's the matter?" I asked.

"So it was you, was it, that crippled Zozinka?" she said. "Don't deny it, I can see her tail nailed up over your window."

"Why so much fuss about a cat's tail?" I asked.

"How dare you do a thing like that?" said she.

"How dare she eat my pigeons?" said I.

"What do your pigeons matter?"

"D'you think your cat's a countess, or what?"

I was then at the age when I had begun to use abusive language, you know.

"Who the hell cares for that blasted cat of yours?" I said.

Then she let go at me. "How dare you speak to me like that? Don't you know it's my cat and the countess herself used to stroke her?" And with that she gave me such a slap across the face with the flat of her hand; now I've been pretty quick with my hands ever since I was a boy and I grabbed a dirty besom from behind the door and caught her such a swipe with it, right across the waist. . . .

Oh, Lord, what a hullabaloo there was after that! They dragged me into the office for judgement and the German steward ordered me to be flogged within an inch of my life and then sent me away from the stables to the English garden to hammer stones into the paths with a mallet. . . . They flogged me something cruel, I couldn't get up afterwards and they carried me to my father on a piece of matting, but I didn't mind that so much—what I didn't like was their condemning me to go down on my bended knees and hammer stones into the ground. . . . The idea tormented me so much that after thinking and thinking and trying hard to find a way out of the trouble I finally decided to do away with myself. From one of the footmen I got a strong rope, the sort they tie up sugar loaves with, and in the evening took a bathe in the river and went to the aspen grove behind the barns, knelt down and prayed for all good Christians, fastened the rope to a branch, made a noose and put my head into it. Then I only had to jump off the branch and in a moment it would have been all over with me. . . . My character being what it is I would have done it all right, but when I leaped off the branch and dropped I found myself lying on the ground and a Gypsy standing over me with a knife in his hand; he was laughing and the dark night made his teeth, white as white, gleam in his ugly black mug.

"What do think you're doing, eh?"

"What's it got to do with you?"

"Maybe," he kept on, "life ain't so good?"

"You can see it isn't too sweet."

"Instead of hanging yourself you'd better come and live with us, maybe you'll get a different hanging if you do."

"What do you do for a living, you're thieves, I suppose?"

"We are," he agreed. "Thieves and vagabonds."

"So I thought," I said. "And you probably murder people, too, don't you?"

"That can happen," he said. "We do that if we have to."

I thought it over for a bit ... what else could I do? At home, day after day, it would be the same thing again—down on your knees and bang, bang, bang, bashing in little stones with a mallet; that trade had already given me calluses on my knees and everybody was laughing at me because a swine of a German had sentenced me to bang a whole mountain of stones into the ground and all on account of a cat's tail! "Call yourself a live-saver," they laughed. "Look who saved his master's life!" I couldn't stand it any longer and, knowing that if I didn't hang myself I'd have to go back to it, I gave up hope, cried a little and joined the highwaymen.

CHAPTER THE FOURTH

The Gypsy was smart and he gave me no time to collect my wits.

"If I'm to believe you won't go back," he said, "you must get me a pair of horses from your master's stable, the best there are, mind you, so that we can be as far away as possible on them by tomorrow morning."

This worried me greatly because I hated the idea of stealing; but needs must when the devil drives and, knowing all the ins and outs of the stables, I was soon able to bring out a pair of swift horses to the barn; they were the sort that didn't know what it meant to tire. The Gypsy took two strings of wolves' teeth from his pocket and hung them round the necks of both horses and we mounted and rode off. The horses scented the wolves' bones and carried us like the wind so that by daybreak we reached the outskirts of the little town of Karachev, a good hundred versts away. We straight away sold the horses to some house porter, took the money and went to the bank of a little stream to share it out. We got three hundred rubles, naturally it was in the banknotes* current in those days, but the Gypsy gave me one silver ruble.

"That's your share," he said.

It seemed unfair to me.

"Why," I said, "I stole the horses and might have suffered more than you. Why do I get such a small share?"

"That's because it hasn't grown any bigger yet," he answered.

"Don't talk nonsense," I said. "Why do you take so much for yourself?"

"That's because I'm the master and you're only my apprentice."

"Apprentice—that's a lie." One word followed another until we finally quarrelled.

"You're a swindler and I don't want to go with you any more," I said.

"Go your own way, for Christ's sake," he said. "You have no passport and getting mixed up with you will only get me into trouble."

We parted and I thought of going to the magistrate and giving myself up as a runaway serf but when I told my story to the magistrate's clerk he said:

"What a fool you are. Why give yourself up? Haven't you got ten rubles?"

---

* In the old currency one silver ruble was worth three rubles fifty kopeks in banknotes.—*Tr.*

"No," I said, "I haven't got ten rubles but I've got one silver ruble."

"Haven't you got anything else, a silver cross round your neck or that thing in your ear—an ear-ring, isn't it?"

"Yes, it's an ear-ring."

"Silver?"

"It is. And I've got a cross," I said, "I got it from St. Mitrofan's. It's silver, too."

"Take them off and give them to me quickly and I'll write out a certificate of liberation for you and you can go to Nikolayev. They're taking on a lot of people there and you can't imagine how many tramps have gone there from here."

I gave him my silver ruble, the cross and the ear-ring. He wrote out the certificate, put the magistrate's seal on it and said:

"You ought to pay extra for the seal, I always make people pay extra for it, but I feel sorry for you, seeing how poor you are, and anyway, I don't want a certificate to leave my hands unless it's in order. Off you go," he said, "and if you know anyone who wants a certificate send him to me."

"All right, good Samaritan," I thought, "he takes the cross off my neck and says he's sorry for me!" I didn't send anyone to him but begged my way along, in the name of Christ, without a kopek in my pocket.

I arrived in the town and went to the market-place to find a job. There were few people looking for jobs at the time, only three men that day who must have been half tramps like myself. There were plenty of employers ready to hire us and they pounced on us, each of them trying to pull a man to himself. One gentleman, a big, burly fellow he was, even bigger than me, pounced on me, brushed all the others aside, grabbed me by my two hands, dragged me away, beating the others off with his fists and using the foulest language imaginable with tears in his eyes. He led me to a hovel built out of God knows what and said:

"Tell me the truth—you're a runaway serf, aren't you?"

"I am," I admitted.

"What are you? Thief, murderer or just a tramp?"

"What do you want to know for?" I asked.

"So that I'll know what work you're good for."

I told him everything, why I had run away, and he fell on my neck and kissed me.

"You're the kind of fellow I want," he said. "Just what I need. If you were sorry for those chicks you'll be able to look after my baby: I want you as a nurse."

I was staggered.

"Nurse?" I gasped, "I'm not the man for such a job."

"That doesn't matter," he said. "That doesn't matter in the least. I can see you'll make a good nurse. I'm in trouble because my wife got fed up and ran away with a cavalry remount officer and left me a baby girl; I haven't time to feed her and I haven't got anything to feed her on. You'll have to nurse her and I'll give you two silver rubles a month for wages."

"But, good Lord, sir," I said, "it isn't the two rubles! How can I manage such a job?"

"Why, man, it's nothing to speak of," he said. "You're a Russian, aren't you? A Russian can manage any job."

"Yes, I'm a Russian all right, but I'm a man and nature hasn't given me what's needed to nurse a new-born babe!"

"Don't let that worry you," he said. "I'll help you by buying a goat from a Jew—you just milk the goat and feed her milk to my baby."

I thought this over.

"Of course," I said, "one could nurse a baby with

the help of a goat. Still, I think you'd better get a woman for the job."

"Never," he said, "and don't you ever mention women to me: they're at the bottom of all the trouble there is and I can't get one, anyway: if you won't nurse my baby I'll go straight away and call the Cossacks and tell them to bind you and take you to the police station and from there they'll send you back. Choose which you like better—knocking stones into your count's garden path or bringing up my baby."

When I thought it over I decided I wouldn't go back and agreed to stay as a nurse. That same day we bought the goat from the Jew, a white nanny it was, with a kid. I killed the kid and my new master and I ate it with noodles, and I milked the goat and began to feed the baby. Such a tiny, miserable and wretched baby it was, squalling all the time. My master, her father, was a Pole, a civil servant, a bit of a rogue who was never at home but spent all his time playing cards with his cronies; I got quite attached to the baby, being alone with her all the time; I busied myself with her so that time wouldn't hang so heavily on my hands. I would put her in a wooden trough and give her a bath and if a rash broke out anywhere on her skin I would sprinkle it with flour; then I would comb her hair and rock her on my knee, and when I got tired of staying indoors I would put on my coat, put her inside it and go down to the lagoon to rinse her linen and the goat had got so used to us she came with us on our walks. That's how I lived until the next summer and the baby first began to crawl and then to stand up on her little legs, but I noticed soon that she was bowlegged. I told my master but he didn't seem to worry much about it.

"It isn't my fault, is it?" was all he said. "Take her to the doctor and let him have a look at her."

I did so and the doctor said:

"She has rickets. You must give her some sand treatment."

I did what he told me—I found a place by the creek where there was good sand, and on a fine, warm day I would take the baby and the goat there. I dug up the warm sand with my hands and buried the baby in it up to the waist and gave her some sticks or some pebbles to play with. The goat would wander about nibbling grass while I sat with my hands clasped round my knees until I dozed off and slept.

The three of us spent days and days like that and I found that it kept me from getting too bored, for I repeat, I was terribly bored, especially in the spring when I first started burying the baby in the sand; when I slept on the beach I used to see all sorts of strange dreams. When I fell asleep with the sound of the lagoon rumbling in my ears, the breeze blowing from the steppe would bring with it some queer spell that made me see horrible visions: I would see steppes such as I had never seen before, with horses there, and all the time somebody calling me and luring me on, even calling my name: "Ivan! Ivan! Come along, Brother Ivan!" I would wake up with a shudder and spit in vexation: "Damn you, what do you want? What are you calling me for?" I would look round and see the same dreary sight—the goat had wandered a long way off nibbling grass, the child was sitting there buried in the sand and nothing else. . . . How dismal it all was! The wilderness, the sun, the lagoon—and I would drop off to sleep again and once more the spell would come with the warm breeze and I'd hear a voice calling me: "Ivan! Brother Ivan, let's go!" And I could not help swearing. "Show yourself for once, the devil take you," I'd say. "Who are you? Why do you call me?" Once when I got angry and was sitting there half asleep looking out across the lagoon, I saw a small cloud rise and come straight towards me. "Whoa!" I said. "Where are you coming, you'll drench me!" And suddenly, who should I see standing in front of me but that old monk with the woman's face that I'd beaten with my whip a long time before when I was still a postillion. "Whoa!" I said. "Get away from me." But he answered in a clear and gentle voice, "Come along, Brother Ivan. You have to pass through many trials before you achieve your end!" I swore at him in my sleep and said, "Why should I go with you? And what end am I supposed to achieve?" But he only turned into a cloud again and through his shade he showed me—well, I don't know what: a steppe, strange, savage people, Saracens, the kind there are in stories about Yeruslan and Prince Bova, all wearing big, shaggy hats and carrying bows and arrows and mounted on wild, terrifying horses. While I was watching I heard shouts, neighing and wild laughter and suddenly . . . a whirlwind, the sand swept up in a cloud and there was nothing left, only somewhere a bell was faintly tolling and the red glow of the sunset lit up the white walls of a big monastery on a hill and winged angels with golden spears were walking along the walls and all round was the sea and every time an angel struck his spear against his shield the sea would rage and foam and from the depths dreadful voices would cry, "Holy!"

"It's the monastery business all over again," I thought. When I woke up I was both vexed and surprised to see a lady kneeling on the sand and bending over my little girl in an attitude of great tenderness and weeping whole rivers of tears.

I watched her for a long time, thinking, quite naturally, that it was my dream continuing, but as she didn't vanish I got up and took a few steps towards her; then I saw that she had dug the baby out of the sand, had taken her in her arms and was kissing her and weeping all the time.

"What do you want?" I asked her.

She came running towards me, clasping the babe tightly to her breast.

"It's my baby, my daughter, it's my daughter," she whispered.

"And what if it is?" I said.

"Give her back to me," she said.

"Why should I give her back to you?" I asked.

"Aren't you a bit sorry for her?" she said through her tears. "Just look how she clings to me."

"That's because she's just a silly infant. She clings to me, too. I won't give her to you, anyway."

"Why not?"

"Because she's been entrusted to my care. That's our goat over there, it always goes with us; I have to take her back to her father."

And she, that lady, started crying and wringing her hands.

"All right, if you won't give me the child, don't tell your master, my husband, that is, that you've seen me," she said. "Bring her to this same place tomorrow so that I can hold her in my arms again."

"That's another matter," I said. "I can promise to do that much."

Sure enough, I said nothing to my master about it and next morning went to the lagoon with the baby and the goat and found the lady waiting for us. She was sitting in a sand pit and jumped up and ran towards us as soon as she saw us. She was laughing and crying together, put toys in the baby's hands and even hung a little bell on a red ribbon round the goat's neck; me she gave a pipe, a pouch of tobacco and a comb.

"You smoke this pipe," she said, "and I'll mind the baby."

We had many meetings like this on the beach; the lady played with the baby while I slept but sometimes she would tell me about herself, that is, how her wicked step-mother had married her to my master against her will and how she'd never been able to love him.... But it seemed that the other man, that remount officer, or whatever he was, him she loved dearly.... "I'm devoted to him," she said, "for you know yourself what a disreputable life my husband leads while the other one...." Well, it seemed that the other one, the one with the moustache, or whatever you call it, was a man of good habits. "And he cherishes me so dearly," she said, "but still I can't be properly happy with him because I'm so sorry for the baby.... Now I've come back to the town with him and we live with one of his friends but I'm always scared my husband may find out. I suppose we shall be leaving soon and then I'll be pining for my darling again...."

"There's nothing much to be done about it," I said. "If you neglect law and religion and have broken your vows you will have to suffer for it."

Then she would start crying again and as the days passed her crying became more pitiful; I was beginning to get sick of her constant plaints when all of a sudden she began to offer me money. In the end she came for the last time to say good-bye.

"Look here, Ivan" (for she knew my name by then), "listen to what I'm going to tell you. *He* is coming here himself."

"Who may *he* be?" I asked her.

"The remount officer," she answered.

"What's that got to do with me?"

Then she told me a long story of how he'd won a lot of money at cards the night before and had decided to give me a thousand rubles, just to please her, if I would give her back her daughter, that is.

"That I shall never do," I said.

"But why not? Why not, Ivan?" she kept on pestering me. "Aren't you sorry for me and for her that's separated from me?"

"Whether I'm sorry or not, I've never sold myself for money, big or little, and never shall, so your remount officer can keep his thousand rubles and I'll keep your daughter."

She began weeping again, but I said to her:

"You'd better stop crying, I don't care, anyway."

"You're heartless," she said, "you're made of stone."

"I'm not made of stone at all," I replied, "I'm flesh and blood like everybody else, but I know my duty and shall do it: I undertook to protect the child and I intend to."

She tried hard to persuade me to change my mind.

"Can't you see the child will be better off with me?" she asked.

"That isn't any of my business," I replied.

"Do you want to say that I'll have to part with my baby again?" she exclaimed.

"Well," I began, "if you neglect law and religion. . . ."

Before I could finish what I wanted to say I saw a sprightly lancer officer coming across the steppe towards us. In the old days officers used to wear real military uniforms and walk with a swagger, not like the officers today that you can't tell from regimental clerks. That lancer came swaggering along, a fine figure of a man, arms akimbo and his greatcoat hanging loose from his shoulders. . . . He wasn't what you would call hefty, but he had plenty of go in him. I looked at the visitor and said to myself, "Why not have a bit of fun with him? I'm bored stiff and a bit of amusement wouldn't hurt." I made up my mind that if he spoke to me I'd be as rude as I knew how, and, God willing, we might even have a fight. That, I thought gleefully, would be just the thing and I didn't listen to what the lady was babbling through her tears, for all I wanted then was a bit of fun with the officer.

CHAPTER THE FIFTH

Once I had decided to get whatever amusement I could out of him I began to wonder how I could best provoke him into attacking me. I sat down, took out my comb and pretended to be combing my hair, while he went straight up to the lady and she started ta-ta-ta-ta... to him, all about how I wouldn't let her have the baby.

He stroked her head and said:

"Don't worry, darling, I've got the right medicine for him. When we show him the money his eyes will pop out of his head and if that doesn't work we'll take the baby, anyway." With these words he came over to me and pushed a roll of banknotes into my hand.

"There are exactly a thousand rubles here," he said. "Give us the baby and you can take the money and go wherever you like."

I didn't answer at once, I tried to be as rude as I could on purpose: first I got up slowly, tucked my comb in my belt, cleared my throat and only then did I say: "Oh no, that medicine won't work." I grabbed the notes, spat on them and threw them on the ground and then said to him as though he were a dog, "Come on, good doggie, grab 'em, fetch 'em!"

He looked hurt, turned deep red and went for me; you can see what a constitution I have—do I need long to deal with any officer? One shove and he was finished, sprawling on the ground with his spurs in the air and his sabre flying out sideways. I immediately put my foot on that sabre and said:

"See how I trample your courage underfoot!"

If the little cavalry officer hadn't got much in the way of muscle, he had plenty of guts. Seeing he couldn't get his sabre away, he unbelted it and came flying at me with his fists. . . . Needless to say he got it good and proper, still I liked him for his proud and noble character: I wouldn't take his money but he wouldn't pick it up himself, either.

When we had stopped fighting I shouted to him:

"Why don't you pick up your money, my lord? It'll do to pay your fares!"

And what do you think? He didn't touch it but ran to get hold of the child; he caught her by one hand and I grabbed the other.

"Let's pull," I said, "and see who gets the bigger half!"

"You dirty swine! You scoundrel!" With that he spat in my face, let go the child and was all set on getting the lady away, but she, in her despair, set up the most pathetic clamour and although she followed him, pulled away by force, she kept her eyes on me and the babe and stretched her hands out towards us. It was quite obvious and I felt it, too, that the poor lady was torn in two—one half of her wanted to follow her lover and the other half her child. . . . Just then I saw my master who had come running from the city with a pistol in his hand and he kept firing it and shouting:

"Ivan! Ivan! Stop them!"

"Not so likely," I thought to myself. "Not for you, I shan't! Let them love each other if they want to." So I ran after the lady and the remount officer and gave them the babe.

"Take the kid," I said, "but you'll have to take me, too, or else he'll have me locked up on account of my fake passport."

"We'll all go together, dear Ivan," she said. "You can live with us."

So off we galloped and with us we took the little girl, my nursling, and my master was left with the goat, the money and my passport.

All the way to Penza with my new masters there was one thing that kept troubling me as I sat on the box of the coach: was it right to hit an officer? After all, he'd taken the oath of allegiance, in wartime he defended our country with his sword, and probably even the Emperor addressed him as "sir" on account of his rank while I, like a fool, had offended him! While I was thinking about this, another thing occurred to me: what did fate have in store for me now?

There was a fair in Penza at that time and the officer came to me and said:

"Listen, Ivan, I suppose you realize I can't have you staying with us?"

"Why not?" I asked.

"Because I'm in government service and you have no passport."

"Well, I did have a passport, only it was a fake."

"But you haven't even got that now, have you? Here are two hundred rubles," he said, "take them and go wherever you like and good luck to you."

Well, I admit I hated the idea of leaving them for I'd got quite fond of the little girl, but there was nothing I could do about it so I said:

"Good-bye, then, and thank you for your kind reward," I said. "But there's one other thing I ought to say."

"What's that?" he asked.

"Just this. I feel it was wrong of me to fight you and be so rude to you."

He just laughed and said:

"Oh, good Lord, that's nothing. You're quite a nice fellow, really."

"I may be a nice fellow," I replied, "but we can't leave it like that, it will always be on my conscience. You're a defender of our country and perhaps even the Emperor calls you 'sir,'"

"That's true," he said. "When we're commissioned the paper says, 'Sir, we commission you and command our people to respect and honour you.'"

"Excuse me," I said, "but I can't stand it any longer...."

"It's too late to do anything about it now. You're stronger than I am and you battered me—that can't be taken back again, can it?"

"It's true I can't take it back," I said, "but to ease my conscience, and, no matter what you think, will you hit me a few times yourself?" And I puffed out my cheeks and stood there in front of him.

"What for?" he asked. "Why should I hit you?"

"For no reason at all," I said, "just to put my conscience at rest, then I shan't have struck an officer of the Tsar without being punished."

He laughed and I puffed out my cheeks again as much as I could and stood there in front of him again.

"What are you blowing out your cheeks and pulling faces for?"

"Like a soldier, according to regulations," I replied. "Please hit me on both cheeks." And again I puffed out my cheeks. But instead of hitting me he jumped up and put his arms round me and kissed me.

"Stop it, Ivan, for the love of Christ, stop it," he said. "I wouldn't hit you for anything in the world only go away quickly before Mashenka comes back with her daughter, they're certain to start crying about your leaving us...."

"That's another thing," I said. "Why make them un-happy."

Although I didn't want to go, there was no other way out, so I made off quickly without taking leave of them and as I passed the gates I stopped and wondered where to go next.

A long time had passed since I had left the count and gone wandering but I had not found a place to set-tle down.... "This is the end," I thought. "I'll go to the police and give myself up! But that's no good, either," the thought occurred to me, "I've got money in my pocket and they'll only take it away from me at the police station; I must at least spend some of it, let me enjoy tea with white buns at some tavern." So off I went to a tavern on the fair-ground, asked for tea and white rolls and sat there a long time drinking it, and when I saw I couldn't sit there any longer I went out for a walk. I went out beyond the River Sura where there are herds of horses in the steppe and where the Tatars that go with them pitch their tents. The tents were all alike except one that was brightly coloured and in front of it many gentlemen were inspecting rid-ing horses. There were all sorts there: civilians, army officers and landowners, they had come especially for the fair and were standing around, smoking their pipes and in the middle, on a brightly coloured rug, sat a tall, grave-looking Tatar, as thin as a lath, in a long patchwork robe and a golden skull-cap. Looking round, I noticed a man who had been drinking tea in the tavern with me and I asked who was the important-looking Tatar, the only man there sitting down. And he said to me:

"Don't you know him? That's Khan Jangar."

"And who may Khan Jangar be?" I asked.

And the man said:

"Khan Jangar," he said, "is the biggest horse-breeder in the steppe. His herds range from the Volga to the Urals and all through the Rhyn Sands. That same Khan Jangar himself is like a tsar in the steppe."

"But isn't the steppe under our rule?" I asked.

"Of course it is," he answered, "only we can't do anything with it because as far as the Caspian there's nothing but salt marshes and grasslands and birds flying high up in the heavens and there's nothing our officials can do with such places, so that's the reason Khan Jangar rules there; and there, they say, in the Rhyn Sands, he has his own sheikhs and sheikhzadas and descendants of Mamai and dervishes and all sorts of others, and he just orders them about as he pleases, and they're glad to obey him."

While listening to these words I noticed a Tatar boy drive a little white mare up to the Khan and say something to him; the Khan got up, picked up a whip with a long handle, stood right in front of the mare's head, stretched out the whip to her forehead and stood stock-still. How shall I describe the way that bandit stood? He was like a beautiful statue that you couldn't help admiring and one look at him told you that he could see right through that mare. I've been observant in these matters since childhood and could see that the mare recognized in him an expert and held herself erect before him— "Look at me and admire me!" And that dignified Tatar looked and looked at the mare without walking round her like our officers do, for they always fuss around a horse and can't stand still for a minute, but he, that Tatar, just kept his eyes fixed on her; suddenly he let the whip fall and kissed the tips of his fingers in silence: "A titbit," he seemed to say. And again he sat down on the rug with his legs crossed under him, and the mare pricked up her ears and began snorting and prancing to show off her paces.

The gentlemen standing round now began to outbid each other: the first bid a hundred rubles, the next a hundred and fifty and so on, each one raising the bid. The mare was certainly a fine animal, not over big, somewhat like an Arab, well proportioned, with a small head, a full eye and sharp ears; her sides were sound, her back dead straight, her legs light and shapely and the swiftest ever. I'm a lover of such beauty and just couldn't take my eyes off that mare. Khan Jangar, seeing that everybody coveted her and that they were raising the price like madmen, nodded to a black-jowled Tatar boy who jumped on the beauty's back and off she went like the wind—he sat her, you know, Tatar fashion, guiding her with his knees and she took wings under him and flew along like a bird, never so much as swaying and whenever he bent over her withers and called to her she disappeared from sight in a whirlwind of sand. "You little snake," I thought to myself, "you little bird of the steppes—oh, where do such horses come from?" And I felt that my soul longed for that beautiful horse with all the passion in me. The Tatar boy brought her back and she just snorted once through both nostrils to blow the wind out of her lungs; she shook off all weariness, and after that not another snort or gasp did she give. "Oh, what a piece of horse flesh," I thought, "how I could love her!" If the Tatar had asked me not only for my own soul but for my father's and mother's as well, I would willingly have traded them for the mare, but how could I even dream of getting such a flier when the gentlemen and army buyers had between them raised her price to God knows what; but even that was nothing compared with what was to come before the auction was over and before anybody got her. We noticed a fast rider on a black horse coming from beyond the Sura, from Seliksa—he flew up waving a wide-brimmed hat, jumped off his horse, went straight to the white mare and stopped dead in front of her, just like the first statue.

"The mare's mine," he said.

But the Khan replied:

"Oh, no, she's not. These gentlemen are offering me five hundred gold pieces for her."

But that horseman, a huge Tatar with a big paunch, a sunburned face with the skin peeling and looking as if it was torn off in places, and with narrow eyes like little chinks, shouted at the top of his voice:

"A hundred more than anybody else!"

The gentlemen were furious and raised their bids while that dry old Khan Jangar sat there smacking his lips; just then another Tatar came riding up from across the River Sura; he was on a roan horse with a whitish tail and long mane—an awfully thin man, all yellow skin and bone, but he was even keener than the first. He slid off his horse and stood in front of the white mare as though nailed to the ground.

"I'm telling you all—that mare's mine!"

I turned to my neighbour and asked him what he thought the final decision depended on.

"It depends on what Khan Jangar decides," he said. "This isn't anything new; he plays tricks like this at almost every fair. First he gets rid of the ordinary horses he has brought for sale and then, on the last day, produces one or two horses like a conjuror, as though he had had them up his sleeve all the time, and the poor connoisseurs go off their heads; the cunning Tatar has a fine time watching the business and gets money for it, too. Everybody knows this habit of his and expects him to produce a titbit at the last moment as he did today; everybody expects the Khan to leave today and he will go tonight but in the meantime he comes out with this mare."

"It's a marvel of a horse!" I said.

"A real marvel," he said. "He brought her here in the middle of a herd so that nobody could see her, only those two Tatars who have just arrived knew about her, and even to them he said that she was not for sale and sent her off with a special herdsman to graze in the woods; now he produces her and offers her for sale and you'll see what strange things will happen on account of her and what money the dog will get for her. If you like we'll have a bet on who'll get her."

"I don't understand you, what can we bet on?" I asked.

"You'll soon see the passions rise," he replied. "These gentlemen will back out soon and one of the two Asiatics will get the mare."

"Are they so very rich, then?"

"Rich? They've got plenty of money, both of them, and they're crazy about horses; they have big herds of their own and won't let anybody else get a horse they've taken a liking to. All the people here know them; the one with the big belly and peeling face is Bakshei Otuchev and the skinny one is called Chepkun Yemgurcheyev and they're both terrors when it comes to horses. They'll be giving us some fun, soon."

I stopped talking and watched: the gentlemen who had been bidding withdrew and stood looking on while the two Tatars kept pushing each other out of the way and slapping Khan Jangar's hands but both of them held fast to the mare, trembling and screaming.

"I'll give five head" (five horses, that is) "over and above the money," shouted one.

The other screamed:

"The devil you will, you ugly brute—ten!"

Bakshei Otuchev shouted:

"I offer fifteen."

And Chepkun Yemgurcheyev:

"Twenty!"

And Bakshei:

"Twenty-five!"

And Chepkun:

"Thirty!"

That was the limit either of them could bid to—Chepkun said thirty and Bakshei also offered thirty and no more. Then Chepkun added a saddle and Bakshei a saddle and a robe, Chepkun also added a robe and then they hesitated, trying to think of how to get the better of each other. Then Chepkun shouted, "Listen, Khan Jangar, I'll send you one of my daughters as soon as I get home," but Bakshei, too, offered a daughter and so they could not outbid each other. Then the whole mob of Tatars who had been watching the bidding suddenly started shouting and screaming in their own lingo. They tried to pull Bakshei and Chepkun apart to prevent them from completely ruining themselves, trying to persuade them to stop.

"What's all the noise about?" I asked the man next to me.

"Those Tatars are sorry for Chepkun and Bakshei; they think they've gone too far and want to separate them and knock some sense into them; somehow or another they hope to persuade one of them to give way."

"How can either of them give up the mare if they both like her so much?" I asked. "They can't do it."

"Oh, no," he replied. "The Asiatics are sensible people who take everything seriously; they realize it isn't fair for either of them to ruin himself and will give Khan Jangar whatever price he asks and decide who's to get the mare by a public flogging match."

"And what d'you mean by a flogging match?" I asked.

But he said:

"Watch, instead of asking questions. It's something you have to see for yourself and it's going to start soon."

So I watched and saw that both Chepkun Yemgurcheyev and Bakshei Otuchev were in a calmer mood and soon they broke away from the Tatar peacemakers, ran up to each other and shook hands. "Good," said one, "it's a bargain!" and the other said just the same, "Good, it's a bargain!"

And with that they both stripped off their robes and their long tunics and their cotton shirts and flopped down on the ground wearing only their baggy striped trousers and sat quite still there, opposite each other, like two sand-pipers.

Never before in my life had I come across such wonders and I watched closely to see what would come next. They grasped each other firmly by the left hand, spread their legs and put their feet firmly together, one against the other, and shouted:

"Give 'em to us!"

I had no idea what they were asking for but the Tatars in the crowd, they knew, and answered back:

"Right now, right now!"

Then a dignified old Tatar stepped out of the crowd with two huge horse-whips in his hands, and he measured them carefully and showed them to the public and to Chepkun and Bakshei.

"Look," he said, "they're both the same length."

"The same," the crowd shouted, "we can see they're both the same and both well made. Let them begin!"

Bakshei and Chepkun were both anxious to grab those whips but the grave old Tatar said, "Wait!" Then he himself handed the whips to them, one to Chepkun and the other to Bakshei, and clapped his hands softly three times, one, two, three.... No sooner had he clapped for a third time than Bakshei lashed out with his whip across Chepkun's bare shoulders and he replied in like manner. And so they kept on at it, regaling each other, staring straight into each other's eyes, the soles of their feet pressed hard together, left hands firmly clasped and lashing out with the whips in their right hands.... But oh, how they flogged each other! One of them would give a real good lash and the other would answer with an even better one. Their eyes glazed, their left hands grew stiff, but neither one nor the other would give in.

"I suppose for them it's like our gentlemen at a duel?" I asked my acquaintance.

"Yes," he replied, "it's a kind of duel except that they're fighting for money and not for honour."

"Can they go on flogging one another like that for a long time?" I asked.

"As long as they please, or as long as their strength lasts."

As they continued slashing away at each other, the people began to argue, some saying, "Chepkun will outflog Bakshei," and the others saying, "Bakshei will outflog Chepkun," and those who liked the idea made bets. Some backed Chepkun and some Bakshei, whichever they fancied. They'd look knowingly at their eyes and their teeth, take a look at their backs for certain signs that would tell them who was the more dependable, and that one they would back. The man I'd been talking to was also a spectator with some experience and at first he favoured Bakshei but later he said:

"Ah, well, that's my twenty kopeks gone! Chepkun's going to beat Bakshei!"

"Who knows?" I responded. "You can't tell yet. They're both sitting pretty."

"They're both sitting tight, all right," he answered, "but they're behaving differently."

"It looks to me as if Bakshei were hitting harder," I said.

"That's the whole trouble," he said. "Yes, the twenty kopeks I put on him are lost. Chepkun will outflog him."

"What a strange business," I thought. "I can't make head or tail of this fellow's arguments, and yet," I said to myself, "he must know a lot about this game or he wouldn't bet."

I got very curious, you know, and kept bothering my acquaintance:

"Tell me, why you're so worried about Bakshei?"

And he said:

"Now aren't you a silly yokel! Just take a look at Bakshei's back!"

I took a look—nothing wrong with it—a fine, strong back, big and plump as a cushion.

"And now d'you see how he's hitting?" he asked me.

I took another look and could see he was hitting with great fury, his eyes were popping out of his head and every time he hit Chepkun he drew blood.

"And now just think how his insides are working."

"What have his insides got to do with it? All I can see is that he's bolt upright, his mouth is wide open and he's taking in plenty of air."

My acquaintance then said:

"That's just what's wrong, you see. He has a broad back and the whole length of the whip-lash lies on it, he hits fast and he's losing his wind; he's breathing through an open mouth and the air he's gasping in will burn up his insides."

"So you think Chepkun more reliable?" I asked.

"He certainly is," he replied. "You see he's as dry as a stick, all skin and bone, and his back is just like a bent shovel so that the whole length of the whip-lash can't lie on it but only catches him in places; and then, you see, he's flogging Bakshei steadily, with a pause after every blow and taking the whip away slowly, not all at once, so as to raise a weal. That's why Bakshei's back is all bloated, and it's as black as a kettle, but it's not bleeding so all the pain stays inside the body; the skin on Chepkun's back is like the crackling on roast pork, as it cracks the blood flows and the pain comes out with it and that's why he'll outflog Bakshei. Now do you understand?"

"Yes," I said, "I see it all right," and, sure enough, I there and then understood this whole Asiatic business and got greatly interested in it: "What would be the best thing for me to do under such circumstances?" I wondered.

"And, you will notice," my acquaintance continued, "the most important thing is the way that damned Chepkun beats time with that ugly mug of his. D'you see him? He lashes out, waits and takes his punishment and shuts his eyes at each blow and then opens them again. That's easier than having his eyes pop out of his head like Bakshei's. He has his teeth clenched and he's bit his lips, too, and that also makes it easier because with his mouth shut there won't be any extra burning inside."

I kept all those curious points in mind, looked more closely at Chepkun and at Bakshei and began to see for myself that Bakshei would certainly go under for his wide-open eyes were already glazed, his lips were drawn out in a thin line and were parted in a fixed grin. . . . And, sure enough, we saw how Bakshei struck Chepkun another twenty blows or so, each weaker than the last, until he suddenly flopped back, let go of Chepkun's hand and continued moving his right hand as though he were hitting with it; but he was already unconscious, in a dead faint. Then my acquaintance said:

"That's that, and my twenty kopeks are gone."

Then all the Tatars started chattering and congratulating Chepkun.

"What a head he's got on him," they shouted. "Chepkun Yemgurcheyev, he's got brains, he's knocked Bakshei right out! The mare's yours, get on her!"

Khan Jangar himself got up from his rug, walked up and down smacking his lips and said:

"It's yours, Chepkun, the mare's yours. Mount and ride her; you can rest on her back."

Chepkun got up; the blood was streaming down his back, but he seemed all right and wouldn't let anybody see he was in pain. He put his robe and long tunic on the mare's back, flung himself across her flat on his belly and rode off in that position; I was left feeling miserable again.

"Well," I thought, "now that's all over my own troubles will be filling my head again." I just hated to have to think about it.

Just then my acquaintance turned to me, and I'm glad he did.

"Wait a bit, don't go," he said. "There'll be something else yet."

"What else can there be?" I asked. "It's all finished."

"No, it isn't," he said. "Just look how Khan Jangar is lighting his pipe. See, he's taking a pull at it, that's a sure sign he's up to some Asiatic mischief!"

And I thought to myself: "If only something of the kind were to start again and somebody were to back me, I wouldn't let the horse go!"

CHAPTER THE SIXTH

Believe it or not, but everything turned out as I had hoped. Khan Jangar sat pulling away at his pipe, while from a nearby wood another Tatar boy came galloping up on a fresh horse, not a mare this time, like the one Chepkun had won from Bakshei, but a black colt that defied all description. Have you ever watched a corn-crake run along the boundary between the corn-fields? Have you seen how he spreads his wings but doesn't spread his tail out in the air like other birds do but just lets it hang down, and his legs hang down, too, as though he had no use for them? He looks as if he is being carried along on air. The new horse, like that bird, seemed to move by some power other than its own.

I'm telling you the truth when I say that colt didn't even fly,—the ground just kept increasing behind it as it went. Never in my life had I seen such a horse, I couldn't even guess how much it was worth, what treasure would be needed to buy it, who, what prince, could acquire it? Least of all did I imagine that he might become mine.

"Did he really become yours?" asked the astounded listeners, interrupting the story-teller.

"Yes, mine, mine by right, even if for one minute only, and if you'll be kind enough to listen I'll tell you how it was."

The gentlemen began bidding for the horse and my remount officer, the one I'd given the baby to, made his bids as well; a Tatar by the name of Savakirei, however, took the field against them all, as though he were their equal; a stocky little man, he was, well-built and with a quick temper, his head was shaven smooth as though it had been turned on a lathe and it was round and smooth like a freshly cut cabbage and his face was as red as a carrot and in general he had a fresh look about him. "There's no sense in wasting money," he shouted. "Let anybody who likes put down as much as the Khan asks and try whipping me for the horse!"

Needless to say the gentlemen could not accept and withdrew at once; how, indeed, could any of them start a whip fight with that Tatar? He, the heathen, would have killed 'em all. My remount officer wasn't in funds at the time, he'd lost at cards again in Penza, but I could see he was crazy to get that horse. So I went up behind him and tugged at his sleeve and told him not to offer any more than the Khan asked but to let me settle with Savakirei. He didn't like the idea but I tried to persuade him.

"Do me a favour," I said. "I'd like to try."

And so we agreed.

"You and that Tatar.... Did you really whip each other?"

"Yes, we settled the matter by a flogging arrangement and I got the colt."

"So you beat the Tatar?"

"Yes, I won. It wasn't easy, but I got the better of him."

"It must have been terribly painful, wasn't it?"

"Well, how can I put it?... At first it did hurt, and very much so, especially as I wasn't used to it and that Savakirei knew how to hit so that your back swelled up but did not bleed. But I thought of a trick of my own to use against his skill: every time he lashed me I'd pull up the skin of my back under the whip-lash and did it so cleverly that the skin broke; so I saved myself from a swollen back and whipped Savakirei to death."

"Do you mean to say you actually killed him?"

"Yes, I did. It was his own stubbornness, you see, and because of his policy, because he acted so foolish, he departed from this world," the story-teller explained, quite good-humouredly and rather casually; seeing that the other passengers looked at him askance, if not in absolute horror, he seemed to feel that there was a need of further explanation.

"You see," he continued, "it was his fault, not mine. Throughout Rhyn Sands he was famous as the strongest man and his pride would not allow him to give in to me for anything in the world; he wanted to take his punishment honourably so as not to dishonour the whole Asiatic nation, but the poor chap couldn't stand it, couldn't stand up against me and I suppose that was because I kept a copper coin in my mouth. That helps wonderfully! I kept biting on it so as not to feel the pain, and to distract my thoughts I counted the blows in my mind and so I was all right."

"How many did you count?" one of the listeners asked.

"I can't say for certain, but I remember I counted up to two hundred and eighty-two and then suddenly got sort of dizzy, lost count for a minute and started hitting without counting. Anyway, soon after that Savakirei aimed his whip at me for the last time but couldn't strike, fell forward on me like a dummy and when they looked at him he was dead. . . . Oh, what a fool he was! What had he suffered so much for? I nearly landed in prison on account of him. The Tatars didn't care a bit—I'd killed him, so well and good, according to the rules he could just as well have whipped me to death. But it was our Russians—it upset me that they simply couldn't understand anything and made a terrible fuss.

" 'What do you want?' I said. 'What's it got to do with you?'

" 'Why,' they said, 'you've killed the Asiatic.'

" 'So what if I did? Wasn't it done by agreement? Perhaps it would have been better for him to kill me?'

" 'If he had killed you,' they said, 'it would have been all right because he's a heathen, but you'll have to be put on trial as a Christian. Come along to the police station,' they said.

" 'Oh, no, my dear friends,' I said to myself. 'It'll be as easy to put the wind on trial as me.' As I don't know of anything worse than the police I straight away dodged behind one Tatar and then behind another and whispered to them:

"'Save me! You saw for yourself it was a fair fight. . . .'

"They took pity on me and pushed me from one to the other and hid me."

"Excuse me, but how did they *hide* you?"

"I fled with them to their steppe."

"To their steppe?"

"Yes, all the way to Rhyn Sands."

"And did you stay there long?"

"Ten whole years: I was twenty-three when they took me to Rhyn Sands with them and I was in my thirty-fourth year when I ran away."

"Did you like living in the steppe or not?"

"I didn't like it. What is there to like? I was fed up all the time but I couldn't get away."

"Why not? Did the Tatars keep you in a pit or watch you all the time?"

"Oh, no, they're kindly people and wouldn't let anybody treat me so dishonourably as to keep me in a pit or in stocks, they just said to me, 'You be our friend, Ivan, we're very fond of you,' they said, 'so live with us in the steppe and make yourself useful, treat our horses and help the women.'"

"Did you doctor them?"

"I did. I was just like a doctor to them, I treated them and their horses and their cattle and their sheep, but most of all I attended their wives, the Tatar ladies."

"Do you know anything about the treatment of illnesses?"

"How shall I put it?. . . Is there anything so wonderful in it, after all? If anybody got ill I'd give him aloe pitch or galangal root and the sickness would pass. Luckily they had plenty of aloe pitch: a Tatar found a whole sackful in Saratov and brought it back with him but until I came they didn't know what to do with it."

"Did you settle down amongst them?"

"No, I didn't, I was always trying to get back."

"Couldn't you really get away from them?"

"No, I couldn't, although if my feet had stayed their proper shape I should soon have got back to my own country."

"What happened to your feet?"

"I was bristled after I tried to run away."

"What's that? Pardon us, but we've no idea what you mean by *bristled*."

"That's a common trick with them: if they take a liking to someone and want to keep him and he gets despondent and tries to escape they do something to prevent his running away. They did it to me after I'd tried to run away and got lost in the steppe. They caught me and said, 'Ivan,' they said, 'you must be our friend and so you won't run away again we'd better cut your heels and stick a few bristles in them.' In this way they crippled my feet and I had to crawl on all fours all the time."

"Please be good enough to tell us how they perform this terrible operation."

"They do it quite easily. About ten of them threw me on the ground and said, 'You shout, Ivan, as loud as you can so that you'll feel better when we start cutting.' They sat on top of me and one of them, a master at the business, cut the skin on my heels in a second, stuck some chopped hair from a horse's mane in the wound, pulled the skin back over the hair and stitched it up with gut. After that, I admit, they bound my hands for about ten days as they were afraid I might make my wounds fester and get the bristles out with the matter. As soon as the skin healed they let me go, saying:

" 'Now, Ivan, you're our friend now and you can never go away from us again.'

"As soon as I tried to stand up on my feet, down I flopped on the ground again, for the chopped hair under the skin of my heels dug into the living flesh and hurt so terribly I couldn't take a single step and couldn't even stand on my feet. I had never wept before in my life but on that occasion I bawled at the top of my voice.

" 'What have you done to me?' I cried. 'You damned Asiatics, I'd rather you killed me outright than make a cripple of me for the rest of my life so that I can't even walk!'

" 'It's nothing, Ivan,' they said, 'you shouldn't make a fuss about a little thing like that!'

" 'What little thing?' I cried. 'You cripple a man and then tell him not to make a fuss!'

" 'You'll get used to it,' they said, 'don't step on your soles but walk bandy-legged, on your ankle bones.'

" 'Oh, you villains!' I thought to myself, but turned away from them and said no more. I made up my mind that I'd rather die than follow their advice and walk bandy-legged on my ankle bones. After that I lay around for a long time until I got fed up with it and started practising and gradually got used to hobbling about on my ankles. They never laughed at me because of that and even said:

" 'That's very nice, Ivan, you walk beautifully now.' "

"What an awful misfortune, but tell us how you tried to run away and how you got caught."

"It was really impossible, the steppe is quite flat, there are no roads and above all one has to eat.... I walked for three days until I grew as weak as a kitten, then I caught a little bird with my hands and ate it raw, but I was soon hungry again and there was no water.... How could I keep going? I collapsed and they found me and brought me back."

One of the listeners remarked with regard to the bristling, that walking on one's ankles must have been most awkward.

"At first it was very difficult," Ivan Severyanich replied, "even when I'd got the knack of it I couldn't walk very far. I can't deny that after that those Tatars tried to make things easy for me.

" 'You can't manage now, Ivan,' they said. 'You can't fetch water or do anything like that, so take yourself a Natasha. We'll give you a good Natasha, any one you like.'

"But I said:

" 'What do I want to choose for? There's only one thing they're any good for. Give me the first one you come across.'

"And without further discussion they married me."

"What? Married you to a Tatar woman?"

"Naturally to a Tatar woman. First to one of the wives of Savakirei, whom I'd beaten at the whipping match, but she, this Tatar woman, wasn't my sort. A queer one, she was, and seemed scared of me and didn't give me any fun. I don't know whether she missed her husband or whether she had something else on her mind, but when the Tatars saw she was a burden to me they brought me another, a little girl, no more than thirteen years old. They said to me:

" 'Take this Natasha, Ivan, she'll be more fun for you.' "

"And was she really more fun?" the listeners asked Ivan Severyanich.

"Yes, she was," he replied, "only sometimes she'd amuse me and at others she'd annoy me with her mischief."

"How was she mischievous?"

"In different ways, just as the fancy took her. She'd jump on my knees, for instance, or when I was sleeping she'd kick my cap off my head, and fling it as far away as she could and then laugh at it. When I'd threaten her she'd roar with laughter and dart about like a pixie and I couldn't catch her because I had to crawl on all fours and I'd slip and start laughing myself."

"Did you shave your head and wear a skull-cap when you lived in the steppe?"

"Yes, I shaved my head."

"Why? Did you want to please your wives?"

"No, it was more for the sake of cleanliness, there are no bath-houses there."

"So you had two wives at the same time?"

"Two in one steppe and afterwards, when another khan, Agashimola, carried me off from Yemgurcheyev, he gave me two more."

"But," one of the listeners questioned him again, "how could they carry you off?"

"By deceit. From Penza I had run away with Yemgurcheyev's Tatars and lived for five years in their camp where all the Tatar princes and sheikhs and sheikhzadas used to foregather for celebrations—even Khan Jangar and Bakshei Otuchev used to come."

"The one Chepkun flogged?"

"Yes, the very same."

"How was that? Didn't he bear any grudge against Chepkun?"

"For what?"

"Because he beat him and took the horse."

"No, in such cases they never bear malice: the match was by common consent and the winner took the prize, that's all. Khan Jangar, though, did once say to me:

" 'Oh, Ivan, Ivan, how stupid of you to sit down and flog Savakirei for that Russian prince when I was just going to enjoy a good laugh watching the prince himself take off his shirt.'

" 'You'd never have lived to see it,' I said.

" 'Why not?' he asked.

" 'Because our princes are faint-hearted and have no courage at all,' I said, 'and their strength isn't much, either.'

"He understood me.

" 'I could see there were no real lovers of sport amongst them,' he said. 'If they want anything they expect to get it for money.'

" 'That's true enough, they can't do anything without money.'

"Anyway that Agashimola lived with his horde a long way off and his herds grazed somewhere near the Caspian. He liked to doctor himself and asked me to come and treat his wife. He promised Yemgurcheyev many head of cattle to let me go. Yemgurcheyev did so. I took my aloe pitch and galangal root with me and off we went. Once he had got me Agashimola moved his horde to another place eight days' ride from there."

"Did you go on horseback?"

"Of course."

"But what about your feet?"

"What about them?"

"That chopped hair you had in your heels, didn't it trouble you any more?"

"Not at all. They had it all thought out, you see. When they bristle a man he can't walk but he can ride a horse better than before because the way he walks makes his legs bandy and they stay that way and fit round a horse's flanks like a hoop so that he can't be thrown off."

"Well, what happened to you in the new steppe?"

"More troubles and worse ones."

"Still you didn't perish."

"As you see, I didn't."

"So please be kind enough to tell us what further troubles you had to bear with Agashimola."

"Gladly."

"As soon as Agashimola's Tatars reached camp they straight away moved on to a new place and wouldn't let me go.

" 'Why do you want to go back to Yemgurcheyev, Ivan,' they said. 'Yemgurcheyev is a thief. Stay with us. You'll like it better and we'll give you lovely Natashas. You only had two Natashas there but we'll give you more.'

"But I refused.

" 'I don't want any more,' I said. 'What can I do with more of them?'

"But they said:

" 'Oh, you don't understand: it's better to have more Natashas to bear you a lot of Kolyas who'll call you daddy.'

" 'How can I bring up Tatar children,' I said. 'If I could baptize them and there was someone to give them Holy Communion it would be different, but as it is, however many children I have, they will all be yours and not Orthodox Christians, and when they grow up they'll cheat Russian peasants!'

"So I took only two wives, no more, for if there are too many women about they only start quarrelling, even Tatar women, and I'd be busy keeping order all the time."

"Did you love those new wives of yours?"

"What?"

"Those new wives—did you love them?"

"Love them? Oh, you mean *that*? Well, the one I got from Agashimola was all right, she always tried to please me and ... well ... I was sort of sorry for her."

"And the young girl, the one who had been your wife before? You must have liked her even more, didn't you?"

"She was all right, I was sorry for her, too."

"You probably missed her when they kidnapped you and took you from one horde to another?"

"No, I didn't."

"But you probably had children by those first wives of yours?"

"Of course. Savakirei's wife bore me two Kolyas and a Natasha and the little one bore me six in five years, once she had two Kolyas at the same time."

"And why, may we ask, do you call them all Kolyas and Natashas?"

"That's Tatar lingo. They call all grown-up Russians *Ivan*, women are *Natasha* and boys are *Kolya*. Although my wives were Tatars they called them Natasha on account of me and the boys they called Kolya. It goes without saying that that's all superficial, because they never received the church sacraments and I did not consider them my children."

"How was that? Why didn't you consider them yours?"

"How could I when they hadn't been baptized or anointed with chrism."

"What about your paternal feelings?"

"What about them?"

"Didn't you love those children even a little? Didn't you ever caress them?"

"Caress them? Sometimes when I was alone one of them would run up to me and I ... er ... I'd pass my hand over his hair and pat his head and say to him, 'Go to your mother!' It didn't happen very often because I had no time for them."

"Why not? Were you very busy?"

"No, it wasn't that, but I sat brooding all the time, I wanted to go home to Russia."

"Couldn't you get used to the steppe, even in ten years?"

"No. I wanted to go home.... The melancholy would

get me, especially in the evenings and even in the day-time when it was a fine hot day. The camp would be quiet, the Tatars would keep out of the heat in their tents and would sleep; then I would raise the flap of my tent and look out into the steppe, first one way and then the other—the same all round.... A cruel burning wilderness ... a great expanse with no end to it ... grass everywhere, feather-grass, white and tufted, rising and falling like the waves of a silver sea and the scent of it was carried on the breeze. There would be a smell of sheep and the sun would blaze and burn and the steppe, like the sorrows of life, seemed endless, just as my yearning was like a bottomless pit. I would stare without knowing what I was looking at and suddenly, I know not where from, a monastery would appear, or a church, and I would remember Christendom and weep...."

Ivan Severyanich was overcome by his memories, stopped, heaved a deep sigh and then continued:

"It was still worse in the salt marshes by the Caspian. The sun glared and burned, the salt marsh glittered and so did the sea. The dizziness from that glitter was even worse than from the feather-grass and you would wonder where in the world you were, whether you were alive or dead and being hopelessly tormented in hell for your sins. Where the steppe is covered with thick feather-grass it is pleasanter; occasionally in some gully you see a patch of blue sage or small bushes of wormwood and savory make a splash of white. But in the salt marsh there is nothing but that glitter. There, sometimes, the grass would catch fire and the flames would race across the steppe—then there would be a general to do: bustards and snipe would take to the air and give us some sport. We'd hunt the great bustards on our horses and lash them to death with long whips; before we could look round we would have to

ian gentlemen out of the public gardens and how he had once gone stark naked to visit the governor's wife. "And now," he said, "I've been cursed for my wilfulness and my entire constitution has turned to stone and I have to soften it, so give me some vodka. I can't pay money for it but instead I'll eat the glass together with it."

So one of the gentlemen ordered a glass of vodka for him to see how he would eat the glass. He emptied the glass in one gulp and quite fair and square began to crunch the glass between his teeth and ate it in front of everybody; the people all stared at him in amazement and burst out laughing. I was sorry for him for he was a man of noble birth so addicted to drink that he would risk his innards for it. So I thought that I ought at least to let him wash the broken glass out of his guts and ordered him another glass at my expense but did not insist on his eating the glass. I said:

"Don't! Don't eat it!"

He was deeply touched by that and offered me his hand.

"I suppose," he said, "you were once a gentleman's servant?"

"I was," I said.

"I could see at once," he said, "that you were different from these swine. *Grand merçi*," he said, "for that."

I said:

"Don't mention it, go your way in peace."

"No," he said, "I'd be very glad to talk to you. Move up a little and I'll sit down beside you."

"All right," I said, "sit down then."

So he sat down beside me and began to tell me what a famous family he came from and what a splendid education he had been given and again he said:

"What's that you're drinking? Tea?"

"Yes," I said, "tea. You may have some with me if you like."

"Thank you," he said, "but I can't drink tea."

"Why not?"

"Because," he said, "my head isn't made for tea, my head's made for desperate things; I'd rather you ordered me another glass of vodka!"

In this way he begged one, then a second and then a third glass of vodka and I was beginning to get fed up with it. But what I disliked most of all was that he said little that was true. He was boasting all the time and showing off, first telling the most monstrous yarns about himself and then debasing himself and weeping quite suddenly and all out of vanity.

"Just think what kind of man I am," he said. "God created me in the same year as the emperor so I'm the same age as he is."

"So what about it?" I asked.

"There's this about it—what is my position in the world, in spite of all that? In spite of all that I'm of no consequence and have turned out a nonentity and, as you have just seen, I am despised by everybody."

Having said that he called for more vodka, a whole decanter this time, and went on to tell me a long yarn about how the merchants made mock of him in the taverns and ended up by saying:

"They're ignorant people. They think it's an easy job to keep on drinking and eating the glass as a titbit. But it's a tough job, brother, even an impossible one for many people, but I've trained my constitution to it because I realize that a man has to make his living and I can bear it."

"But why," I said, "do you let this habit get the better of you? Why not give it up?"

"Give it up!" he exclaimed. "Why, my dear fellow, that's impossible."

"But why?" I asked.

"It's impossible," he replied, "for two reasons. Firstly because I should never get to my bed unless I were full of spirits but would go wandering the streets and secondly and principally, my Christian sentiments do not permit it."

"What on earth are you talking about?" I exclaimed. "I can well believe that you wouldn't get to bed because you'd be hunting all the time for a drink, but I cannot possibly believe that Christian sentiments won't allow you to drop that harmful filth."

"I see that you don't want to believe it," he said. "That's what everybody else says, too. But what do you think would happen if I were to drop my boozing habit? Would not somebody else pick it up? And would he thank me for it or not?"

"God forbid," I said. "I certainly don't think he would like it."

"Aha," he said, "so you see how it is, and since it's necessary that I should suffer at least you ought to honour me for it and order me another decanter of vodka."

I stood him another decanter and sat and listened to him, for I was beginning to find him amusing; he went on in the following way:

"It is fitting that this torment should end with me, for I," he said, "am a man of good family and upbringing and when I was still a little boy I could say my prayers in French. But I knew no mercy, I tortured people, I lost my serfs at cards, I separated mothers from children, I married a rich woman and tormented her to death and, finally, although I was myself the cause of all my troubles, even murmured against my

167

Creator for having given me such a nature. And so he has punished me by giving me another nature and I haven't got any pride left. You may spit in my eye or slap my face as long as I can get drunk and forget myself."

"Don't you ever grumble now," I asked, "because you have your present nature?"

"No," he answered, "I don't for although it is worse yet it is better."

"I don't understand you, I don't know what you're talking about—worse yet better!"

"And yet it's so simple," he replied. "Now I know only one thing: although I'm ruining myself I can no longer ruin others since everybody turns away from me. Today," he said, "I am like unto Job smitten with boils and therein lies my happiness and my salvation." Having said that he drank up his vodka and asked for another decanter, saying:

"Remember, my friend, never to scorn any man, for nobody can tell why a man is tormented with a passion and has to suffer. We, the possessed, suffer that it may be easier for others. If you, too, sorrow on account of some passion, do not wilfully abandon it lest another should pick it up and be tormented, but instead look around for a man who would be willing to take the weakness upon himself."

"But where can I possibly find such a man?" I asked. "Nobody would ever agree to such a thing."

"Why not?" he replied. "You haven't even far to go for such a man sits before you. I am that man."

I said:

"You're joking, surely."

But he suddenly jumped up and said:

"No, I'm not joking and if you don't believe me you can test me."

"How can I test you?" I asked.

"Very easily. Do you want to know what kind of gift I possess? For, brother, I possess a great gift: as you see I'm drunk.... Am I drunk or am I not?"

I looked at him and could see that his face was purple, that he was quite fuddled and unsteady on his legs.

"Yes, of course you're drunk," I said.

But he replied:

"Now turn towards that icon and say the Lord's Prayer to yourself."

I turned away and just had time to say the Lord's Prayer over once to myself, looking at the icon, when that drunken gentleman again called to me:

"Look at me now: am I drunk or not?"

I turned round: he stood there smiling and looked as sober as if he had never had a drink.

I said:

"What's the secret? What does it mean?"

"It's no secret," he replied, "it's something called magnetism."

"What's that?" I asked.

"It is a certain will power that is given to a man," he said, "and he cannot lose it by drinking nor in sleep since it is a gift. I have demonstrated it to you so that you may understand that I could stop drinking this minute if I wanted to and never start again, but I don't want any man to start drinking instead of me while I, with my mended ways, should again forget God. But I'm willing and can in one minute remove from any man his desire for drink."

"Do me a favour and remove it from me," I said.

"Do you drink?"

"I do, indeed," I said. "There are times when I drink quite a lot."

"Don't you be afraid," he said, "it is in my hands and I want to repay you for treating me to all that drink. I shall remove it all from you."

"Oh, be so kind, I pray you. Set me free."

"With pleasure, my dear fellow," he said, "with pleasure. I'll do it for your having treated me: I'll remove it all from you and take it on myself."

With that he called for more vodka and two glasses.

"What do you want two glasses for?" I asked.

"One for me and the other for you," he answered.

"I'm not going to drink," I said.

"Shush! *Silence!* Not a word! Who are you, may I ask? You're a sick man."

"Have it your way," I said, "I'm your patient."

"And I," he said, "am a doctor, you will carry out my orders and take your medicine."

He then poured himself and me a glass of vodka and started to make passes with his hands over my glass like the precentor of a church choir.

After he had made a few passes he said:

"Now drink!"

It is true I had my misgivings but I quite frankly wanted a drink of vodka very badly and, as he had ordered me to drink, I said to myself, "Let's try it and see what happens," and drink it I did.

"Well?" he asked. "Did you like it? Did it taste all right or was it bitter?"

"I don't rightly know what to say," I said.

"That's because you haven't had enough," he said, poured out another glass and made more passes over it. He waved and waved his hands, gave them a final shake, made me drink this second glass and again asked what it was like.

I tried a joke on him.

"This one seemed a bit heavy," I said.

He just nodded his head and started making passes over the third glass. "Drink!" he ordered, and I drank.

"This one was a bit lighter," I said.

After that I got hold of the decanter myself and began pouring out for both of us and we went on drinking. He didn't try to stop me but he wouldn't let me drink a single glass until he had made his passes over it and whenever I got my hand on the glass he'd take it out of my hand and say:

"Shush! *Silence! Attendez!*" Then he would wave his hand over it and say, "Now it's ready, *thou canst receive it as it is written.*"

The cure by the former gentleman continued at that tavern until late in the evening. I wasn't troubled about it because I knew that I was drinking to end drinking and not for the pleasure of it. I felt for the money inside my coat and it was there all right, in its proper place, and then went on drinking.

The gentleman I was drinking with told me all about himself, how in his time he had boozed and made merry and he spoke particularly about love and tried to pick a quarrel with me because I knew nothing about love.

"What can I do if I'm not interested in all that nonsense?" I asked. "It's quite enough that you do know all about it and have turned out such a wreck."

But he said:

"Shush! *Silence!* Love is sacred!"

"Nonsense," I said.

"You're a yokel and a rascal, too," he said, "if you dare laugh at what is sacred to the heart and even call it nonsense."

"But it is nonsense."

"But you," he said, "don't know the meaning of beauty, nature's perfection."

"Yes I do," I said. "I understand beauty in horses."

Now he jumped up and tried to strike me.

"Do you call a horse 'beauty,' the 'perfection of nature'?" he said.

As it was getting late he had no time to prove his point and the barman, seeing that we were both drunk, winked to the waiters and six of them rushed up to us and said:

"It's time you got out of here," and they took us under the arms and put us into the street, slamming the doors behind us and locking up for the night.

It was after that that I became so possessed that although many years have passed since then I am to this day not sure what really took place and what forces were acting upon me, but I underwent adventures and temptations such as are not to be found in any one of the Lives of the Martyrs.

CHAPTER THE TWELFTH

The first thing I did after I was thrown out of the tavern was to feel inside my coat to see if my money was safe. So far it was. "Now," I thought, "the whole trouble is how to get the money home safely."

The night was the darkest you could possibly imagine. Near Kursk, you know, we get such nights in summer, pitch dark but exceedingly warm and calm, the stars hang in the sky like lamps before icons and down below the darkness is so thick that you get the impression that someone is touching you all over. At fair time hundreds of wicked people roam the streets and there are many cases of robbery and murder. Although I was fully aware of my own strength I also knew that, firstly, I was drunk and, secondly, if a dozen or so men were to attack me, even my great strength would not prevent my being robbed and, moreover, bold as I was from drink, I still remembered that every·time I got up to pay for drinks my companion, the ragged gentleman, must have seen that I had plenty of money on me. It then occurred to me, you know, that he was perhaps contemplating some evil towards me. Where was he, anyway? We had been thrown out together, so where had he disappeared to so hurriedly?

I stood there peering quietly round me and as I did not know his name I called to him softly:

"Hi, you, magnetizer, where are you?"

Suddenly he rose right up before my eyes like a jack-in-the-box and said:

"Here I am."

It seemed to me that it wasn't the same voice and in the pitch darkness even his mug looked different.

"Come closer," I said, and as he did so I took him by the shoulders and peered down at him but I couldn't make out just who he was. When I touched him I suddenly lost my memory and for no reason at all. All I could hear was him mumbling something in French, "Dee-ka-tee-lee-ka-tee-pay," and I couldn't make head or tail of it.

"What are you mumbling about?" I asked.

And he repeated his French:

"Dee-ka-tee-lee-ka-tee-pay."

"Stop it, idiot," I said. "Tell me in Russian who you are, I've forgotten you."

Again he said:

"Dee-ka-tee-lee-ka-tee-pay: I'm the magnetizer."

"Oh, it's you, you villain," I said. For a brief moment I seemed to remember who he was, but as soon as I looked at him more closely I saw that he had two noses ... two noses, sure enough, and when I began to wonder why that was I again forgot who he was.

"Damn you," I thought to myself, "where the hell could a rascal like you have sprung from?" And again I asked, "Who are you?"

And again he said:

"The magnetizer."

"Get thee behind me," I said, "for you may be Satan himself!"

"I'm not exactly the Devil," he answered, "but something like it."

I struck him on the forehead and he didn't like that and said:

"What are you hitting me for? I'm being so good to you curing you of your passion for drink and you hit me."

No matter how hard I tried I couldn't remember who he was and again I said:

"Who are you?"

"I'm your friend of the evening," he answered.

"All right," I said, "we'll say you're my friend, but you can still do me an injury."

"No, I won't," he said. "I'm going to show you such a *petit-comme-peu* that it will make a different man of you."

"Please stop telling lies," I said.

"But it's true," he said, "really, a *petit-comme-peu....*"

"Will you stop talking French at me, you devil," I said. "I've no idea what your *petit-comme-peu* may be."

"I'll give your life a new meaning for you," he said.

"Well, then, let's say you can, but what sort of new meaning will it be?"

"I will make you able to understand beauty, nature's perfection."

"And how will this understanding come to me so suddenly?"

"Come with me and you'll see."

"Very well," I said, "let's go."

And off we went. Both of us staggered as we walked but still we kept on our feet; I didn't know where we were going but I'd suddenly remember that I didn't know who my companion was and I'd ask again:

"Stop! Tell me who you are or I shan't go with you!"

And so he would tell and I'd seem to remember it for a time and when I did I'd ask him:

"Why is it that I keep forgetting who you are?"

"That," he would reply, "is the effect of my magnetism, but don't you be afraid, it'll soon pass off but in the meantime let me give you a bigger dose of it."

He got hold of me, turned me with my back towards him, took me by the nape of the neck and ran his fingers through my hair. It was uncanny: as he fumbled about behind me it seemed to me that he was trying to crawl inside my head.

"Look here," I said, "whoever you may be, what are you fiddling about behind me for?"

"Just stand still and wait a minute, will you?" he answered. "I'm putting magnetism into you."

"It's very good of you to transfer your power to me," I said, "but are you sure you don't want to rob me?"

This he denied.

"Then I'll see if my money's all right," I said.

I felt under my coat for it—the money was safe.

"Well, I can see you're not a thief," I said, but by that time I'd again forgotten who he was and by now I couldn't even remember how to ask him, so completely was I occupied by the strange feeling that he had gone through the back of my neck and was crawling around inside me looking at the world through my eyes and that my eyes were just plain glass to him.

"What a trick to play on me!" I thought, and asked him:

"What's happening to my eyesight?"

"You have none," he said.

"What nonsense is that?" I said. "What do you mean—I haven't got any eyesight?"

"It's true," he said, "with your own eyes you'll only see what isn't there."

175

"That's another yarn you're telling me," I said. "All right, let me try hard."

I strained my eyes very hard and seemed to see all sorts of ugly mugs on spindly shanks peering at me from behind dark corners and running across the road in front of me or standing at the cross-roads and saying:

"Let's kill him and take away his money!"

Then my gentleman again stood in front of me, his hair bristling and his face shining with a bright light and behind me I heard an awful noise and commotion, voices and twanging instruments and howling and screaming and roars of merry laughter. I looked round and saw that I was leaning against a house with open windows, all lit up inside and that the noise, and the voices, and the twanging of a guitar all came from there and my gentleman was again making passes in front of my face and then over my chest; his hands stopped at my heart and pressed against it, then he seized my fingers and shook them gently, then went back to the hand waving, and so hard that I could see the sweat break out on him.

As the light from those windows shone on me I felt that I was regaining consciousness; I was no longer afraid and said to him:

"Listen to me, whoever you are—Satan, or one of his devils or just a minor imp—be kind enough either to awaken me or make yourself scarce."

In reply to that he said:

"Wait! The time has not yet come, there's still a danger that you may not be able to stand up to."

"What won't I be able to stand?"

"That which is happening in the aerial spheres," he said.

"What?" I said. "I can't hear anything in particular."

He insisted that I wasn't listening properly and spoke to me in the sacred tongue.

"To hear it," he said, "thou must follow him who playeth upon the harp, who inclineth his head to the earth and straineth his ear to the singing and striketh the strings with his hand."

"This is something new," I thought, "this isn't the speech of a drunken man, the way he's talking now."

And he stared at me and quietly made passes over me, all the while exhorting me to obey him.

"The strings sing together," he said, "as they are cunningly struck one with the others, and the harp giveth forth song and the player rejoiceth in its honeyed sweetness."

Believe me, it was just as if I heard no words at all, but as if living water were streaming past my ear and I said to myself:

"Is this a drunkard? See how well he speaks the sacred tongue."

By this time my gentleman stopped fidgeting and said:

"That will be enough for now. Awaken and fortify yourself," he said.

At that he bent down and rummaged for a long time in his trousers' pocket and at last got something out. I looked at it and saw something fuzzy, a fuzzy little piece of sugar, all covered in dirt, from lying so long in his pocket, I suppose. He scratched the dirt off with his thumbnail, blew on it and said:

"Open your mouth."

"What for?" I asked but I opened my mouth wide all the same.

He thrust the piece of sugar between my lips and said:

"Suck, suck boldly, for this is the *magic sugar-mentor* which will give you strength."

Although he used these strange words, I gathered that he was talking about magnetism so I didn't ask any more questions but busied myself sucking the sugar but when I did so I could no longer see the man who had given it to me. Whether he went away somewhere in the darkness or whether he disappeared through the ground, the devil alone knows, but I was left alone with my senses completely restored.

"What's the use of waiting for him," I asked myself, "I must get home now."

The trouble was that I didn't know what street I was in and what kind of house I was standing in front of.

"Is this really a house?" I said to myself, "or am I just seeing things? Maybe it's more witchcraft.... It is night, people are all asleep so why should there be a light here? Still I'd better try.... I'll go in and see what's going on; if they are real people in the house I'll ask them the way home, and if it is only a delusion and there are no living people here what danger can there be? I'll say:

"This is holy ground. Get thee behind me, Satan," and everything will vanish....

CHAPTER THE THIRTEENTH

With bold determination I walked up the front steps, crossed myself and uttered a short prayer, but nothing happened: the house remained standing. It didn't even sway, the doors were open and at the end of a long, wide passage, a lantern with a lighted candle in it hung on the wall. I looked round and saw two more doors on the left, both covered with matting, and over them were strange candlesticks with star-shaped mirrors behind them.

"Well," I wondered, "what sort of house is this? It doesn't look like a tavern, but I can see it is a guest-house of some sort," but just what sort I couldn't make out.

As I listened I heard the strains of a song through one of the doors, a soft sweet song that came straight from the heart and the voice that sang it was as clear

as a bell so that you felt it gripped your heart and you
fell under its spell. I listened without moving and a
moment later the farther door opened and out came a
tall Gypsy in wide silken breeches and a short velvet
jacket: he was showing somebody out of the house
through a special door under the distant lantern, a door
that I had not noticed before. Although I must admit
that I couldn't be quite sure whom he was showing out
of the house, it did seem to me that it was my magnetizer and the Gypsy said to him as he left:

"All right, all right, old friend, don't be angry about
the fifty kopeks, come again tomorrow and if we get
any benefit from *him*, we'll add something for bringing
him here."

With these words he bolted the door and rushed towards me as though he hadn't noticed me before; he
opened the door under the mirror and said:

"Welcome to our house, sir merchant. Come in and
hear our songs. We have some beautiful singers."

He quietly pushed the door wide open before me and
... I don't know what happened to me but everything
seemed so familiar to me that I felt quite at home there.
The room was big but low, the ceiling was sagging and a
big bulge hung down in the middle; it was dark and sooty
and the tobacco smoke was so thick that the big chandelier
under the ceiling was only visible because the candles
were lighted. In the dense smoke below there was a
crowd of people, an awfully big crowd, and in front of
them a young Gypsy girl was singing in that wonderful voice I had heard outside. As I went in she was just
finishing the last bars of her song and her voice sus-
tained the last note and then let it gradually die away.
When her voice died away everything in the room
seemed to die, too. But an instant later everybody jumped
up like mad and began clapping and shouting. I
looked on in absolute bewilderment: where had all the

crowds of people come from, I wondered. It seemed that more and more faces were constantly appearing from out of the smoke.

"Ugh," thought I, "are they not perhaps demons in human shape?"

Then I saw some gentlemen I knew, horse-breeders and remount buyers and prosperous land-owners and merchants whom I knew to be keen horse-lovers. The Gypsy girl was moving about amongst them, such a ... well, it is quite impossible to describe her as a woman, she was like a brightly coloured serpent moving on its tail, her whole body bending lithely and fire blazing in her black eyes. A most charming figure! She was carrying a large tray with glasses of champagne around the edge of it and in the middle was a huge pile of money. There was no silver in the pile, only gold coins and banknotes—blue tits, grey ducks, red heath-cocks, only the white swans were missing.* She would offer a glass of wine to a man and he would drink it and throw some money on the pile, a gold piece or a banknote, according to his whim, and then she would stoop down and kiss him on the lips and curtsey to him. The guests were sitting in a sort of semi-circle and she walked round the first row, then the second and then the third and last, beyond which I was standing behind a chair. She was about to turn back, not wishing to offer me a drink, but the old Gypsy who was walking behind her suddenly let out such a shout:

"Grusha!" and indicated me with his eyes.

She just flickered her eyelashes at him. Lord, what lashes they were! They were long and black and seemed to live a life of their own, fluttering like little birds on

* Blue tits—blue five-ruble banknotes. Grey ducks—grey twenty-five-ruble banknotes. Red heath-cocks—red ten-ruble banknotes. White swans—white hundred-ruble banknotes.—*Tr.*

her cheeks. When the old man shouted his order I saw her eyes blaze up as if her whole being were aroused in anger. She was angry, of course, at being ordered to offer me a drink, but she did her duty, came up to me behind the last row of chairs, bowed and said:

"Drink my health, my dear guest."

So completely did she captivate me that I couldn't even find words to reply to her; she charmed me immediately, that is, when she bowed to me over the tray and I saw the parting of her black hair running like a silver thread over her head and disappearing down her back; I went raving mad and lost my reason completely. I drank her offering and looked at her over the rim of the glass but I couldn't tell whether her skin was dark or fair, all I could see was that the colour glowed beneath her thin skin like a plum in the sunlight and that a vein was throbbing on her lovely temple.

"So that," thought I, "is the real beauty that is called nature's perfection! The magnetizer had spoken the truth: such beauty is not like that of a horse, an animal to be bought and sold."

I drained the glass and banged it down on the tray while she stood waiting to see what value I'd put on her kiss. I put my hand into my pocket but there was nothing there but a few twenty- and twenty-five-kopek silver coins and other small change. "That's not enough," I thought, "that would be an unworthy present for such a beauty, beside I should only lower myself in the estimation of the others."

I could hear the gentlemen saying to the old Gypsy, without troubling to lower their voices:

"Really, Vasily Ivanov, why did you order Grusha to serve the lout? It's an insult to us!"

But he answered them:

"We give place and honour to every guest, gentlemen, and my daughter knows the customs of her Gypsy forefathers. You have no reason to feel resentful for you don't yet know how some of the common people value beauty and talent. I've seen many such examples, gentlemen."

When I heard that I thought to myself:

"May the wolves get you! Surely you don't think you have more feeling than I because you're richer? What is to be, will be. I'll pay the prince back later but now I'll not disgrace myself nor will I throw dishonour upon this unbelievable beauty by my stinginess."

At that I straight away put my hand inside my coat, took out a hundred-ruble white swan from my roll and flicked it on to the tray. The Gypsy girl then took the tray in one hand and with the other wiped my lips with a white handkerchief; she touched my lips with hers so lightly that she didn't even kiss me but instead seemed to smear my lips with some poison and then went away.

When she had gone I would have remained standing where I was but the old Gypsy, Grusha's father, and another Gypsy took me by the arms, dragged me to the front and sat me down next to the police captain and the other gentlemen.

I must admit I didn't like it and wanted to leave but they wouldn't let me, they entreated me to stay and called to Grusha:

"Grusha, sweetest, don't let our dear guest leave us."

She came to me and ... the devil alone knows what she could do with those eyes: one glance and she seemed to infect me.

"Don't offend us," she said, "stay a little longer in our house!"

"Who would dream of offending you," I said and sat down again.

She kissed me again and once more I had the feeling that she touched my lips with a poisoned brush that made my blood burn with pain right to my very heart.

After that the singing and dancing began again and another girl went round with the champagne. She, too, was beautiful, but nothing to compare with Grusha! She wasn't even half as lovely and to show what I thought of her I pulled a handful of silver twenty-five-kopek coins out of my pocket and flung them on the tray. The gentlemen made fun of that but I didn't mind, I was looking only at Grusha, waiting for her to sing alone, without the choir, but she did not. She sat amongst the other Gypsies and sang together with them, but never alone and I couldn't hear her voice. I could only see her dainty little mouth with its white teeth. . . .

"Oh," I thought, "what a miserable fool I am, I came in here for a minute, lost a hundred rubles and won't even hear her sing alone!"

It was my good luck that I was not the only one who wanted to hear her sing: others, important gentlemen, joined voices after a time, shouting:

"Grusha! Grusha! *The Skiff! The Skiff!*"

Then the Gypsies cleared their throats, her younger brother took up his guitar and she began to sing. Their singing, you know, is always something that reaches out for you, something that reaches for your heart and when I heard the voice that had had so much attraction for me even from behind closed doors I was deeply moved, so much was it to my liking! She began, perhaps, somewhat harshly, a little mannishly, something like this: "*The sea is ho-ow-ow-ling, the sea is mo-o-o-oaning. . . .*" and you could really hear the sea moaning and see the little skiff struggling against it. But her voice changed suddenly when she appealed to the star: "*Herald of the day, beautiful morning star, human sorrow cannot touch me whilst thou art there. . . .*" Then came another and unexpected change—all their songs are full of these appeals, they weep and languish, tear your soul out of your body and then they suddenly burst into something quite different, something to make your heart light and merry again. So it was then—she had begun by dashing the skiff against the raging waves but the others suddenly burst out in chorus on a high note:

Ja-la-lá, ja-la-lá,
Ja-la-lá, pringalá!
Ja-la-lá, pringalá!
Hey da chepuringalá!
Hey hop-hi, ta hará!
Hey hop-hi, ta hará! . . .

and then Grusha went round with the tray offering wine and kisses again so I gave her another swan from my roll. People began to look askance at me, for my magnificent gifts lowered their prestige and they felt ashamed to give money after me, but I didn't regret it, I wanted to show what my heart felt, and my soul, and I did. Every time Grusha sang I gave her a swan for her song, I soon lost count and handed them out one after the other so that when any of the others asked for a song she would excuse herself by saying that she was "tired" but I nodded to the old Gypsy, meaning "Can't you make her sing?" and he would turn his eyes on her and she would sing another song. She sang a lot, each song more entrancing than the last, and I kept throwing her swans without counting them until at last—I don't know what hour it was, but day was breaking—she seemed to be really tired and worn out. She cast a meaning glance at me and began to sing, *"Go away, look no more, vanish from my sight."* These words seemed intended to drive me away, but she followed them up with words of inquiry: *"Wilst play with my brave heart and try what power my beauty has o'er thee?"* So I gave her another swan. She kissed me again, unwillingly, as though she were stinging me, and her dark eyes were blazing; it was an evil hour when the other Gypsies burst out in a farewell chorus:

Oh, feel my love, and feel it well,
My darling, as I feel your spell...

and everybody joined in that chorus and looked at Grusha, and I looked at her, too, humming to myself: "Feel my love...." Then the choir broke into a dance chorus —"Dance, house! Dance, stove! The master has no place to lay his head...." The Gypsies and their girls danced and the gentlemen danced, all of them caught up in a whirl as though the house really was dancing. The Gypsy girls pranced in front of the gentlemen and these raced after them, the young ones with wild shouts and the older ones grunting.... I looked round and there was not a man left in his seat. Even those who had reached riper years and from whom I never expected such ribaldry, even they had left their seats. At first some of the more important-looking remained seated, apparently ashamed to join in that riot; they just followed the action with their eyes or pulled at their moustaches until one imp jerked their shoulders and another started tugging at their legs and up they'd jump and throw their legs about although they couldn't dance. The police captain, a man of immense girth and with two married daughters, joined in with his sons-in-law and paced round the room gasping like a huge fish and stamping his feet heavily; a rich hussar remount officer, a fine upstanding young captain and a dashing dancer, made the best showing; arms akimbo, he sent his feet flying left and right, squatting and rising in the dance, simply showing off, and he'd cut all sorts of capers and every time he got near to Grusha, he'd toss back his mop of hair, throw his cap at her feet and shout, "Step on it, crush it, my beauty!" And she ...

what a dancer she was! I've seen actresses dancing on the stage but their dancing was like some unimaginative officer's charger prancing on the parade ground and going through his paces just for the sake of show, without any life in him at all! But Grusha—how she danced, sailing along like a swan, never once swaying, and you hear how inside her, inside that serpent, the tendons were cracking and the marrow flowing from bone to bone and then she would stop dead, her back straight, a shoulder quivering and her eyebrow in line with the toe of her foot. What a picture! Her dance was enough to turn the head of every man in the room; all were drawn towards her in a headlong rush, some had tears in their eyes, others grinned, but all shouted:

"Take everything we have and dance!"—and they threw their money at her feet, some of them gold coins, others, banknotes. The dancing crowd grew continually denser until only I was sitting out and I didn't know how long I'd be able to hold out for I could not bear to see how she kept stepping on that hussar officer's cap. She stepped on it and the devil would pull at my heart-strings; she'd step on again and he'd pull once more, until at last I said to myself, "Why should I torment myself for nothing? I'll let my soul rejoice as it wishes." So I jumped up, pushed the hussar officer out of the way and leaped and squatted in the dance in front of Grusha. To make sure that she would not step on the hussar officer's cap again I invented this:

"You're all shouting that you don't mind giving away all you have," I thought, "but that doesn't astound me at all, and I'll show you that I truly mean it." And I jumped in front of her, took a swan out of my pocket and threw it under her feet, shouting, "Crush it, step on it!" But she wouldn't, she wouldn't, although my swan was more valuable than the hussar's cap she wouldn't even look at it but tried to follow

the hussar; but the old Gypsy—I thank him for it—
saw it in time and stamped his foot at her in anger.
She took the hint and followed me. She sailed after
me with her eyes cast on the ground and she blazed
so with anger that she almost set the ground on fire
like the dragon in the fable, while I kept leaping in
front of her like an imp and every time I leapt I flung
another swan under her feet. I held her in such rev-
erence that I kept repeating to myself, "Didst not thou,
accursed one, create heaven and earth?" and to her
I shouted, "Faster, come on, faster!" all the while
throwing swans to her until at last I felt inside my
coat and found that there were only about ten of them
left. "Well," I thought, "to the devil with them!" and I
crumpled them into a ball and threw them in one
heap at her feet, snatched a bottle of champagne from
the table, knocked off the neck and shouted, "Get out
of the way, sweetheart, or I'll splash you!" and in one
gulp drank it all down to her health, for I felt terribly
thirsty after the dance.

CHAPTER THE FOURTEENTH

"And what happened after that?" we asked Ivan
Severyanich.
"After that everything went the way *he* had prom-
ised."
"The way who had promised?"
"The magnetizer, the man who cast a spell over me.
He had promised to free me of the drink devil and he
did. He did it remarkably well for I've not tasted a
drop since then."
"Well, ye-e-es.... But how did you settle with the
prince for the swans you set free?"
I don't quite know myself, but it all turned out very
simple. I don't remember how I got back home from

the Gypsies, nor how I went to bed, but I remember hearing the prince knocking at my door and calling to me. I wanted to get up from the wooden chest on which I slept but couldn't find the edge of it and so I couldn't get off it. I crawled to one side, no edge, I crawled to the other, again no edge. I lost my way on top of that chest. The prince kept calling me, "Ivan Severyanich" and I answered him, "Just a moment," and kept crawling from side to side and still couldn't find the edge. At last I said to myself, "If I can't get down I'd better make a jump for it." I took a flying leap, intending to jump as far as possible, and something hit me in the face, everything all round me began to ring and crash to the ground and the same behind me, everything there was rattling and crashing to the ground, too. I heard the prince say to his batman, "Get a light, quick!"

I stood still for I didn't know whether this was happening to me in reality or in a dream, for I believed that I still had not reached the edge of my bed; but when the batman brought a light I saw that I was standing on the floor and had poked my head through the door of my master's cabinet and broken all the glass in it.

"How did you manage to get lost like that?"

Very easily: I thought I was sleeping on the chest as usual but apparently I had fallen asleep on the floor when I got home from the Gypsies and had been crawling about looking for the edge and then, when I took that leap, I crashed into the glass cabinet. My wandering about the room was due to that magnetizer: he had driven out the drink devil and in its place had put the vagabond devil in me. Then I remembered his words: "Mind," he said, "it may be worse for you if you leave off drinking," and I went to look for him to tell him he had better demagnetize me back to my old state, but I was too late. He had taken too much on himself and proved unable to stand it; he drank so much at the pub opposite the Gypsy house that night that he died.

"So you remained magnetized?"

"Yes, that's how I remained."

"And did the magnetism affect you for a long time?"

"Why a long time? It's probably still working today."

"It would be interesting to know how you settled with the prince. Surely there must have been some trouble between you about those swans."

"Of course, I had to give an account of what I had done with them, but it didn't seem to matter. The prince also came back after losing at cards and began asking me for money to try his luck again."

"You're wasting your time," I said, "I have no money."

He thought I was joking but I said:

"It's true, while you were away I had a very big outing."

"How could you get rid of five thousand in one outing?" he asked.

"I threw it all to a Gypsy girl ..." I said.

He didn't believe me, but I said:

"Don't believe me if you don't want to, but I'm telling you the truth."

He lost his temper and said:

"Shut the door and I'll show you how to waste government money." But he suddenly changed his mind and said, "Never mind; I'm the same sort as you are, a wastrel."

He went back to his room to finish his night's sleep and I went to sleep in the hayloft. When I next came to my senses I found myself in hospital and was told that I had had delirium tremens and had tried to hang myself, but, thank God, they put me into a straight jacket. When I recovered I went to see the prince in his village, for he had by then retired from the army, and I said to him:

"Your Highness, I want to work for you until I've paid you back."

But he said:

"You can go to the devil."

I could see that he was very angry with me so I went up to him and stood with bowed head in front of him.

"What does that mean?" he asked.

"At least give me a good beating," I said.

But he said:

"Why do you think I'm angry with you? Perhaps I don't even think you were at fault."

"Mercy," I said, "how was I not at fault if I threw all that money away? I know myself that hanging would be too good for a scoundrel like me."

But he replied:

"What can we do about it, my dear chap, if you are an artist?"

"I'm a what?" I asked.

"Yes, I mean it, my dear Ivan Severyanich, my semi-respected sir, you are an artist."

"I can't understand what you are talking about," I said.

"Don't think I mean anything bad," he said, "I, too, am an artist."

"I can understand that all right," I thought to myself, "I'm not the only one who drank himself into D.T.'s."

But he got up, knocked out his pipe on the floor, and said:

"It doesn't surprise me that you threw her all the money you had when I, my dear old chap, gave more for her than I have or ever have had."

I could only stare at him in amazement.

"But, for mercy's sake, Your Highness," I said, "what are you saying? It frightens me even to hear you talk like that."

"You needn't get scared," he said, "for the Lord is merciful and I may find some way out of it, but the fact is that I've paid fifty thousand to the Gypsy camp for that Grusha."

I simply gasped.

"What?! Fifty thousand for a Gypsy girl?! D'you think she's worth it, the serpent?"

"Now, my semi-respected friend," he said, "you're talking more like a fool than an artist. Not worth it! Why, a woman's worth the entire world, for she puts such a curse on you that you can't get cured of it for a whole kingdom while she can cure you of it in a minute."

"Well," I thought, "that's true enough," but all the same I shook my head and said:

"It's an awfully big sum—fifty thousand."

"Yes, yes," he said, "and don't keep repeating it, for I was glad enough when they accepted that much for her and I should have given even more. I'd have given them whatever they asked."

"You should have just spat on the ground, that's all."

"I couldn't, my dear fellow," he said, "I couldn't just spit on the ground."

"Why not?"

"Because I had been so affected by her beauty and talent that I had to get cured or go mad. But tell me truly, she's beautiful, isn't she? Eh, it's true, isn't it? She has something to drive a man mad, hasn't she?"

I just bit my lips and nodded silently: it was true enough.

"Do you know," the prince said, "that I would willingly die for a woman? Can you understand that I'd think nothing of dying for a woman?"

"Why, there's nothing to understand," I said. "Beauty is nature's perfection."

"What do you understand by that?"

"As I understand it, beauty is nature's perfection," I said, "and for a man who has fallen under its spell death may even be a joy!"

"You're a fine fellow, my almost semi-respected and greatly-little-significant Ivan Severyanich!" my prince exclaimed. "That's just it—to die is a joy and that's why I'm so happy that I have turned my life upside down for her sake: I've retired from the army and mortgaged my estate and I shall in future live here and see no one but just look into her face alone."

Here I lowered my voice and whispered:

"What do you mean by 'look into her face'? Is she here?"

And he replied:

"What do you think? Of course she's here."

"Is it possible?" I breathed.

"Just wait here and I'll bring her right now," he said. "You're an artist and I won't hide her from you."

With that he left me and went away. I stood there waiting and thinking to myself:

"It's a bad sign if you insist you don't want to look at any face but hers: you'll soon get tired of her!"

I didn't ponder over all the implications of the prince's words, however, for I began to go hot and cold all over as soon as I realized she was in the same house. "Shall I really see her now?" I wondered. Suddenly they both of them came in, the prince walking ahead, carrying a guitar with a wide scarlet ribbon in one hand and pulling Grusha along with the other, her two hands squeezed between his: she walked with her head bowed, resisting him and not looking at him, only those long, black eyelashes were fluttering on her cheeks like the wings of a bird.

The prince led her into the room, picked her up in his arms and sat her down with her legs under her in the corner of a wide divan; he put a velvet cushion behind her back and another under her right elbow, placed the ribbon of the guitar over her shoulders and her fingers on the strings. He, himself, sat down on the floor beside her and rested his head on her scarlet, morocco-leather slipper and nodded to me to sit down, too.

I dropped quietly to the floor by the door and tucked my feet up under me and there I sat looking at her. So great was the silence that it was sickening and I sat still so long that my knees began to ache but every time I looked up she was still sitting in the same position and when I looked at the prince I saw that he had chewed the ends of his moustache away out of sheer agony of soul—but he spoke no word to her.

I nodded my head to him, indicating that he should ask her to sing and he answered me in pantomime that she wouldn't obey him.

Thus the two of us remained sitting on the floor until suddenly she began to sigh and sob as though in a delirium, tears hung on her eyelashes and her fingers began to hover and hum over the guitar strings like wasps. All at once she began to sing in a very soft voice that seemed as if she were not singing but weeping: "Good people, list to the sorrows of my heart. . . ."

The prince whispered to me, "Well?"

In reply I whispered in French:

"*Petit-comme-peu*," I said and could say no more for at that moment she burst out in a loud voice: "But for my beauty they'll sell me, they'll sell me," and she hurled the guitar far across the room, tore the kerchief from her head and threw herself down on the divan, her face buried in her hands, and began to sob bitterly, and the prince and I, looking at her, began to weep, too. The prince picked up the guitar and did not so much sing as intone a litany: "If only thou knewest the fire of love, how my soul is consumed with yearning...." he groaned and sobbed. Then he sobbed and sang: "Oh, give repose to restless me, give happiness to unhappy me...." He was so utterly wretched that she, I noticed, was beginning to take heed of his tears and his singing; she grew more composed and resigned and then, quite suddenly, she withdrew her hands from her face, and put her arm tenderly round his head like a mother....

Naturally I realized that at that moment she pitied him and would comfort him and heal his burning soul of its great yearning, so I got up and left the room unobserved.

"And then, I suppose, you entered the monastery?" one of the listeners asked.

"No, not then, but later," Ivan Severyanich replied, adding that he was still destined to see a great deal of that woman while he remained in his secular state, that is, until everything fate held in store for her came to pass and his own destiny was fulfilled.

His listeners naturally besought him to relate the story of Grusha, even if only in outline, and Ivan Severyanich complied with their request.

CHAPTER THE FIFTEENTH

You see, Ivan Severyanich began, my prince was a good man at bottom but his character was unstable. If he wanted anything you just had to give it to him immediately or he'd go off his head, and in that state he would give everything in the world to get what he wanted but once he had got it he did not set any value on his good fortune. That was exactly what happened with the Gypsy girl; Grusha's father and the

rest of the Gypsies in his camp had a pretty good idea
of the prince's character when they asked that terrific
price for her, much more than his property warranted,
for although his estate was a good one it had gone to
rack and ruin. The prince did not have such a sum as
the Gypsies asked for Grusha in ready money so he
had to run into debt and resign from the army.

Knowing his habits I did not expect that much good
would come of it for Grusha, and so it turned out. For
a time he was kind and gentle to her and would not
let her out of his sight, he could not bear to be without
her, but suddenly he fell to yawning in her presence
and began asking me to share their company.

"Sit down," he used to say, "and listen."

I would take a chair, sit down somewhere near the
door and listen. And it often happened for when he
asked her to sing she would say:

"Who shall I sing for? You have grown cold and I
want my singing to set a soul ablaze and torment it."

That's why the prince would send for me and he
and I would listen together; after a time Grusha began to ask him to send for me. She grew quite friendly
with me and after she had sung I would often remain
in her apartments with the prince for tea, although I
always sat at a separate table or somewhere near the
window except when the prince was not there and she
would sit me down beside her. Some time passed in
this manner but I could see the prince was getting
more and more worried until one day he said to
me:

"Do you know, Ivan Severyanich, things are in a
bad way."

I said:

"What is there so bad about them? Thank God, you
live as you ought and you have everything you want."

Then he got angry with me.

"What a fool you are, my semi-respected sir," he said. 'You have everything!' What is it that I *have*?"

"Everything you want," I answered.

"It isn't true," he said, "I've grown so poor that I have to think twice before I order a bottle of wine for dinner. Is that the way to live? Is that the way to live, I ask you?"

"Oho," I said to myself, "so that's what's worrying you," and aloud I said, "Even if you do go short of wine it won't hurt you very much for you've got something that's sweeter than wine or honey."

He knew that I was referring to Grusha and looked a bit ashamed of himself and he began to pace the room and wave his hands about.

"Of course ... of course ... naturally ... but only..." he began, "but you see, I have spent the last six months here and not a soul has been near me."

"What do you want with strangers when you've got your heart's desire?"

The prince flared up.

"You understand nothing at all, my dear fellow. It's good if you have both the one and the other."

"Aha," I thought, "so that's the way the wind's blowing," and aloud I said:

"What are we going to do about it?"

"Let's do a bit of horse-dealing," he said. "I'd like to see horse-breeders and remount buyers in my house again."

Horse-dealing is no good and not meant for a gentleman, but I thought that it did not matter what I did to humour the child as long as it did not cry and I said:

"As you will."

We began buying up horses to get into condition for the fairs, but no sooner had we started than the prince got carried away by his new passion: he would raise money and immediately buy up horses, taking anything that came without listening to my advice. We bought up a whole herd but there were no sales. The prince soon got tired of that, dropped the horse business and began trying everything that came into his head: first he got excited about a marvellous flour mill that he was going to build, then he opened a saddler's shop, all of which led to more losses and greater debts, and, what was more serious, his worries increased. He wouldn't stay at home but kept rushing off to one place or another, always on the look-out for something, while Grusha was left alone in a bad way, for she was with child. She was bored to death. "I hardly ever see him," she complained, but she made every effort to put on a bold face: as soon as she saw that he was bored after a day or two at home she would herself suggest:

"You ought to go somewhere, my precious jewel, and enjoy yourself. Why sit with me, I'm a simple, uneducated woman."

Such words would make the prince ashamed of himself and he'd kiss her hands and stick it out for another two or three days, but after that, when he kicked over the traces again, there would be no holding him and he'd leave her for me to look after.

"Take good care of her, my semi-respected Ivan Severyanich," he'd say. "You're an artist, not a wastrel like me, an artist of the highest degree, that's why you know how to talk to her and you are happy in each other's company, but those 'precious jewels' of hers send me to sleep."

I said:

"Why should they? They're terms of endearment."

"They may be terms of endearment but they're stupid and boring, all the same," he said.

I said nothing after that but went to see her regularly: whenever the prince was away I'd visit her in her apartments twice a day, have tea with her and amuse her as well as I could.

She needed cheering up, for if ever she talked at all it was only to complain.

"My dearest Ivan Severyanich," she'd say, "jealousy, my friend, is weighing heavily on me."

I, of course, did my best to talk her round.

"Why worry so much?" I'd say, "wherever he goes he always comes back to you, doesn't he?"

Then she would cry and beat her breast and say:

"Please tell me the truth, dear friend, hide nothing from me—where does he spend his time?"

"With gentlemen," I would say, "with neighbours and in the town."

"But isn't there some woman who keeps him away from me?" she'd ask. "Tell me, perhaps he loved some woman before he knew me and has gone back to her, or perhaps the wretch intends to get married to somebody else." And as she said that her eyes would blaze up so that she frightened me.

I would comfort her but I thought to myself:

"Who knows what he's up to?" for it was very rarely that we saw him at that time.

When the idea occurred to her that the prince might be wanting to marry someone she said to me:

"Go down to town, my dear friend, Ivan Severyanich, go and find out everything for certain and come back and tell me. Don't hide anything from me."

She got more and more persistent in her demands and in the end I felt so sorry for her that I thought: "Come what may, I'll go, although if I do learn that he's unfaithful to her, I shan't tell her; but I'll have a look so that I know what's going on."

As an excuse for going to town I said that I had to

go to the herbalist's myself to buy medicine for the horses, but I didn't just go casually. I had a cunning plan all worked out.

Grusha did not know, and the servants had been strictly forbidden to tell her, that before he knew her the prince had had another mistress, a woman of good breeding, Yevgenya Semyonovna, the daughter of a highly placed civil servant. She was known all over the town as a fine pianist, was a very kind-hearted lady, good-looking, too, and had had a daughter by the prince, but she had grown rather stout and it was said that he had thrown her over on account of that. At that time, however, he still had plenty of money and he had bought a house for the lady and her daughter and they lived on the income from it. After rewarding her in that way the prince never again visited her but our servants still remembered her for her kindness and whenever they were in town used to call on her because they loved her and she was very kind to them and because she was still interested in the prince.

So when I got to town I went straight to her, to this kind-hearted lady and said:

"Yevgenya Semyonovna, I'd like to stay at your place, madame, if I may."

"Of course you may, I'll be very glad," she replied, "but why don't you stop at the prince's flat?"

"Is he here in town?" I asked.

"Yes," she replied, "he's been here for a week or more, getting something going."

"What's he thought of now?" I asked.

"A cloth mill," she said, "he wants to rent it."

"Good gracious, madame," I exclaimed, "what has he got into his head?"

"Why?" she asked, "is that bad?"

"It's not bad," I answered, "only I'm surprised."

She smiled.

"That's not really surprising," she said, "but here's something to surprise you: the prince sent me a letter asking me to receive him today and saying he wants to see his daughter."

"And you, Yevgenya Semyonovna, did you give him permission, madame?"

She shrugged her shoulders.

"Why not? Let him come and look at his daughter." She sighed and sat with her head bowed, deep in thought, still so young and fair and robust, and her manners were so different from Grusha's.... Grusha knew nothing but her "precious jewel" and this one, she was so different. It made me feel jealous on account of Grusha.

"Oho," I thought to myself, "I hope that when he looks at the girl he won't take a glance at you as well, with that insatiable heart of his! If he does no good will come of it as far as Grusha is concerned."

I pondered over this while I was sitting in the nursery where Yevgenya Semyonovna had told the nurse to give me a cup of tea; suddenly I heard the doorbell ring and a parlourmaid rushed in and said to the nurse:

"The prince has arrived!"

I was about to go into the kitchen but the nurse, Tatyana Yakovlevna, a talkative old woman from Moscow who loved a bit of gossip and hated to be deprived of a listener, said to me:

"Don't go away, Ivan Golovanich, let's go into the dressing-room and sit there behind the wardrobe. She won't take him in there and you and I can have a cosy little chat together."

I agreed for I hoped to learn something useful to Grusha from this talkative old Tatyana Yakovlevna and, as Yevgenya Semyonovna had sent me a little flask of rum for my tea I decided, as I had already given up the drink by then, to give it to the dear old soul in her tea and, bless her heart, she would let out something she would otherwise never have told me.

We left the nursery and sat down behind the cupboards in the dressing-room, which was very narrow, just a mere passageway, if the truth be told, with a door at one end that led straight into the room where Yevgenya Semyonovna was receiving the prince and was right behind the couch on which they sat down. In a word, only that closed door, with hangings on the other side, separated me from them, so that it was the same as being in the room with them, for I could hear every word they said.

The prince came in and said:

"How do you do, my old and trusted friend?"

And she replied:

"How do you do, prince? To what do I owe this visit?"

And he said:

"We'll talk about that later, but first accept my greetings and let me kiss your head." And I could hear him give her a smacking kiss on the head; then he asked about his daughter.

Yevgenya Semyonovna told him that she was at home.

"How is she?"

"She is well."

"She must have grown up, eh?"

She laughed and said:

"It stands to reason that she's grown."

"I hope you're going to show her to me," said the prince.

"Why not," she said, "I'd be delighted!" and she got up, went into the nursery and called the nurse, Tatyana Yakovlevna, who was drinking tea with me.

"Nurse, please bring Lyuda to the prince," she said,

"Tatyana Yakovlevna was annoyed, put her saucer down on the table and said:

"A plague on you all, I just get into a nice chat with a person and you call me away and spoil all my pleasure." She quickly covered me over with some of her mistress's skirts that were hanging on the wall and said, "Sit still"; then she went away to fetch the girl while I sat behind the cupboards and could hear how the prince kissed the child twice and took her on his knees.

"Would you like, *mon enfant*, to go for a ride in my carriage?" he asked her.

The girl did not answer and the prince turned to Yevgenya Semyonovna.

"*Je vous prie*," he said, "please let her go out with the nurse in my carriage."

Yevgenya Semyonovna said something to him in French, why and *pourquoi*, but he said something like "absolutely necessary" and having exchanged a few phrases in this way Yevgenya Semyonovna said reluctantly to the nurse:

"Dress her and take her for a ride."

Off they went for their ride and those two stayed together with me eavesdropping on them, for I could not possibly leave my hiding place and, besides, I said to myself, "My time has come, now I'll find out who has harm for Grusha in mind."

CHAPTER THE SIXTEENTH

Once I'd made up my mind to eavesdrop I didn't stop at that but determined to see with my own eyes whatever was to be seen and I managed to do so. I climbed very quietly on to a stool and found a chink in a groove above the door to which I pressed my eye eagerly. I saw the prince sitting on the divan and the lady standing by the window, probably watching her girlie being put into the carriage.

The carriage drove off and she turned to the prince and said:

"I've done all you asked me to, prince, so now tell me what brought you here."

And he answered:

"The devil take the business; business isn't a bear that will run away to the forest. Come over here and sit down beside me and let's have a good talk like we used to in the old days."

Yevgenya Semyonovna, however, stood with her hands behind her back, leaning against the window and frowning in silence. The prince implored her:

"What's the matter? Come, I beg you, I want to talk to you."

She obeyed and went over to him; seeing that, he again said jokingly:

"That's right, let's sit together as we used to," and he tried to put his arm round her but she pushed him away and said:

"Tell me your business, prince. What do you want? What can I do for you?"

"Good Lord," said the prince, "do you want me to put all my cards on the table without any preliminaries?"

"Of course," she said, "tell me straight out what you want. We're old friends, aren't we?"

"I want money," said the prince.

Yevgenya Semyonovna looked at him but said nothing.

"But not much money," added the prince.

"How much?"

"For the time being, twenty thousand."

Yevgenya Semyonovna did not answer and the prince went on to describe very eloquently how he was buying a cloth mill although he hadn't a kopek in his pocket,

"But," he said, "if I buy it I shall be a millionaire; I'll rebuild it, get rid of all the old stuff and start making brightly coloured cloths to sell to the Asiatics at Nizhny-Novgorod. If I weave them in bright colours, from rubbish, even, they'll sell quickly and I'll make a lot of money, but at the moment I want twenty thousand to pay as a deposit on the factory."

Yevgenya Semyonovna said:

"And where will you get it?"

And the prince replied:

"I don't know, but I must get it, for my plan's absolutely certain. I have a man, Ivan Golovan, a fine judge of horseflesh, rather dull, but a fine fellow, honest and dependable, and he was a captive amongst the Asiatics for years and knows their tastes well. There's a fair in Nizhny-Novgorod, going on now, so I'll send Golovan down there with samples to get me contracts, and there'll be advances on the orders and then ... well, first of all I'll pay back those twenty thousand...."

He stopped and the lady did not say anything for a while; at last she sighed and said:

"Yes, prince, your plan is a sure one."

"Yes, isn't it?"

"Absolutely sure," she said. "That's what you'll do, you'll pay a deposit on the factory, everybody will regard you as a manufacturer, people in society will say that your affairs have improved...."

"Yes."

"Yes, and then...."

"...And then Golovan will get hundreds of orders and advances at the Nizhny-Novgorod Fair and I'll repay my debt and be a rich man!"

"Please don't interrupt me; first of all this business will so deceive the Marshal of the Nobility that he will think you are rich. You'll marry his daughter and when you get her dowry you will be rich indeed!"

"You think so, darling?"

Yevgenya Semyonovna replied:

"Do you think differently?"

"As you understand the situation so well, God grant your words may come true and bring joy to us all."

"*Us?*"

"Of course," the prince said, "we shall all benefit, you'll mortgage your house for me and I'll pay our daughter ten thousand interest on the twenty thousand!"

"The house is yours. You gave it to her and you can take it back if you need it," said the lady in reply.

He began saying that the house wasn't his, "But I ask you, as her mother . . . that is, of course, if you trust me. . . ."

"Is that all I've trusted you with, prince?" she said, "haven't I trusted you with my honour and my life?"

"Oh, I see," he stuttered, "you mean. . . . Well, thank you, thank you, excellent. . . . May I send the mortgage for your signature tomorrow?"

"Send it and I'll sign," she said.

"But aren't you afraid?"

"After what I've lost already," she said, "there's nothing more to be afraid of."

"But aren't you sorry? Tell me, aren't you sorry? I believe you still love me a little, don't you? Or is it just pity?"

She merely laughed at his words and said:

"Stop talking nonsense, prince! Won't you have some soaked cloudberries and sugar? They're delicious this year."

The prince must have been offended at that. He probably didn't expect anything like it, but he got up and smiled.

"No," he said, "you may eat your cloudberries yourself, I don't feel like sweets. Thank you and good-bye," and he stooped to kiss her hand just as the carriage returned.

Yevgenya Semyonovna got up and gave him her hand in farewell and said:

"What are you going to do with your black-eyed Gypsy girl?"

The prince slapped himself on the forehead and said:

"Why, of course. How clever you always are! Believe it or not, I never forget how clever you are and thank you for having reminded me of that jewel."

"Do you mean to say you have forgotten all about her?" she said.

"Honestly, I had," he said, "it had slipped my mind. Of course, I must do something for that silly little fool."

"Do something and let it be something good," said Yevgenya Semyonovna, "she isn't a Russian girl. A mixture of tepid blood and new milk. She won't take it easily and she'll never forgive you for old times' sake."

"Don't worry, she'll calm down."

"Is she in love with you, prince? I've been told she's terribly fond of you."

"I'm sick and tired of her. Thank God, she's very friendly with Golovan."

"How does that help you?" Yevgenya Semyonovna asked.

"I'll buy them a house, register Ivan in the Merchants' Guild and they'll marry and live happily."

Yevgenya Semyonovna shook her head and smiled.

"How hopeless you are, my poor prince," she said. "And where's your conscience?"

"Leave my conscience alone," he said, "I've no time for it at the moment: I must send for Golovan to come to town today if possible."

Then the lady told him that Ivan Golovan was in town already and even staying at her house. The prince was very glad to hear this, asked her to send me to him as quickly as possible and left her immediately.

After that things began to move fast, just as in a sto-

ry-book. The prince gave me power of attorney and cer-
tificates to the effect that he was the owner of a factory.
He taught me to say what kinds of cloth he manu-
factured and sent me straight from the town to Nizhny-
Novgorod so that I did not get a chance to see Grusha;
all the time I was angry with the prince for how could
he say that she must be my wife? I had good luck at the
Fair, I got orders and samples and money from the Asiatics; I sent the money to the prince but when I got back
to the estate I couldn't recognize it. Everything seemed
to have been changed by magic. It had all been redeco-
rated like a peasant's cottage at holiday time and not
a trace was to be seen of the little lodge where Grusha
had her apartments. It had been levelled to the ground
and a new building stood in its place. I gasped with
astonishment and rushed off to find Grusha, but nobody
knew anything about her: the servants were all new,
all hired people who gave themselves such airs and
wouldn't let me get near the prince. Before that the
prince and I had been like two regular army men; our
relations had been simple, but now everything was in the
grand style and if I wanted to tell the prince anything
it had to be through his valet.

I can't stand that sort of thing and I wouldn't have
stayed there another minute but would have left immediately if it hadn't been that I was sorry for Grusha and
couldn't find out where she was. No matter which of the
old servants I questioned, I could get no answer. They
had all obviously received strict orders on that point.
With great difficulty I got an old maidservant to tell me
that Grusha had been there shortly before—"It's only
some ten days or so ago that she left with the prince in
a carriage and didn't come back," she told me. So I
went to see the coachmen who had driven them, but they
could tell me nothing: all they knew was that the prince
had changed horses at the first stage, sent them back

and driven off somewhere with Grusha on hired horses. Wherever I went, I could find no trace at all of her: whether the villain had stuck a knife into her, or shot her with a pistol and thrown her body into a ditch and covered it with leaves, or whether he had drowned her.... Anything was possible with a man of such passion, for she certainly stood in the way of his marriage and, as Yevgenya Semyonovna had warned him, Grusha loved him, the villain, with all the passion of her unrestrained Gypsy love, and she would not put up with it and humble herself like Yevgenya Semyonovna, a Russian Christian lady who let her life burn out before him like a lamp before an icon. I imagined that when the prince told Grusha about his marriage the Gypsy blood in her must have blazed up like a smouldering fire; God knows how she must have cursed him and he had killed her.

The more I thought it over the more convinced I became that it could not have been otherwise and I could not bear to watch the preparations being made for his marriage to the daughter of the Marshal of the Nobility. When the wedding day came and the servants were given brightly coloured kerchiefs and new clothes to wear, each according to his station, I didn't put on my new suit or kerchief but took everything to my storeroom in the stables and left it there; early in the morning I went into the woods and wandered about aimlessly till evening, wondering all the time whether I might not come upon her dead body. When evening came I left the forest and sat down on the steep bank of the little river beyond which I could see the prince's house in a blaze of lights and the festivities were well underway; the guests were enjoying themselves and the band was playing and the music could be heard a long way off. I sat there without looking at the house but with my eyes fixed on the lights reflected in the rippling water—they looked like columns as though some watery palace had been opened up. And I grew so miserable and sick at heart that I did what I had never done before, not even as a captive, I started talking to the unseen powers; as in the fairy-tale of Sister Alyonushka, whom her brother kept calling, so I called her, my lovely Grusha, in a plaintive voice:

"Oh sister, my sister," I cried, "little Grusha, answer me, speak to me, say just one word to me, come to me for a moment."

And what do you think? I moaned like that three times and then terror seized me: it seemed to me that someone was running towards me, and had reached me and begun to circle round me, whisper in my ear, peer into my face over my shoulder and then, all at once, something rushed at me out of the darkness of the night ... and hung round my neck, shaking convulsively....

CHAPTER THE SEVENTEENTH

I was so frightened that I nearly fell to the ground, but I didn't lose consciousness and felt that something alive and light was fluttering beside me like a wounded crane, sighing but uttering no word.

I muttered a silent prayer and then I saw poor Grusha's face before me!

"My dear," I said, "my poor, poor darling! Are you alive or have you come to me from the next world? Don't hide anything from me. Tell me the truth; I shan't be afraid of you even if you are dead!"

She heaved a deep, deep sigh, from the very depths of her bosom.

"I am alive," she said.

"Thank God for that!"

"But I have run away and come here to die."

"Good Lord, Grusha," I said, "why should you die? Let us live happily together: I shall work for you, build a little place for you and you'll be like a sister to me."

But she answered:

"No, Ivan Severyanich, no, my dearest friend, please accept my last blessing for your kind words but I, miserable Gypsy girl that I am, cannot go on living because I might bring death to an innocent soul."

"What are you talking about?" I asked her. "Whose soul is it that you pity so?"

"I'm sorry for her, the young wife of that villain of mine," she answered, "for hers is ia young and innocent soul but, even so, my jealous heart cannot tolerate her and I shall kill her and myself."

"Cross yourself," I said. "You were baptized, weren't you? What will happen to your own soul?"

"I'm not even sorry for my own soul, let it go down into hell—here it is worse than in hell!"

I could see that the woman was not in her right mind, so terribly upset was she, so I took her by the hands and held her and looked at her: I was amazed at the terrible change in her, where had her beauty gone? Her body seemed to have shrunk to nothing, only her eyes blazed in her dark face like those of a wolf at night, eyes that seemed twice ias big as they were before, and her belly bulged horribly for her time was near and her face was no bigger than my fist and her black locks fluttered down over her cheeks. I looked at the dress she was wearing and saw that it was of cheap, dark cotton and all in holes and she wore her shoes on her bare feet.

"Tell me where you have come from," I said. "Where have you been and why are you in such a state?"

Suddenly she smiled iand said:

"What? Am I not beautiful? Beautiful! This is the way my sweetheart fitted me out to repay me for the great love I bore him, for giving up one whom I loved more than him, for giving myself to him entirely, body and

soul! He hid me away in a safe place and ordered his
guards to take care of my beauty...."
· Then she suddenly burst out laughing and said in
great anger:
"Oh, prince, what a foolish head you've got! As though
a Gypsy girl is one of your young ladies that she can be
kept locked up. Why, if I wanted to, I could at this very
moment throw myself at your young wife and set my
teeth in her throat."

I could see that she was shaking all over from her fit
of jealousy and thought to myself: "I must try to distract her thoughts by sweet memories and not by threats
of hell," so I said to her:

"But he really loved you. Oh, how he loved you, how
he used to kiss your feet.... He used to kneel beside the
couch when you were singing and kiss your scarlet slipper all over, top and bottom...."

She began to take heed of my words and her long
black eyelashes fluttered over her dry cheeks. Looking
down at the water she said in a soft, hollow voice:

"He loved me, he loved me, the villain, he loved me
and didn't begrudge me anything as long as I didn't
love him, but the moment I fell in love with him he jilted
me. And what for? Is my rival better than me? Will she
love him more than I did? He is so foolish, so foolish....
As the winter sun has no warmth compared with that
of summer so will he never again know a love like
mine. You tell him so, tell him that before her death
Grusha prophesied that such would be his fate!"

I was glad that she had begun to talk and I started
questioning her.

"What happened between you? What was the cause of
it all?"

She threw up her hands and said:

"It didn't happen for any reason at all, except that
he was unfaithful to me.... He didn't like me any more,

that is the only reason." As she said this she began to weep bitter tears. "He had dresses made for me to suit his own taste, dresses with narrow waists that were no good to a woman with child. If I put them on for him he'd get angry and say, 'Take it off, it doesn't suit you.' But if I didn't wear them and came out to him in a loose dress he'd get twice as angry. 'What d'you think you look like?' he'd say. Then it was that I realized that I had lost him for ever, that I made him sick...."

She now began to sob continuously, looking straight in front of her.

"For a long time," she whispered, "I felt that he didn't like me any more, but I wanted to find out what his conscience was like. I mustn't plague him, I thought, I must wait for him to pity me, and pity me he did!"

She told me such a strange, fanciful story of her last parting with the prince that I could make nothing of it and still cannot understand it: how could a wicked man ruin a woman for ever and all for nothing?

CHAPTER THE EIGHTEENTH

After you had gone away and disappeared, Grusha began,—that is when I went to the Fair—the prince didn't come home for a long time but I heard rumours that he was to be married. I cried terribly on account of those rumours and lost all my good looks. My heart ached and I could feel my child moving within me. It will die in the womb, I thought. Then one day, I suddenly heard them say, "He's coming." I trembled all over and rushed to my room to dress myself as prettily as possible for him, I put on my emerald ear-rings and took down from behind a sheet on the wall his favourite sea-blue dress, trimmed with lace and with a low-cut bodice. I hurried and the back wouldn't fasten, so I left it as it was and threw a red scarf over my shoulders so that he would not notice that it was unfastened and rushed out to meet him on the porch. I was still trembling and before I knew what I was doing I exclaimed, "Oh, my darling, my sweet, my fair, my precious jewel!" And I threw my arms round his neck and fainted....

She was nauseated at the time.

When I came to, she went on, I was in my room, lying on the divan and trying to remember whether I had embraced him in reality or in a dream. And I felt awfully weak, she said. She did not see him for a long time after that, she kept sending for him but he wouldn't go to her.

At last he appeared and she said to him:

"Have you thrown me over altogether and forgotten me?"

"I have a lot to do," he said.

"Why are you so busy now when you weren't ever busy before, my precious jewel?" And she stretched out her arms to embrace him but he pulled a wry face and tugged with all his might at the silken cord round her neck.

Luckily, she said to me, the cord wasn't very strong, it had frayed and broke easily for I had been wearing an amulet on it for many years, otherwise he would have strangled me, which is what I believe he meant to do, for he turned quite white and hissed at me:

"Why are you wearing such a dirty cord?"

"Why should you worry about my cord? It used to be clean but it got dirty because I worry so much that I perspire."

"Phew, phew, phew," he said, spat and went out but late in the afternoon he came back, looking angry, and said:

"Let's go out in my carriage." And he pretended to be nice to me, he kissed me on the head and I suspected nothing. I got into the carriage with him and we drove away. We drove for a long time, changed horses twice, but where we were going I could not get him to say. I saw that we had reached a wooded place, all marshy, wild and dreadful. We soon came across some beehives in that forest and behind them there was a house out of which three buxom farm-girls in madder-red dresses came to meet us and addressed me as "madame." I got out of the carriage and they immediately took me under the arms and carried me into a room that had been made ready for me.

All that troubled me greatly, especially those girls, and my heart contracted with pain.

"What posting station is this?" I asked the prince.

"This is where you're going to live from now on," he replied.

I began to cry and kiss his hands, imploring him not to leave me there, but he showed no mercy, pushed me away and left me there.

At this point Grusha stopped and bowed her head, then she sighed and continued.

I wanted to run away. I tried a hundred times to escape, but those girls kept a close watch over me, never letting me out of their sight. Although I felt so wretched there I made up my mind to deceive them and I pretended to be happy and carefree and told them I wanted to take a walk in the woods. They took me for a walk but they wouldn't take their eyes off me. I kept looking up at the trees, at the tops of the branches, and at the bark to see which was the southern side and all the time I was trying to think of a way to give the girls the slip. Yesterday I carried out a plan I had thought of. After dinner I went out with them to a clearing in the forest.

"Come on, girls," I said to them, "let's play blind man's buff in this glade."

They agreed.

"But instead of covering our eyes," I said, "let's tie our hands and bump each other with our behinds."

There was no objection to this either.

We did as I suggested. I tied the hands of one of them tightly behind her back and ran off with another behind a bush and tied her up and the third I tied up in sight of the other two; they shouted for help but I ran away swifter than a racehorse, although I am with child, and I ran through the forest all night until, in the morning, I collapsed beside some beehives where the forest was thickest. Here an old, old man came to me and muttered something I couldn't understand; he was all covered with beeswax and smelt of honey, and bees were swarming in his yellow eyebrows. I told him I wanted to find you, Ivan Severyanich, and he said:

"Call to him, girlie, once with the wind and once against the wind and he'll miss you and start looking for you and you'll meet."

He gave me some water to drink and some honey on a cucumber to give me strength. I drank the water and ate the cucumber and continued my way calling once with the wind and once against the wind until we met.

"Thank you," she said and embraced me and kissed me. "You're like a brother to me."

"And you're like a sister to me," I said, and, overcome by my feelings, I began to weep.

She, too, wept and said:

"I know, Ivan Severyanich, I know everything. I know that you alone love me truly, my dear friend. Show me your last love and do what I shall ask you in this dreadful hour."

"Tell me what you want me to do," I said.

"First you must swear to me by the most awful thing in the world that you will do what I ask."

So I swore to her by the salvation of my soul.

"That's not enough," she said, "for my sake you might

break such an oath. Swear to me by something more awful."

"But," I said, "I can't think of any more terrible oath than that."

"All right," she said, "I've thought of something for you. Say it after me quickly and don't think about it."

Foolishly I promised her I would and she said:

"Damn my soul as you have sworn by your own if you don't obey me."

"Very well," I said and I straight away damned her soul.

"Now listen to me," she said, "for you must hurry to become the saviour of my soul. I have no more strength to go on living in torment, seeing his treachery and his disgraceful treatment. If I live one more day I'll kill *him* and *her* and if I take pity on them I'll kill myself and damn my soul for ever more. Take pity on me, dear brother, and thrust a knife into my heart."

I jumped aside and made the sign of the cross over her and then stepped back from her but she threw her arms round my kness and wept and prostrated herself before me.

"You," she said, "will live and pray to God for forgiveness for my soul and yours, but don't ruin me, don't let me lay hands on myself.... Go on."

Ivan Severyanich frowned sternly, bit his moustache and seemed to be forcing the words out of his heaving breast.

She got my knife out of my pocket, opened it, straightened the blade... put it into my hands... and carried on so terribly that I couldn't bear it.

"If you don't kill me," she said, "I'll repay all of you by becoming the worst of all harlots."

I trembled all over and told her to pray but I did not stab her. I took her by the shoulders and pushed her over the steep bank into the river....

It was when we heard this last confession by Ivan Severyanich that all of us began to doubt the veracity of his
tale; we maintained complete silence for some time until,
at last, somebody coughed and said:

"Did she drown?"

"The water closed over her."

"What did you do after that?"

"In what way?"

"You must have suffered a lot."

"Naturally."

CHAPTER THE NINETEENTH

I ran from that place without realizing what I was
doing or whither I was going. I only remember that someone seemed to be chasing me, someone terribly tall and
big and shameless, too, and naked, and his whole body
was black and his head was small and like a chicken's
gizzard; he was all covered with hair and I guessed that
if it was not Cain it must have been the foul fiend himself,
so I kept running and calling upon my guardian angel. I
came to my senses somewhere on the highway, under a
willow-tree. It was a dry and sunny autumn day, but it
was chilly and the wind raised the dust and tossed the
yellow leaves about. I had no idea of the time or what
place it was or where the road led to, and there was a
horrid emptiness within me and I had no feeling or con-
ception of what I ought to do. I could think of one thing
only—Grusha's soul was damned and it was my duty
to suffer for her and to save her from hell. I did not know
how I was to do that and was greatly distressed on that
account, but, suddenly, something touched me on the
shoulder. I looked up and saw that it was a dead twig
that had fallen from the willow-tree and was being
carried far away by the wind and as I watched Grusha
suddenly came along, only she was very small, six or

seven years old and there were tiny wings on her shoulders, but no sooner had I noticed her than she flew away from me swift as a bullet and there was only the swirl of dust and dry leaves that followed her.

I thought that this must certainly be her soul watching over me and that she was probably beckoning me and showing me the way. So I followed her. I walked for a whole day without any idea of where I was going and I was already dead tired when some people overtook me, an old man and woman travelling in a cart.

"Get in, poor fellow," they said, "we'll give you a lift."

I did so. They drove on and I could see they were suffering great anxiety.

"We are in great trouble," they said, "our son is being taken into the army and we have no money to pay another man to take his place."

I felt very sorry for the old couple and I said:

"I'd go for you without any pay, but I have no papers."

But they said:

"That doesn't matter. Leave that to us, and you call yourself by our son's name, Pyotr Serdyukov."

"All right," I said, "that will do for me, I'll pray to my own saint, St. John the Baptist, and can call myself anything you like."

It ended with that; they took me to another town, enlisted me in place of their son, gave me twenty-five rubles for the road and promised to help me as long as they lived. I deposited the money they had given me at a poor monastery for prayers for the repose of Grusha's soul, and then requested the authorities to send me to the Caucasus where there would be a greater chance to lay down my life for my faith. So they did and I spent more than fifteen years in the Caucasus; I never revealed my true name and occupation to anybody and was known as Pyotr Serdyukov, but on St. John's day I prayed for myself to God through St. John the Baptist. I had almost forgotten my past life and occupation and was serving my last year in this way when it suddenly happened that on that very St. John's day we were in pursuit of the Tatars who had been giving us a lot of trouble and had retreated beyond the River Koisa. In those parts there are several Koisas: one flows along the Andian valley and is called the Andian Koisa, the second is in the Avarian valley and is called the Avarian Koisa and the third and fourth are known as the Korikumuiskaya and Kuzikumuiskaya, and all of them meet to form the River Sulak. They are all four very rapid and cold, especially the Andian Koisa beyond which the Tatars had retired. We had killed more of those Tatars than we could count but some of them did succeed in getting across the River Koisa where they hid behind boulders and fired at us every time we exposed ourselves. They fired so skilfully that they did not waste a single shot but reserved their fire for a sure mark, since they knew that we had more ammunition than they had; they were so anxious to do certain damage to us that they never once fired in our direction although we were in full view of them. Our colonel who liked to act as another Suvorov, set us examples by his personal courage and was always exclaiming, "God have mercy." He sat down on the bank, bared his legs and put them into the ice-cold water up to the knees and started praising it.

"God have mercy," he said, "how warm the water is, just like new milk fresh from the cow. Which of you, my good men, will volunteer to swim over to the other side with a rope so that we can put a bridge across?"

While our colonel was sitting there talking to us like that, the Tatars laid the barrels of two guns in a crack but did not fire from them. But as soon as two men volunteered and began to swim across, their guns spurted flame and the two soldiers disappeared in the waters of the Koisa. We pulled out the rope and another pair set out while we showered bullets on the boulders behind which the Tatars were hiding, but we couldn't get them, for our bullets struck the stones; but those devils let fly at our swimmers, the water became red with blood and another two soldiers disappeared. A third pair followed, but neither did they reach the middle of the Koisa before the Tatars sent them to the bottom. After that third pair there were few willing to volunteer for everybody could see that it was not war but plain murder and the murderers had to be punished. The colonel said:

"Listen to me, my good men, isn't there one among you who has a mortal sin on his conscience? God have mercy, what a chance he now has of washing away his sin in blood."

And I thought to myself:

"What better chance of ending my life can I hope for? May the Lord bless my undertaking!" and I stepped forward and stripped off my clothes. I said the Lord's prayer, bowed in all directions to my comrades and my superiors, said to myself, "Well, Grusha, whom I call sister, may my blood expiate our sin," and then took a string, the other end of which was tied to a rope, into my mouth, took a flying leap from the bank and plunged into the river.

The water was terribly cold: I got shooting pains under my arm-pits, my chest contracted painfully and I felt cramp in my legs, but I swam on. Our bullets flew overhead and Tatar bullets were plopping into the water all round me, but they did not touch me and I didn't know whether I was wounded or not, but I did reach the far bank. There the Tatars couldn't fire at me for I was standing under the wall of a ravine and in order to shoot at me they would have had to leave cover under the heavy fire which our soldiers kept up from the other bank. So I stood under the rocks and pulled away at the rope until it came across and we threw a bridge over the river; our men got across quickly, but I was still standing there quite beside myself for I was wondering all the time: "Did anybody else see what I had seen?" As I swam I had seen Grusha flying above me and she was now a maiden of about sixteen, and her wings were huge and bright, they covered the whole river and she protected me with them. As nobody else said a word about it to me I thought that I should have to tell about it myself. How the colonel started embracing, kissing and praising me!

"God have mercy, Pyotr Serdyukov, what a fine fellow you are."

"I'm not a fine fellow, sir," I said, "I'm a great sinner such as neither earth nor water will receive."

He began to question me.

"What was the nature of your sin?"

"I have been the ruin of many innocent souls in my time," I answered, and in his tent that same night I told him what I have just told you.

He listened for a long time, fell into a reverie and then said:

"God have mercy, the things you have gone through! But all the same, my lad, whether you like it or not, you must be made an officer. I shall send in my recommendation straight away."

"As you will," I said, "but won't you also send and find out whether I really did kill that Gypsy girl?"

"Yes, I'll make that inquiry," he said.

He did so but the paper with the colonel's request went from one town to another and came back with a denial. It was said that there had never been any incident with a Gypsy girl in those parts and that, although Ivan Severyanich had been employed by the prince he had since purchased his freedom by proxy and had died at the house of the Serdyukovs, state-owned peasants.

What more could I do to prove my guilt?

The colonel said to me:

"Don't you dare tell me any more lies about yourself, my friend. When you swam across the Koisa the icy water and the fright must have turned your head a bit. And I'm glad," he said, "that what you said about yourself isn't true. Now you'll be an officer and, God have mercy, that's splendid."

After that I even got all mixed up myself: I didn't know whether I had really pushed Grusha into the water or had imagined it all on account of my great longing to see her.

They made me an officer for my bravery but as I insisted on the truth of my story of my past life they retired me from the army with a St. George's Cross so that I should no longer worry myself about it.

"Accept our congratulations," the colonel said, "you are now a member of the nobility and can get a civil service job, God have mercy, what an easy life." He gave me a letter to an important man in St. Petersburg. "Go and see him," he said, "he'll help you with your career and see that you're all right."

I got to St. Petersburg with the letter but I had no luck with my career.

"Why not?"

"I couldn't get a job for a long time and then I got Theta and that made it even worse."

"*Theta?* What do you mean by that?"

The man to whom I was sent about my career got me a job as information clerk at the Address Bureau and at that office each clerk had his own letter of the alphabet on which he had to give information. Some letters are good, for instance, the letters B or P or K with which many surnames begin, and the clerk who has these letters can make quite a good living; but they gave me Theta, the most insignificant letter in the Russian alphabet, one that is seldom used at all, and those whose surnames normally should begin with this letter do their best to get rid of it as soon as they rise in the world: they write their names with an F which is pronounced exactly the same as Theta. You look and look for a name under Theta, but all in vain, the owner has spelt his name with an F. There's nothing to be made out of such work but, still, you have to be at the office all day. I could see that was a bad business and tried to get another job—as a coachman, my old trade, but nobody would employ me: "You're an officer, with a military medal," they said, "and we can't even curse you, let alone beat you!" I felt like hanging myself, but, thank God, I did not do anything so desperate but took a job as an artist in order not to die of hunger.

"What kind of artist?"

"I acted in plays."

"At what theatre?"

"In a booth on Admiralty Square. They didn't scorn the nobility and took anybody who came along: they had army officers and heads of civil service departments, students and, especially, people who came from the Senate, a lot of them."

"How did you like that life?"

"Not at all."

"Why not?"

"In the first place, you see, we had to learn our parts and rehearse during Passion Week or at Shrovetide when they sing in the churches: 'Open unto me, ye gates of repentance,' and, secondly, the part I had to play was too difficult."

"What did you play?"

"I had to play the devil."

"What is there difficult about that?"

"Quite a lot; I had to dance during two intervals and turn somersaults; this somersaulting was a tricky business for I was covered from head to foot in a shaggy grey goatskin and had a long tail on a wire that kept getting between my legs; and I had horns that got tangled up in everything, besides which I was getting on in years and was no longer young and agile; to make things even worse I had to be beaten all through the play. They weren't real sticks they beat me with, they were hollow and made of canvas with cotton wool inside, but still I got fed up with their continually beating me; some of the actors, either because they were cold or maybe just for the fun of it, contrived to hit me quite hard. This was especially the case with the Senate men who had experience and hung together; when an army man came their way they made an awful nuisance of themselves; they started beating me in front of the public at noon, as soon as the police flag was hoisted, and kept it up till midnight, and every single one of them made his blows resound as hard as possible to amuse the public. There was nothing very pleasant about that job. On top of it all here, too, an unpleasant incident occurred that compelled me to leave the job."

"What happened to you?"

"I pulled a prince's hair."

"A prince's?"

"He wasn't a real prince, of course, just a theatrical one, a Senate official who played that part at our theatre."

"What did you beat him for?"

"He deserved more than that. He was one of those jokers, a tricky fellow who was always playing practical jokes on everybody."

"On you as well?"

"Yes, on me, too, a lot of them: he spoiled my costume; in the little room where we used to sit over a charcoal brazier and drink tea to warm ourselves up, he'd steal up behind me and fasten my tail to my horns or do something else to make the people laugh and I wouldn't discover it till I ran out on the stage in front of the public and then our manager would get angry with me. I did not touch him as long as he played his tricks on me but soon he began to annoy one of the fairies. She was a very young girl from an impoverished nobleman's family who played the goddess Fortune, and had to save the prince from me. In her role she had to go on the stage in nothing but a tulle dress and her wings, and there were hard frosts at the time and her hands got blue with the cold; he would keep on worrying her, thrusting his attentions upon her; one day, when we all three of us dropped through a trapdoor into a cellar at the climax of the play he started pinching her. I felt awfully sorry for her and gave him a good thrashing."

"How did it all end?"

"Nothing happened to me, there were no witnesses in the cellar except the fairy but the Senate crowd went on strike and wouldn't have me in the company and, as they were the chief actors there, the manager had to sack me to please them."

"Where did you go then?"

"I should have been left without food or shelter if it hadn't been for the fairy who fed me out of gratitude, but my conscience wouldn't let me keep taking food from her when she hardly had enough to eat herself. I racked my brains to find a way out, I didn't want to go back to the Theta business again, and, anyway, the place was taken by another man down on his luck, so I took and entered a monastery."

"Was that the only reason?"

"What else could I have done? I had nowhere to go and it's all right where I am now."

"So you like the monastery life?"

"Yes, very much. Everything is so quiet, just like it was in the regiment. In fact there's a great resemblance—everything's provided, clothes, boots and food, and the authorities look after me and demand only complete obedience."

"But isn't obedience a bit irksome?"

"Why should it be? The more obedient a man is the

easier it is for him to live. I have no fault to find with my life as a lay brother, I don't have to go to church unless I want to and I perform my duties by force of habit. If they say to me, 'Harness the horses, Father Ishmael,' (I'm called Ishmael now) I harness them up, and if they say, 'Unharness the horses, Father Ishmael,' I unharness them."

"Just a minute," we said, "it seems that in the monastery you are still with the horses?"

"Yes, I have the permanent job of coachman. They don't mind my officer's rank in the monastery, you see, for I'm regarded as a real monk although I haven't taken my final vows."

"Will it be long before you do?"

"I shan't take them at all."

"No? Why not?"

"I—er—don't consider myself worthy."

"On account of your past sins and transgressions?"

"Well—er—ye-e-es. And then, why should I? I'm very content as a lay brother and I live in peace."

"But have you ever told anybody else the whole story of your life the way you've told it to us?"

"Yes, I've recounted it several times but what's the use when there's nothing to prove it? They don't believe me; so I've brought a worldly untruth into the monastery with me and they think I am of noble birth. It doesn't matter, however, how I live out the remainder of my life for I'm getting on in years."

The enchanted wanderer's story was obviously drawing to a close, and there was only one thing of interest left for us—how had he fared in the monastery?

CHAPTER THE TWENTIETH

As our wanderer's life's voyage had brought him to his haven, the monastery, to which he firmly believed he had been destined from birth, and everything seemed to be going well with him, we thought that no more misfortunes had come the way of Ivan Severyanich; this, however, was not the case. One of the passengers recalled that according to legends the lay brethren suffered constantly from the devil.

"Tell us, please," he said, "hasn't the devil been troubling you in the monastery? I've been told that he is always tempting monks."

Ivan Severyanich peered at him calmly from under his eyebrows and said:

"Of course he has. If the Apostle Paul could not escape—for does he not say in his epistle, 'There given me a thorn in the flesh, the messenger of Satan to buffet me,' —then how could I, a weak and miserable sinner, hope to escape him?"

"What did you suffer from him?"

"Many things."

"What sort of things?"

"Oh, various abominations, and in the early days, before I got the better of him, he even tried to tempt me."

"Do you mean to say you got the better of *him*, of Satan?"

"Naturally, what else would you expect? That is your vocation in a monastery, although, to be frank, I couldn't have done it alone; an old hermit helped me because he had great experience and knew the remedy for all temptations. As soon as I revealed to him that Grusha appeared to me so vividly that the air seemed to be filled with her, he thought it over and said:

" 'James the Apostle saith: "Resist the devil and he will flee from you," so you resist him.' And he gave me instructions how to do it: 'As soon as you feel the spirit weakening within you,' he said, 'and you think of her, then you must know that Satan is drawing nigh unto you and you must give him battle. First of all fall down on your knees. A man's knees,' he said, 'are the first instrument to use against the devil because when you kneel your soul flies upwards and being thus exalted in spirit you prostrate yourself to the ground until you are exhausted, and wear yourself out with fasting, even unto starvation, for when the devil sees you are ready for martyrdom he won't be able to stand it and will run away at once for he fears to bring a man more quickly to the bosom of Christ by his intrigues, and says to himself, "If I leave him alone and tempt him no more then he's more likely to stumble." ' I did as he told me and everything passed."

"Did you have to torment yourself like that for a long time before the imp of Satan left you alone?"

"Quite a long time, and only by wearing myself out did I conquer the enemy since this is the one thing he fears: at first I prostrated myself about a thousand times and abstained from food and drink for four days on end, and then *he* realized that he was no match for me, lost heart and weakened; as soon as he saw me throw my bowl of food out of the window and take up my beads to count my prostrations he knew that I was in dead earnest and was again quite ready for martyrdom and away he ran. He's terribly afraid of bringing a man to a state of joyful bliss."

"Well, that is ... *he* er-er.... That is, you overcame him but you must have suffered a lot from him, didn't you?"

"That wasn't so important—I was oppressing the oppressor and it caused me no inconvenience."

"Have you got rid of him altogether?"

"Absolutely."

"And he never appears to you?"

"He never appears any more in an alluring female form, and if he does occasionally appear somewhere in the corner of my cell, he's a pitiful thing to look at: he squeaks like a stuck pig and I have stopped tormenting him, I just make the sign of the cross over him and prostrate myself once and he stops his squeaking."

"Well, thank God, you've overcome all that."

"Yes, I've conquered the temptations of the big devil, but I must confess, although it is against the rules, that the little imps are bothering me with tricks even worse."

"Is that so? Have the little imps been annoying you as well?"

"Of course, even if they're of the lowliest rank they don't give me any rest...."

"What could they do to you?"

"They're only babes, of course, but there are so many of them in hell, and they get full board and lodging and have nothing at all to do, so they keep asking for permission to visit earth and learn how to make a nuisance of themselves; they simply enjoy themselves on earth, and the more important a man's position, the more they annoy him."

"In what way? Give us an instance of how they can annoy people."

"Well, they put something in your way, or shove it under your feet and you knock it down or break it and annoy or anger somebody else: that gives them great satisfaction and they're happy; they clap their hands and rush off to their superior: 'Look, we've caused trouble down there, give us a penny for it.' And that's what they're after all the time ... just babes."

"How did they manage to annoy you?"

"There was the case of the Jew who hanged himself in the forest near our monastery and all the lay brethren said it was Judas Iscariot and that he walked the monastery at night and moaned and there were many who had seen him. He meant nothing to me, for, I said to myself, haven't we still got enough Jews left? But one night, when I was asleep in the stables, I heard someone come and shove his head through the upper flap of the door and moan. I immediately breathed a prayer but he remained standing there. Then I made the sign of the cross but he still stood there and moaned. 'What can I do for you?' I asked myself. 'I can't pray for you because you're a Jew and even if you weren't I still have no dispensation to pray for suicides, so get out of here and go to the forest or the wilderness.' I put that sort of curse on him, he went away and I fell asleep; but next night the scoundrel was there again with his moaning.... He just wouldn't let me sleep. 'Phew, you beast,' I said to myself, 'isn't there room enough in the forest or on the church porch without your poking your nose into my stables? It seems there's no help for it, I shall think up something effective for you,' and next morning I drew a big cross on the door with a clean piece of charcoal; at night I lay down calmly to sleep thinking that he wouldn't come again after that but no sooner had I fallen asleep with that thought in my mind than there he was, standing at the door and moaning. 'Phew, the jailbird,' I said. 'Will nothing get rid of him?' He kept me scared all that night and in the morning, as soon as the bell began to toll for morning service, I jumped up and rushed to complain to the abbot, but on my way I met Brother Diomedes, the bellringer.

" 'What are you so scared about?' he asked me.

" 'Such and such,' I said, 'is what I had to put up with last night so I'm going to tell the abbot.'

"But Brother Diomedes said:

" 'You needn't bother: the abbot put a leech on his nose yesterday and is now in a very bad temper and won't help you in this business, but I can help you more than he can, if you want me to.'

" 'It's all the same to me,' I said, 'only please do help me and I'll give you my old warm mittens for that: they'll be useful to you when you have to ring in winter.'

" 'All right,' he said.

"I gave him the mittens and from the belfry he brought me an old church door on which was a picture of St.

Peter holding the keys to the Heavenly Kingdom in his hand.

" 'That's the important thing, the keys, I mean,' said Brother Diomedes. 'You stand this door up to screen you and nobody can pass it.'

"So filled with joy was I that I almost bowed to his feet but I thought to myself, 'Why stand this door like a screen and have to keep taking it down again, when I can hang it properly so that it will always serve as a barrier?' So I hung the door on strong hinges and to make doubly sure I fixed up a heavy block with a big stone on the end of the rope. All this I managed quietly in one day and by evening, when all was ready, I lay down to sleep and—what do you think? I heard that breathing again! I couldn't believe my own ears, but sure enough, I wasn't imagining it—he was standing there and I could hear his breath. He didn't only breathe but he was pushing against the door. The old door had had a lock on the inside but I had hoped to depend entirely on the sacredness of the new one and hadn't put a lock on it, and in any case, there hadn't been time for it. There he stood, pushing more and more boldly at my door till I seemed to see his snout appear, then the block slammed the door to and he jumped back.... He jumped away, seemed to be scratching himself, waited a bit and then began pushing the door open again, still more energetically, the snout just got inside when the block slammed the door with a still bigger bang. It must have hurt him for he quietened down and didn't try any more. I fell asleep but soon woke up and saw that the scoundrel was at it again, and more cunningly this time: he didn't try to get in by butting the door but pushed it slowly open with his horns and, as my head was covered with a sheepskin coat, he had the cheek to tear it off and suddenly licked my ear.... That was more impudence than I could stand: I reached under the bed, got hold of an axe and ... smack!... I heard him bellow and then collapse where he stood. 'Serve you right!' I thought, but in the morning, instead of the Jew, I found the monastery cow lying there for those little imps had put it in his place."

"Did you injure it?"

"I killed it with the axe. There was a terrible hullabaloo in the monastery about it."

"That probably made things very unpleasant for you, didn't it?"

"It certainly did. The abbot said that I had imagined it all and that it was because I didn't go to church often enough, so he gave me his blessing and told me to stand by the screen to light candles every evening after I had finished my work with the horses. But those little imps played an even better trick on me. During the night service on the eve of the Fast of the Assumption, when the abbot and the dean, as became their rank, were standing in the middle of the church for the communion, an old lady devotee handed me a candle and said, 'Put it up for me, father, for the festival.'

"I went over to the lectern where the icon of Christ upon the Waters stood and stuck the candle in place and as I did so knocked down another. I stooped to pick it up and was fixing it when I knocked down two more, I started putting them back when four fell down! I shook my head at that, thinking: 'It's those little imps playing pranks on me again, and pulling candles out of my hands....' I bent down to pick them all up and as I raised my head I banged it under the candlestick and brought the candles showering down. That made me mad and I knocked the remaining candles down with my hand. 'If they are that cheeky,' I thought, 'I'd better knock them all down with my own hand as quickly as I can.'"

"And what happened to you then?"

"They wanted to indict me for that, but a hermit, a blind old monk living in seclusion, interceded for me.

"'Why put *him* on trial for it?' he said, 'it is the servants of the Devil that led him astray.'

"The abbot listened to him and without giving me any trial gave me his blessing and had me confined in an empty cellar."

"Did they keep you in the cellar long?"

"The abbot didn't put me there for a definite period, he only said, 'Put him there,' so I was kept there all summer long until the first hoar-frosts began."

"I suppose it must have been more miserable and tormenting in the cellar than in the steppe?"

"Oh, no, how can you compare them, here I could hear the church bells ringing and friends would come to see me. They came and stood above the cellar and we talked; the Father Treasurer had a quern lowered into the cellar on a rope so that I could grind salt for the refectory. How can you compare it with the steppe or any other place?"

"Why did they release you? I suppose it got too cold when the frosts began?"

"No, that wasn't the reason, there was a different one —I began to prophesy...."

"Prophesy?"

"Yes, while I was sitting in that hole I fell into meditation and pondered over the meanness of my spirit and the suffering I had endured on account of it and how I never seemed to improve; I sent a lay brother to that old teacher, the hermit, to ask whether I could pray to God to grant me a more suitable spirit. He sent back the answer: 'Let him pray ardently and await that which he has no right to expect.'

"I did as he had ordered: three nights I knelt in the cellar on that instrument, the knees, and prayed with all my soul and began to await the perfection of my spirit.

There was a monk there by the name of Gerontius, a well-read man who had books and newspapers; once he gave me the life of the holy Tikhon Zadonsky to read and when he happened to pass my prison he would pull a newspaper from under his robe and drop it down to me.

" 'Read it,' he would say, 'and seek what may be of use to you, it will fill in your time in that hole.'

"While I was waiting for the 'impossible' answering of my prayer I began, for the time being, to occupy my mind with reading. As soon as my day's salt-grinding stint was over I took up a book, usually beginning with the life of Tikhon; there I read how the Holy Virgin accompanied by Peter and Paul had visited his cell. It was written that the saint had asked the Holy Virgin to prolong peace on earth, but the Apostle Paul said in a loud voice, 'This sign I give unto you when peace shall come to an end: when everybody will say, "It is peace" and confirm it, then sudden ruin will befall the world.'

"I pondered over the apostolic words but at first could not understand them: what was the meaning of the revelations made to the saint by the apostle in these words? But I read in the papers that people in our country and in foreign parts never grew tired of saying that there was peace throughout the world. It was then that my prayer was granted and it came to me that the sign was being fulfilled: 'When everybody will say, "it is peace," then sudden ruin will befall the world.' I was filled with fear for my Russian nation and I began to pray; those who came to visit me I implored: 'Pray that under our Tsar every enemy and foe be vanquished, for the day of destruction is at hand.' And tears were granted unto me in great abundance.... I wept continuously for my country. Then the abbot was told about it.

" 'Our Ishmael is shedding tears in his cellar,' they said, 'and he is prophesying war.'

"The abbot then had me confined in an empty hut in the kitchen-garden where he ordered them to place an icon of the Blessed Silence, that is, the Saviour in the shape of an Angel with gently folded wings, not in his crown of thorns, but as the Lord God of Hosts, with his hands crossed serenely on his breast. I was bidden to prostrate myself daily before the icon until the spirit of prophecy left me. I was locked in the hut and remained there till spring, praying all the time to the Blessed Silence, but directly I saw a man, the spirit would arise in me and I would speak.

"The abbot sent a doctor to look at me and find out whether I was right in my head or not. The doctor spent a long time in my hut and listened to my story as you are doing, but he just spat and said:

" 'You are like a drum, brother, they beat and beat you but they can't beat you to death!'

"Said I:

" 'What can I do? I suppose it has to be that way.'

"When the doctor had listened to everything I had to tell him he went to the abbot and said:

" 'I can't tell just what he is—a harmless, good-natured soul, a lunatic or really a prophet. That's your business, for I know nothing about prophesying, but I advise you to send him away to visit remote places, perhaps he's been too long in one place.'

"They let me go and now I'm on my way to the Solovki Monastery* to pray to Zosim and Sabbatai, for which I have been blessed by the abbot. I've been to most places, but those I haven't seen yet and I want to kneel to them before I die."

"Why do you talk about dying? Are you ill?"

"No, I'm not ill but it may soon be necessary to fight."

---

* A monastery on Solovetsky Island in the White Sea, founded in 1436.

"Just a moment, are you talking about war again?"

"Yes."

"So the Blessed Silence didn't help?"

"I don't know: I try, but the spirit overcomes me."

"What does the spirit tell you?"

"Always the same: gird your loins for battle."

"Do you intend to go and fight yourself?"

"Of course I do. Absolutely: I want to die for my people."

"How can you go and fight in your cowl and cassock?"

"I shan't, I'll take off my cowl and put on a uniform."

At this the enchanted wanderer seemed to feel the spirit of prophecy descending upon him and he fell into a quiet meditation which none of his fellow-passengers dared interrupt by further questions. And what more, indeed, could we have asked him? He had told us the tale of his past life with all the forthrightness of his simple soul and as for his prophecies, they remain in the hands of the one whose works are hidden from the learned and the wise and are at times revealed to babes and sucklings.

1873

LEFTY

BEING THE TALE OF CROSS-EYED LEFTY OF TULA AND THE STEEL FLEA

CHAPTER THE FIRST

WHEN TSAR ALEXANDER PAVLOVICH had finished with the Vienna Council* he got the idea of travelling about Europe to see what the different countries had to show him. He went to many countries, was very friendly and had heart-to-heart talks with all sorts of people; they all had something to impress him with and win him over to their side, but he had with him a Cossack from the Don, Platov** by name, who did not like all these goings on; Platov was homesick for his farm on the Don and kept worrying the tsar to go back to Russia. Whenever Platov saw the tsar getting interested in something foreign, with all his following standing by in silence, he would go up to him and say, "That's all right, of course, but ours at home are just as good." Then he would get up to some trick to distract the tsar's attention.

By the time the tsar got to their country the English had heard all about this and they thought up some pretty tricks calculated to capture his fancy by their very foreignness and so take his mind off the Russians. In many cases they succeeded, especially where there were big assemblies and Platov could not say what he wanted to in French. As a matter of fact he was not interested in French, for he was a married man and thought all French talk too trifling to bother his head about. The English invited the tsar to their warehouses and arsenals and soapworks and everywhere else to show that they were so much better at everything than the Russians and were thus able to boast. Then it was that Platov made up his mind:

* The Vienna Congress, September 1814-June 1815.
** Matvei Ivanovich Platov (1751-1818), a famous ataman of the Don Cossack army, a popular hero during the Napoleon wars of 1812-1815.

"That's enough. I've put up with it so far but—no more! Even if I can't talk French I'm not going to let our people down!"

No sooner had he said this to himself than the tsar spoke to him:

"You and I are going to see their arms museum tomorrow," he said. "They have many things of great perfection there and once you've seen them you'll stop arguing when you hear it said that we Russians are no good at anything."

Platov did not answer the tsar, he merely buried his big ugly nose in his shaggy cloak and went back to his quarters. There he ordered his batman to get a bottle of Caucasian vodka out of his hamper, knocked back a full glass, said his prayers before a travelling shrine, rolled himself up in his cloak and snored so terrifically that none of the Englishmen in the house could get any sleep.

"I must sleep on it," he thought.

CHAPTER THE SECOND

The next day the tsar went to the museum with Platov; he could not take any other Russians with him because the carriage they gave him was a two-seater.

They arrived at a huge building with an indescribable entrance, corridors without end, rooms one after another, and, in the middle of the last big room, where there were all sorts of big busts, there stood a statue of the Apollo Belvedere under a canopy.

The tsar kept glancing at Platov as they walked along to see whether he showed surprise and to find out what he was looking at. But Platov strode along with his eyes fixed on the floor as though he wasn't looking at anything at all and kept twisting the end of his moustache into a ring.

240

The English immediately started showing them all kinds of marvels and explaining what things they had for use in wartime: naval barometers, camel-hair cloaks for the infantry, and waterproof cloaks for the cavalry. The tsar was very pleased with all this, everything seemed so good to him, but Platov was still waiting, nothing of this meant anything to him.

"How can you be like that?" said the tsar. "Why don't you say something? Isn't there anything here that impresses you?"

And Platov replied:

"There's only one thing that impresses me: my Cossack boys fought without any of this and drove twelve nations out of our country."

The tsar said:

"That's all prejudice."

To which Platov replied:

"I don't know what it's called, but I don't dare argue and must keep my mouth shut."

But the Englishmen, noticing the dissension between them, took them straight to the statue of Apollo Belvedere and took a Mortimer musket from one of his hands and a pistol from the other.

"Look," they said, "what we can make," and handed the musket to the tsar.

The tsar did not show any great interest as he looked at the Mortimer musket for he had some like it at Tsarskoye Selo, so they gave him the pistol and said:

"This pistol is of unknown, incomparable make—one of our admirals snatched it from the belt of a pirate captain at Calabria."

The tsar examined the pistol and couldn't take his eyes off it.

"Oh," he gasped in amazement. "It is—how can anyone possibly do such wonderful work!" And he turned and said to Platov in Russian, "If I had just one such craftsman in Russia I would be very happy and proud and I would make that craftsman a lord on the spot."

When he heard that, Platov put his right hand into the pocket of his big, baggy trousers and pulled out a gunsmith's screwdriver. The Englishmen told him that the thing didn't open but he paid no attention to them, and picked at the lock. He gave the screwdriver a turn or two and pulled the lock out. He showed the tsar the cocking piece that had an inscription on it in Russian: "Ivan Moskvin in the town of Tula."

The Englishmen were surprised and nudged each other:

"Oho, we've been had."

But the tsar said sadly to Platov:

"Why did you have to upset them; I'm sorry for them now. Let's go."

They got back into their two-seater carriage and drove off. The tsar attended a ball that day but Platov knocked back a still bigger glass of Caucasian vodka and slept the sound sleep of a Cossack.

He was glad he had upset the English and brought the Tula craftsman to the tsar's notice, but one thing vexed him: why had the tsar felt sorry for the English under the circumstances?

"What has made the tsar sorry for them?" Platov wondered. "I can't understand it at all."

Thinking deeply about this he got up twice, crossed himself and drank vodka until he forced himself to fall sound asleep.

The English couldn't sleep either because they were just as worried. While the tsar was having a good time at the ball they got such a new marvel ready for him that even Platov's imagination was staggered.

CHAPTER THE THIRD

Next day, when Platov went to say "Good morning" to the tsar, the emperor said to him:

"Tell them to harness up the two-seater and we'll go and look at some more museums."

Platov even made bold to ask, "Haven't we had enough, looking at foreign things?" he asked. "Wouldn't it be better to get back home to Russia?"

But the tsar said:

"No, there are some more new things I want to see: they've been boasting about the first-class sugar they make."

Off they went.

The English showed the tsar what fine goods they made and Platov kept looking at them and then said:

"Show us some *Molveaux* sugar from your factories."

The Englishmen didn't know what *Molveaux* was. They whispered and winked at each other and kept repeating, "*Molveaux, Molveaux*" and didn't realize that it's a kind of sugar we make in Russia and they had to admit that they had all the sugars there are, but no *Molveaux*.

Platov said:

"Then you haven't got anything to boast about. Come and visit us and we'll treat you to tea with real *Molveaux* from Bobrinsky's factory."*

But the tsar tugged at his sleeve and said softly:

"Don't you go upsetting my politics."

Then the English invited the tsar to see the very last of their museums where they have minerals and insects gathered from all over the world, from the biggest pyramid of Egypt down to the tiniest flea that can't be seen with the naked eye but gets under the skin and bites.

The tsar went there.

* Y. N. Molveaux's sugar refinery was near St. Petersburg and that of A. A. Bobrinsky in Tula Gubernia.

They looked at the Egyptian pyramids and mummies and when they were leaving Platov thought to himself:

"Thank God everything went off all right—there was nothing there to astonish the tsar."

But when they reached the very last room they saw there workmen in sleeved waistcoats and aprons holding a tray on which there was nothing.

The tsar was surprised at their offering him an empty tray.

"What does this mean?" he asked, and the English workmen said, "This is our humble gift to Your Majesty."

"But what is it?"

"Can you, please, see that speck?"

The tsar looked and sure enough there was the tiniest speck of dust lying on the silver tray.

And the workmen said:

"If it please Your Majesty, lick your finger and take it in your hand."

"What do I want a speck of dust for?"

"It isn't a speck of dust: it's a flea."

"Is it alive?"

"Oh, no, it's not alive," they said, "it's made out of pure English steel, we forged it in the form of a flea and inside there's clockwork with a spring. Be kind enough to turn the key and it'll do a dance."

The tsar was curious and asked:

"Where's the key?"

And the English workmen said:

"The key's there, in front of your eyes."

"Then why is it I can't see it?" asked the tsar.

"That's because you need a microscope."

They brought a microscope and the tsar saw that there really was a key lying on the tray next to the flea.

"Be pleased to take it on your hand," they said, "there's a special orifice in its belly; you turn the key seven times and it will begin to dance. . . ."

pipe that held a pound of Zhuko
get back in the carriage and s
silence. The tsar would look o
stick his pipe out of the other
carry the smoke away. In this
tersburg, but the tsar didn't ta
Priest Fedot.

"You aren't fit for spiritual c
you smoke too much, my hea
pipe."

Platov remained behind offe
couch and sulked and smoke
while.

CHAPTER TH

The remarkable flea of Eng
Alexander Pavlovich's whaleb
Taganrog having given it to
over to the empress when she
When the empress saw the
them but didn't do anything

"Mine is a widow's lot," sh
me any more," and when she
she handed it to the new tsar
of his inheritance.

Emperor Nikolai Pavlovich
tention to the flea because c
ascended the throne,* but one
casket left him by his broth
and out of the snuffbox came
the nut, the steel flea, but it
long time and didn't work bu
it had gone stiff.

* The Decembrist Uprising in

2

The tsar could hardly get hold of the key, with difficulty
he held it between finger and thumb and took the flea between the thumb and finger of his other hand; as soon as
he put the key in he felt its whiskers wiggling, then it
began to move its feet and at last it gave a sudden jump,
cutting a caper as it flew through the air; after that it
did two variations on one side and two on the other and
so on until it had danced a full quadrille of three move-
ments.

The tsar immediately ordered that a million be given to
the Englishmen in any money they liked, silver five-kopek
pieces or in small banknotes—anything they wanted.

The Englishmen asked for silver as they had a poor opinion of banknotes; then they showed another cunning trick
of theirs: they gave the tsar the flea but there wasn't any
box to put it in and he couldn't keep either the flea or the
key without a box as they'd soon get lost and thrown out
with the dust. The workmen had made a case out of a
whole diamond as big as a nut with a place for the flea
carved out of the middle. But they didn't give him the
case, they said, because it belonged to the Exchequer
and the English were strict about such things and they
couldn't give it away even to the tsar.

Platov got all worked up over this.

"What's all the swindling about?" he said. "You made
the tsar a present and got a million for it and that's still
not enough for you! You always get a box with everything
you buy."

But the tsar said:

"Don't you go upsetting my politics. You leave matters
alone; it's not your business. They have their own customs," and he asked, "How much does the nut cost, to
put the flea in?"

The English asked another five thousand for it.

Tsar Alexander Pavlovich said, "Pay them," and himself put the flea in the nut and the key together with it

and in order not to los
box which he ordered t
all inlaid with mother-
took leave of the Engl
said:

"You are the first
people can do nothing

They were very plea
ing Platov could say t
the microscope and w
pocket, for, he thought
and, besides, they had

The tsar knew nothi
Russia, and they left
melancholy on account
go to the Priest Fedot
was little pleasant con
for their minds were fill
of the opinion that the
Platov insisted that ou
saw, only they hadn't
to the tsar that the E1
of life for everything,
and that every man ha
thing so that things l

The tsar didn't wan
of thing and Platov, s
they travelled in silenc
get out to drown his v
nibble a salt biscuit;

* "Priest Fedot" is no
Alexander Pavlovich, bef
the Rev. Alexei Fedotov-
self "His Majesty's Con
purely accidental occurre
ently the legendary Pries

The tsar looked at it and wondered.

"What rubbish is this and why did my brother take such care of it?"

His courtiers wanted to throw it away but the tsar said:

"No, there must be some meaning to this."

From the chemist's opposite Anichkov Bridge they called a chemist who was used to weighing poisons on tiny scales and showed it to him and he put it on his tongue and said:

"It feels cold, like some hard metal." Then he tried it lightly with his teeth. "And if it please you, it isn't a real flea, it's a model, it's made of metal, and it's not our handiwork, not Russian."

The tsar immediately ordered that inquiries be made as to where it had come from and what it meant.

They hurried to look through records and registers but did not find any mention of it. They began asking one person after another, but nobody knew anything about it. Fortunately the Don Cossack Platov was still alive; he was even then lying sulking on his couch and smoking his pipe. As soon as he heard that there was such trouble in the palace he rose up from his couch, threw away his pipe and appeared before the tsar wearing all his medals.

"What do you want of me, my brave old man?" asked the tsar.

"I don't want anything for myself, Your Majesty," Platov made reply. "I have my fill of meat and drink and am satisfied. I have come to report about the insect that has been found. It happened in such and such a way," he went on to say, "and it took place before my eyes in England. There's a key to it and I have their microscope for you to see it through. If you take the key and wind it up through its belly it will jump as far as you like and do all sorts of dancing pranks."

When they wound it up it began to jump about.

"True enough, Your Majesty," said Platov, "it's a deli-

248

cate and interesting piece of work but we mustn't let our admiration get the better of us; we must let our master craftsmen at Tula or Sesterbek" (Sestroretsk was called Sesterbek in those days) "have a good look at it and see whether they can't do something better so that the English won't be able to show they're better than the Russians."

Tsar Nikolai Pavlovich had great confidence in his Russian people and did not like to elevate any foreigner over them so he said to Platov:

"That was well said, my brave old man, and I will trust you to prove it. I don't need this box now. I've trouble enough without it, so you take it with you and don't lie on your couch and sulk any more but go to your quiet Don and have a heart-to-heart talk with my Cossacks there about the way they live and about their loyalty and anything else they would like. And when you pass through Tula show this insect to my craftsmen there and let them think about it. Tell them that my brother was impressed with it and praised the foreigners who made the insect very highly, but I rely on my own people and think they are no worse than any others. They won't disregard my words and will do something about it."

CHAPTER THE FIFTH

Platov took the steel flea and as he passed through Tula on his way to the Don showed it to the Tula gunsmiths, told them what the tsar had said and asked them:

"What are we going to do about it, good folk?"

The gunsmiths answered:

"We, sir, are moved by the tsar's gracious words and will never forget him because he has faith in his own people, but what we're going to do in the present case can't be decided in a minute, for the English nation aren't fools, either. They are quite clever, in fact, and their art has a lot of sense to it. To beat them," they said, "we have to think and ask the Lord's blessing. And if you, sir, have as much faith in us as the tsar has, then go home to your quiet Don and leave us the flea as it is, in its case and in the tsar's gold snuffbox. Have a good rest on the Don so that the wounds you received in defence of your country may heal, and when you go back through Tula stop here and send for us: by that time, God willing, we shall have thought of something."

Platov wasn't very pleased that the Tula people wanted so much time and hadn't said definitely what they hoped to arrange. He asked them this way and that, and chatted with them in the cunning manner of the Don Cossacks. The men of Tula, however, were no less cunning than he and they had immediately got hold of such an idea that they couldn't even hope that Platov would believe them and wished to put their bold plan into execution before they disclosed it.

"We don't know ourselves what we're going to do," they said, "only we'll put our trust in the Lord and we hope the tsar will have no reason to regret his kind words about us."

Platov tried cunning arguments but he had met his match in the men of Tula.

He tried one artful move after another but when he saw that he couldn't get the better of them he handed them the snuffbox with the insect in it and said:

"There's nothing more I can do about it. Have it your way. I know what you're like, so there's nothing I can do but trust you, but you had better look out for yourselves. Don't try to replace the diamond and don't spoil the fine English work, and don't be too long about it because I travel fast. Before a fortnight has gone I'll be leaving the Don for St. Petersburg again, so be sure you have something for me to show to the tsar."

The gunsmiths did their best to console him.

"We shan't spoil the fine work," they said, "and we won't replace the diamond. Two weeks is time enough for us and when you come back there'll be *something* for you to show the tsar that is worthy of His Majesty."

But *what*, exactly, they were clever enough not to say.

CHAPTER THE SIXTH

Platov left Tula and three of the gunsmiths, the most skilled amongst them—one cross-eyed and left-handed, with a birthmark on his cheek, whose hair had been pulled out above his temples when he was serving his apprenticeship—took leave of their workmates and families, packed their bags, took some food with them and left the town without a word to anybody.

It was seen, however, that they did not leave by the Moscow Toll-Gate, but by the opposite one, in the direction of Kiev and it was thought that they had gone to Kiev to pray at the tombs of the saints or to seek the advice of the holy men always to be found there in large numbers.

Although this was close to the truth it was not the truth itself. Neither the time nor the distance would allow the Tula gunsmiths to walk three weeks to Kiev and after that do a job that would put the English nation to shame. They would have done better to go to Moscow to pray, since it was only "twice ninety versts" there and there were saints enough in the city. In the other direction it was also "twice ninety versts" to Orel but from Orel to Kiev was a good five hundred versts more. That was a journey they couldn't do in a hurry and if they had done it they would have needed a long time to rest, with their feet swollen and their hands trembling.

Some people even thought that the gunsmiths had merely boasted to Platov, had then thought better of it, got scared and run away altogether taking with them the tsar's gold snuffbox, the diamond and the flea in its case that had caused so much bother.

But such a suggestion was quite groundless and unworthy of the craftsmen on whom the honour of the nation now rested.

CHAPTER THE SEVENTH

The people of Tula, clever people skilled in the art of metal work, are also well-known experts on matters religious. They enjoy this fame not only in their own country but also at holy Mount Athos: not only do they sing well, putting in all the trills, but they know how to paint the picture *Evening Bells*, and if any of them dedicate themselves to service and join a monastery they become famous as stewards and make the most skilled collectors of funds. At holy Mount Athos it is known that the men of Tula bring in the best results; if it were not for them the dark corners of Russia would probably never have seen many of the holy relics from the distant East, and Athos would have been deprived of much evidence of Russian generosity and piety. The "Athos Tulans" carry the sacred relics all over the country and are clever enough to collect funds even where there is nothing to collect. Your Tulan, then, is devoted to the church and is a great religious practitioner, so that the three gunsmiths who had undertaken to give their support to Platov and all Russia had made no mistake in leaving for the south instead of going to Moscow. They had no intention of going to Kiev but to Mtsensk, a district town of their own Orel Gubernia where there was a "graven stone image" of St. Nicholas that had come floating down the River Zusha on a stone cross in the most ancient days. That "menacing and terrifying" icon was a life-size depiction of the Saint in silver robes and with a dark face, a temple in one hand and in the other a sword called "Victory in Battle." The whole secret of the business was in that "victory": St. Nicholas in general, and the Mtsensk Nicholas in particular, was the patron of commerce and war and so, as gunsmiths, they went to pray to his icon. They held a service before the icon itself, another before the stone cross and returned home from there by night; without a word to anybody they set about their work in dead secret. They got together in Lefty's house, locked themselves in, closed the shutters, lit the lamp in front of the icon and began work.

They remained there a day, a second and a third; none of them left the house but all the time they were tap, tap, tapping away with their little hammers. They were forging something but what it was nobody knew.

Everybody was curious but nobody could find out anything for the workers spoke to nobody and did not show themselves outside the house. All sorts of people went knocking at the door with all manner of excuses, asking for a light or for some salt, but the craftsmen wouldn't open the door under any pretext; what they ate all that time, nobody knew. Attempts were made to scare them by cries that the house next door was on fire in the hope that they would run out and reveal what they were forging. Nothing, however, could trick the cunning gunsmiths. Once Lefty did stick his head and shoulders out and shout:

"Burn as much as you like, we're busy," and again slammed the shutter to and got on with his work.

Through chinks in the shutters it could be seen that a fire was burning and the people outside could hear little hammers ringing on the anvils.

In short the whole business was done in such great secrecy that nobody could find out anything, and this went on until the Cossack Platov returned from the quiet Don on his way back to the tsar; all that time the gunsmiths spoke to nobody and saw nobody.

CHAPTER THE EIGHTH

Platov travelled with great speed and ceremony: he sat in his carriage and two Cossack orderlies sat on the box on either side of the coachman and belaboured him with their whips mercilessly so that he would keep going at a gallop. If either of the Cossacks dozed off Platov in his carriage would give him a reminder with the toe of his boot to speed up the gallop. So great was the effect of this method of encouragement that the horses could not be halted at any of the stations but always overshot the halting places by a hundred lengths. Then the Cossacks would reverse the operation with their whips and the coachman would drive back to the inn.

They entered Tula in the same way. At first they dashed a hundred lengths past the Moscow Toll-Gate, then the Cossacks operated on the coachman with their whips until he drew up at the inn and fresh horses were put in. Platov did not get out of the carriage but told one of the orderlies to bring to him, as quickly as possible, the gunsmiths with whom he had left the flea.

One of the orderlies ran off to tell the gunsmiths to come as fast as they could and bring with them the work that was to disgrace the English, but before he had gone far Platov sent more and more Cossacks to hurry them up.

He sent off all the Cossacks and then started sending people from the crowd of onlookers, and himself even put his legs out of the carriage in his impatience and wanted to run there himself; he ground his teeth with rage—they all seemed too slow to him.

In those days everything had to be done with speed and precision, so that not one minute should be lost that might be of value to Russia.

CHAPTER THE NINTH

The Tula craftsmen who were doing a wonderful piece of work were at that time just finishing it off. The orderlies ran, panting, to their destination but the people from the crowd didn't get far for they were not used to it and their legs gave way and they flopped to the ground and after that, out of fear of Platov, hurried home and hid wherever they could.

When the orderlies reached the house they called out loudly and as the gunsmiths didn't open the door they tried to break open the shutters. These, however, were strong and would not give, so they tried the door but that was held fast inside with an oaken beam. Then the orderlies took a log that was lying in the street, put it under the eaves the way firemen do and in a moment ripped the roof off that tiny house. They got the roof off but were knocked off their feet themselves by the foul air that burst out, for the gunsmiths had been working continuously in the little closed room and the atmosphere had become so thick that a man used to fresh air couldn't stand a single whiff of it.

"What are you doing in there, you so-and-so's, you bastards," the messengers screamed, "and how dare you make such a stink to knock us out. Isn't there any fear of God in you?"

The gunsmiths answered:

"We're just knocking in the last nail and when it's done we'll bring our work."

"He'll eat us alive by that time," said the messengers, "and leave nothing to remember us by."

But the gunsmiths reassured them.

"He won't have time to swallow you because we've knocked in the last nail while you've been talking," they said. "Run and tell him we're coming."

The orderlies ran off, but they weren't too sure of

things. They thought the gunsmiths might be deceiving them, so that they kept looking back as they ran; but the craftsmen ran after them and were in such a hurry that they had not had time to dress in a manner fitting the important person they were to appear before, but hooked up their coats as they ran. Two of them had nothing in their hands, but the third, Lefty, held the tsar's casket in a green cover with the English steel flea inside.

CHAPTER THE TENTH

The orderlies ran up to Platov and said:
"Here they are themselves!"
Platov immediately turned to the gunsmiths.
"Is it ready?"
"Everything's ready," they answered.
"Let me have it!"
They gave it to him.
The horses were already harnessed up and the coachman and postillion were in their places. The Cossacks had taken their places beside the coachman and were holding their whips over him in readiness.
Platov pulled off the green cover, opened the casket, took out the gold snuffbox and out of that the diamond nut. He looked at it. The English flea was lying there but apart from that there was nothing else.
"What's the meaning of this?" asked Platov. "Where's the work you wanted to please the tsar with?"
"Our work's there as well," the gunsmiths answered.
"What sort of work have you done?" asked Platov.
"Why explain it?" said the gunsmiths. "It's all there in front of your eyes. You have a good look at it."
Platov shrugged his shoulders and roared:
"Where's the key to the flea?"
"It's there," they answered, "the key's where the flea is, in the same nut."

Platov tried to pick up the key but his short, stumpy fingers wouldn't hold either the flea or the key to its belly mechanism no matter how he tried, and he began to let out a stream of real Cossack profanity.

"You scoundrels haven't done anything," he shouted, "and you've probably spoilt the whole thing! I'll have your heads for this!"

"There's no need to insult us like that although we have to put up with it because you're the tsar's envoy but since you doubt us and think that we are capable of playing a trick on the tsar even, we shan't tell you the secret of our work; be kind enough to take it to the tsar. He'll see what kind of people he has and whether he has cause to be ashamed of us."

But Platov screamed back at them:

"You're lying, you scoundrels, but I'm not letting you go like that. One of you will come to St. Petersburg with me and there I'll make him tell me the secret."

With that he stretched out his hand, seized cross-eyed Lefty by the collar with his stumpy fingers so that all the hooks flew off his coat, and threw him down at his feet in the carriage.

"You can sit there like a poodle all the way to St. Petersburg," he said, "and you'll be responsible for all of them. And you," he said turning to his orderlies, "get a move on. Don't doze and see that I'm in St. Petersburg at the tsar's palace the day after tomorrow."

The craftsmen dared only say on behalf of their workmate that Platov shouldn't take him away like that without any paper because he wouldn't be able to get back. Instead of answering them Platov showed them his fist, a terrible, red, gnarled fist covered with ugly scars, shook it at them and said, "There's a paper for you!"

And to the Cossacks he said:

"Off you go, lads."

The Cossacks, the coachman and the horses all worked

with a will and carried off Lefty without any papers and, in two days, as Platov had ordered, galloped up to the tsar's palace at such speed that they flew past the columns.

Platov got out, put on his medals and went to the tsar leaving the Cossack orderlies to keep watch over Lefty at the palace gates.

CHAPTER THE ELEVENTH

Platov was afraid to appear before the tsar, for Nikolai Pavlovich was a man who noticed and remembered everything, and never forgot a thing. Platov knew that he was certain to ask about the flea. And he, who had never feared any enemy in the world, took fright: he went into the palace with the casket and quietly placed it behind the stove in one of the rooms. Once he had hidden the casket Platov appeared before the tsar in his study and began his report on the heart-to-heart talks he had had with the Cossacks on the quiet Don. "I'll keep the tsar busy with this," he thought, "and if he remembers the flea and talks about it I'll have to answer him, but if he doesn't say anything I'll keep quiet, and I'll tell the valet who looks after the study to hide the casket and Tula Lefty can go into a fortress where he can remain until he's wanted."

Tsar Nikolai Pavlovich, however, had not forgotten anything, and as soon as Platov had finished telling him about his heart-to-heart talks he straight away asked him:

"And what did my Tula craftsmen do that's better than the English flea?"

Platov answered what he believed to be the truth.

"The flea, Your Majesty," he said, "is just where it was and I've brought it back, but the Tula craftsmen couldn't do anything more wonderful."

"You're a brave old man," said the tsar, "but what you've told me can't be true."

Platov assured him that it was, and told him the whole story of what had happened. When he got to where the Tula gunsmiths asked him to show the flea to the tsar, Nikolai Pavlovich tapped him on the shoulder:

"Bring it here," he said, "I knew my people wouldn't let me down. They've done something that is beyond all understanding."

CHAPTER THE TWELFTH

They brought the casket from behind the stove, took off the cloth cover, opened the gold snuffbox and the diamond nut—and there lay the flea just as it had done before.

The tsar looked at it and said:

"What the devil!" But his faith in his Russian workmen was not shaken and he told his people to call his favourite daughter, Alexandra Nikolayevna, and said to her, "You have delicate fingers. Take the little key and wind up the machine in the insect's belly."

The princess began to turn the key and the flea immediately wiggled its whiskers but its feet didn't move. Alexandra Nikolayevna wound it up as far as it would go, but the insect didn't dance and didn't cut any of the capers it did before.

Platov turned quite green and shouted:

"Oh, those dirty swindlers! Now I know why they didn't want to tell me anything there. It's a good thing I brought one of the fools with me."

At that he rushed to the palace gate, caught Lefty by the hair and banged his head back and forth until some of the hair came out. When Platov had stopped beating him, Lefty said:

"I lost enough hair when I was an apprentice, and I don't know why that has to be repeated now."

"I'll tell you why," answered Platov, "it's because I trusted you and vouched for you, and you've spoilt a rare piece of work."

"We are very pleased that you vouched for us," answered Lefty, "but we did nothing to spoil it: look at it under the most powerful microscope and see for yourself."

Platov ran back to tell the tsar about the microscope but threatened Lefty in parting:

"And you, you so-and-so, I'll give you what for."

He ordered his Cossacks to tie Lefty's elbows back still tighter and as he ran panting up the stairs muttered a prayer to himself, "Oh, King of Kings, Oh, pure and holy Virgin...." and so on to the end. The courtiers standing on the staircase turned away from Platov for they thought that he was in trouble and would be sure to be kicked out of the palace, and they couldn't stand him on account of his bravery.

CHAPTER THE THIRTEENTH

When Platov told the tsar what Lefty had said the tsar exclaimed joyfully:

"I knew my Russian people wouldn't let me down," and ordered a microscope to be brought to him on a cushion.

In a moment it was brought in and the tsar took the flea and put it under the glass, at first back upwards and then on its side and then belly uppermost, but whichever way he turned it he could not see anything. But still the tsar did not lose faith and just said:

"Bring that gunsmith who is downstairs to me right away."

"He ought to be properly dressed," said Platov, "he's wearing what I took him in and he's rather tousled."

anyway, I'd ge[...]
married."

"You'll get u[...]
and we'll find y[...]

"That can nev[...]

"Why not?"

"Because," he[...]
faith; our ances[...]

"But you don'[...]
"We have the s[...]
same Gospel."

"The Gospel i[...]
"only our books[...]
fuller."

"What makes [...]

"We have eve[...]

"What proofs [...]

"We have thes[...]
have others that[...]
have nothing Yo[...]
except Sunday, a[...]
be embarrassing[...]
even if we were [...]

"Why should i[...]
our women. They[...]
housewives."

But Lefty said:[...]

"I don't know [...]

"That doesn't [...]
arrange a rendez[...]

Lefty felt asham[...]

"Why trouble [...]
refused them. "A[...]
doesn't become u[...]
Tula they'd make [...]

This made the E[...]

sect immediately examined it under the most powerful microscope and sent a description to the newspapers so that it would be published next morning for everybody's information.

"And that craftsman," they said, "we want to see him."

The messenger took them to the hotel room and from there to the dining-room where our Lefty had already got a good load on, and said, "There he is!"

The Englishmen patted Lefty on the shoulder and shook hands with him as an equal.

"Kamerad," they said, "Kamerad, fine craftsman— we'll talk to you later on but in the meantime we'll drink your health."

They ordered a lot of wine and offered Lefty the first glass, but he politely refused to drink first: "They might want to poison me because I have them beat," he thought.

"No," he said, "that's not right: the host must drink first, then I'll drink."

The Englishmen tried all the wines before he drank and then began to fill his glass. He stood up, crossed himself with his left hand and drank the healths of all of them.

They noticed that he crossed himself with his left hand and asked the messenger:

"What is he, a Lutheran or a Protestant?"

"He's neither a Lutheran nor a Protestant," answered the messenger, "he's Russian Orthodox."

"Then why does he cross himself with his left hand?"

"He's left-handed, he does everything with his left hand."

This astounded the English still more and they began pouring wine into Lefty and the messenger and kept it up for three whole days and then said, "Enough." They drank a siphon of soda water each and quite refreshed began to question Lefty: where and what he had learned, how far had he gone in arithmetic?

"Our le
Book of I
don't leari
    The Eng
    "How v
    "That's
answered
    "And wl
Dreams?"
    "It's a t
reading of
Book of P
tional expl
    "That's
know at th
it would be
Dreams. Th
is calculate
very clevei
a tiny mac
precision
That's why
more."
    Lefty agr
    "There's
very strong
    The Engl
    "Stay hei
and you'll t
    To this, h
    "I have p
    The Engli
but he woul
    "We are
father's an
they're used

"If you don't have a rendezvous," they asked, "how do you manage to make sure of a good choice?"

Lefty explained to them how we do things.

"When a man wants to make known his intentions towards a girl," he said, "he sends an old woman, a matchmaker, and she makes the proposal, then they go together to the girl's home and see her publicly, in front of all her relations."

They understood what he had told them but said that they had no matchmakers and no such custom but Lefty said:

"So much the better, for to do anything of the sort one must have honourable intentions and as I don't feel well disposed towards a foreign nation why should I trouble the girls?"

The Englishmen approved of his opinions and again patted him on the shoulders and knees very affably and asked:

"There's something we want to know out of curiosity: what faults have you discovered in our girls that you're so anxious to avoid them?"

Lefty answered that question quite frankly.

"I don't want to find fault only I don't like the way their clothes billow around them and you can't tell what they've got on and for what purpose; here she has something and underneath it there's something else pinned on and she has some sort of stockings on her hands. And their velvet talmas are like those they put on little monkeys."

"How does that hinder you?" asked the Englishmen, laughing.

"It's no hindrance, only I'm afraid I'd feel ashamed watching her and waiting till she gets out of it all."

"Can it be that your fashions are better?" they asked.

"Fashions in Tula are simple," he answered, "each

wears her own lace and even the great ladies wear our lace."

They showed him their ladies, poured him out tea and asked:

"What are you turning your nose up at?"

"We're not used to anything so sweet."

So they gave him a piece of sugar to hold in his mouth, Russian fashion.

They thought that would be worse but he said:

"To our taste it's better."

The Englishmen couldn't do anything to make him fancy the English way of life; they could only persuade him to be their guest for a short while during which time they would show him their factories and their skill in making things.

"And then," they said, "we'll take you in one of our own ships and *bring you alive to St. Petersburg.*"

To that he agreed.

CHAPTER THE SIXTEENTH

The English took Lefty under their own protection and sent the Russian messenger back to Russia. Although the messenger was a man of rank and knew different languages, they were not interested in him, but in Lefty, whom they took round and showed everything. He saw all their metal factories and their soap factories and he liked them; he liked the way things were done and especially the way the workers lived. Every worker had enough to eat all the time and wasn't dressed in rags but in a good sleeved waistcoat and thick leather boots with iron tips so that he wouldn't hurt his feet if he trod on anything; he didn't work from fear of the whip but had been properly taught and understood what he was doing. The multiplication tables hung in front of every worker and to hand he had a slate: whenever a craftsman did anything he looked at the multiplication tables and checked what he was doing with understanding. Then he would write something on the slate and rub something else out and got everything right; whatever was written in figures came out in the work. And on holidays they'd gather in couples, walking sticks in hand, and walk along sedately, in proper style.

Lefty had a good look at the way they lived and at their work but he paid the greatest attention to something that astounded the English. He wasn't so interested in the way they made new muskets as he was in the condition of the old ones. He would look at the new guns, praise them and say:

"We can make them as well as that."

Whenever he came across an old musket he'd stick his finger in the muzzle, run it round the walls of the barrel and say:

"That beats ours by a long shot."

The Englishmen couldn't make out what Lefty had got his eye on.

"Could you tell me whether our generals have seen this or not?" he asked them.

"Those that were here must have seen it," they told him.

"And were they wearing gloves or not?" he asked.

"Your generals are always in full dress," they told him, "and always wear gloves so they must have worn them here."

Lefty didn't answer. But he suddenly became miserable and terribly homesick.

"I thank you humbly for your hospitality," he said to the English. "I've been very pleased with everything and I've seen all I wanted to see, now I want to get home as quickly as I can."

They couldn't persuade him to stay any longer. They couldn't let him go overland because he didn't know languages and it wasn't advisable to go by sea as it was autumn and stormy, but he insisted: "Let me go."

"We have looked at the barometer," they said, "there's going to be a storm; you may get drowned, for this is the real sea, this isn't your Gulf of Finland."

"It's all the same where a man dies," he answered, "it's the will of God and I want to go home before I go off my head."

They didn't hold him back by force. They gave him food, provided him with money, presented him with a gold repeater watch as a memento and a woollen coat with a hood to protect him from the cold at sea. They dressed him very warmly and placed him on board a ship bound for Russia. They gave him the best cabin, like a real gentleman, but he didn't want to sit below decks with the other gentlemen but went up on deck, sat down under a tarpaulin and asked:

"Where is our Russia?"

The Englishman he asked would point in the direction with his hand, or indicate it with his head and Lefty would turn his face that way and gaze impatiently in the direction of his native land.

When they sailed out of the bay into the open sea his longing for Russia grew so great that he could not be consoled. The tossing was terrible but Lefty didn't go down to his cabin, he sat under his tarpaulin, pulled his hood down and stared towards home.

Many times the English tried to take him down to a warm place but he lied to them so that they would leave him alone.

"No," he said, "I'm better up here. If I go down under the roof I'll get seasick."

All the time he didn't go below except for an important reason, and this was to the liking of a certain English skipper's mate, who, to Lefty's sorrow, could speak Russian. This sailor was greatly surprised that a Russian landlubber could stand all that bad weather.

"Good boy, Russ!" he said. "Let's have a drink."

Lefty had a drink.

"Another," said the mate.

Lefty took another drink and they both got tipsy.

The mate asked Lefty:

"What's the secret you're taking back to Russia from our country?"

"That's my business," answered Lefty.

"If it's that way," said the mate, "then let's make a bet, English fashion."

"How?" asked Lefty.

"We bet never to drink alone but always together and the same drink; and whoever outdrinks the other wins the bet."

"The sky's cloudy, my belly's rowdy, I'm bored to death, there's a long way left, and I can't see my home for the waves—the bet'll make me cheer up a bit," thought Lefty to himself.

"All right," he said, "it's a go."

"But play fair."

"Don't worry about that," said Lefty.

They agreed and shook hands on it.

CHAPTER THE SEVENTEENTH

Their bet began in the open sea. They kept on drinking till they reached the Riga Dünamünde keeping perfectly level, neither falling behind the other, and so well matched were they that when one of them looked at the sea and saw the devil creeping out of the water, the devil would immediately appear to the other, except that the sailor saw a red-headed devil and Lefty saw one that was dark, like a blackamoor.

"Cross yourself and turn away," said Lefty, "that is the devil rising out of the deep."

The Englishman argued with him:

"It's a diver."

"If you like," he said, "I'll chuck you into the water and you needn't be afraid, he'll give you back to me at once."

"If that's so you can chuck me into the water," said Lefty.

The Englishman picked him up and carried him to the rail.

The other sailors saw them and stopped them; they told the captain and he ordered them to be locked in a cabin together and that rum and wine and cold food be given them so that they could keep their bet—he didn't give them hot pudding with flames because it might set fire to the spirit inside them.

So they were brought safely locked up to St. Petersburg, and neither of them won the bet and in port they were laid out on different carts and the Englishman was taken to the English Embassy on the English Quay and Lefty to a police station.

From then on they suffered greatly different fates.

CHAPTER THE EIGHTEENTH

As soon as the Englishman was brought into the Embassy a doctor and an apothecary were sent for, the doctor ordered him to be given a hot bath in his presence, the apothecary there and then rolled a pill and put it in his mouth, then the two of them took and laid him out on a feather bed, covered him with a heavy coat and left him to sweat and gave orders that nobody in the Embassy should sneeze in order not to disturb him. The doctor and the apothecary waited until the mariner had fallen asleep, then they made another pill for him, placed it on the table beside his head and went away.

Lefty was dumped on the police station floor where they asked him:

"Who are you and where have you come from? Have you got a passport or any other document?"

On account of sickness, the drink and the tossing of the ship he was so weak that he did not say a word, but only groaned.

They searched him, took off his fine clothes, took away his repeater watch and his money and the police captain ordered him to be taken to the hospital free of charge in the first sleigh they could find.

A policeman took Lefty out to put him in a sleigh but it was a long time before he could find one, for sleigh-drivers avoid the police. All this time Lefty was lying on the cold, stone steps; then the policeman caught a cabby but the sleigh was without a fur rug for in such cases the cabbies hide the fur rugs under them so that the policeman's legs will get frost-bitten more quickly. So they took Lefty uncovered and transferred him from one sleigh to another, dropping him and picking him up again and pulling his ears to bring him round. They took him to one hospital but they wouldn't accept him without a document, so they took him to a second and a third and a fourth and so they kept on until morning, dragging him round all the distant alleys and byways and moving him from one sleigh to another until he was all beaten black and blue. Then a doctor's assistant told them to take him to the Obukhov Free Hospital where people of unknown origin were taken in to die.

They told the policeman to sign something and to sit Lefty on the floor in the corridor until they could deal with him.

In the meantime the English petty officer, since it was already morning, got up, swallowed the other pill, made a light breakfast of chicken and rice, washed it down with soda water and asked:

"Where's my Russian comrade? I'm going to look for him."

He dressed and went out.

CHAPTER THE NINETEENTH

In some amazing way the petty officer very soon found Lefty and they still hadn't got him to bed, he lay on the floor in the corridor and complained to the Englishman.

"There are a couple of words I must say to the tsar," he said.

The Englishman ran to see Count Kleinmikhel* where he created a disturbance.

"How can you allow it? Hasn't he got a human soul under his ragged coat?" he said.

For this wise thought the Englishman was driven away so that he wouldn't dare mention a human soul again. Then somebody told him he ought to see the Cossack Platov, whose feelings were simple and human.

The Englishman found Platov who was back on his couch again, sulking. He listened to the petty officer and remembered all about Lefty.

"Why, brother," said Platov, "I know him very well, I've even pulled his hair, only I don't know how to help in this present misfortune because I've finished with the service and have quite retired. Nobody respects me any more, but you go to the Commandant Skobelev.** He has power and he's had this sort of experience so he'll do something for you."

The petty officer went to Skobelev and told him every-

* Count Kleinmikhel, Minister for Foreign Affairs, Imperial Chancellor under Nikolai I.
** General Skobelev, a general under Nikolai I, for many years commandant of the Fortress of Peter and Paul.

thing, what kind of disease Lefty was suffering from and how it had happened. Skobelev said:

"I know that illness. Only the Germans can't cure it, what you need is a doctor from a priestly family, because they've known such cases from childhood and can help: right now I'll send you the Russian doctor, Martin-Solsky."

The only thing was that when Doctor Martin-Solsky arrived Lefty was already dying for the back of his head had been split open on the pavement and all he could gasp was:

"Tell the tsar that the English don't clean their musket barrels with brick-dust; we shouldn't clean them that way, either, for if there should be a war, which God forbid, they won't be any use for shooting."

And with that expression of loyalty Lefty crossed himself and died.

Martin-Solsky immediately reported the matter to Count Chernishev* so that he should bring it to the tsar's notice but Count Chernishev shouted at him:

"You look after your emetics and purgatives and keep your nose out of what doesn't concern you—there are generals in Russia for that."

So nobody ever told the tsar and the muskets were cleaned that way right up to the Crimean War. And then, when they started loading the muskets, the bullets rattled in them because the barrels had been enlarged through being cleaned with brick-dust. Then Martin-Solsky reminded Chernishev of Lefty's words and the count said to him:

"You can go to hell, sawbones, and mind your own business, or I'll deny that you ever said anything of the sort to me and you'll get into trouble."

* Count Chernishev, Minister for War and President of the State Council.

"He'll deny it, sure enough," thought Martin-Solsky and kept his mouth shut.

If Lefty's words had been conveyed to the tsar in time things would have turned out differently during the war in the Crimea.

CHAPTER THE TWENTIETH

All this is now "a matter of days long past," a "legend of the days of old," but the days aren't so very old, either, so we need not be in a hurry to forget the legend, despite the air of fable it has about it and the epic character of the hero. Lefty's real name, like those of many of the world's greatest geniuses, has been lost for posterity; he is, however, interesting as a myth created by the fantasy of the people and his adventures can serve to recall a whole epoch that has here been precisely and faithfully rendered.

Needless to say, there are no craftsmen like the fabulous Lefty in Tula any more: machines have served to smooth out inequalities in talents and endowments and genius cannot do battle against industry and accuracy. Although machines favour an increase in wages they do not favour that artistic daring which, at times, broke down all barriers and which inspired the popular fantasy to compose legends like this present story.

The workers, of course, can appreciate the advantages they gain from devices put at their disposal by science but they remember the days of old with pride and affection. This is their epic and one with a very "human soul."

1881

Amongst the blessed will their souls find rest.
A Dirge

THE MAKE-UP ARTIST

(THE STORY OF A GRAVE)

*(In sacred memory of the blessed day
of February 19th, 1861)*

CHAPTER THE FIRST

THERE ARE MANY amongst us who hold that artists must be either painters or sculptors, and of these only those on whom the Academy has conferred the title, others being deemed unworthy. To many people Sazikov and Ovchinnikov are mere "silversmiths." Such is not the case with other nations. Heine recalls a tailor who was an "artist," a man who "had ideas," and ladies' dresses made by Worth are today called "artistic creations." It was recently claimed for one of them that "the cut of the bodice contained a world of imagination."

In America the artistic field is understood in an even broader sense. The famous American writer Bret· Harte tells of a man who gained great fame there as an "artist" who "worked on the dead." He gave the faces of the late lamented various "comforting expressions" which attested the more or less happy state of their departed souls.

There were several degrees of this art—I can recall only three: 1) composure, 2) exalted contemplation and 3) the bliss of direct intercourse with God. The fame of the artist was as great as the high perfection of his work, that is, it was enormous, but unfortunately he fell victim to the rude mob which had no respect for free creative art. He was stoned to death for giving an "expression of blissful intercourse with God" to the face of a fraudulent banker who had robbed the whole town. The grafter's happy heirs had wanted to express their gratitude to their dear departed relative but the artist paid for this order with his life.

In Russia we once had an artist who was also a master in an unusual field.

CHAPTER THE SECOND

My younger brother's nurse was a tall, dried-up but stately old woman known as Lyubov Onisimovna. She had been an actress of the Orel Theatre which formerly belonged to Count Kamensky, and that which I am about to relate also took place in Orel in my boyhood days.

My brother is seven years younger than I, so that when he was two years old and in Lyubov Onisimovna's hands, I had already turned nine and could readily understand the stories I heard.

Lyubov Onisimovna was not very old at that time, but her hair was pure white; she had finely cut, delicate features and her tall figure was remarkably slender and upright, like that of a young girl.

When my mother and my aunt chanced to glance at her they would say that in her time she had undoubtedly been a real beauty. She was honest to a fault, gentle and sentimental; she loved the tragic in life and ... she sometimes drank.

She used to take us for walks to the cemetery at the Church of the Holy Trinity where she would sit down on a simple grave mound adorned with an old cross and quite frequently would tell me stories.

It was there that I heard from her the story of the "make-up artist."

CHAPTER THE THIRD

He had been our nurse's colleague at the theatre: the difference was that she "acted on the stage and performed dances" while he was the "make-up artist," that is the hairdresser and make-up man who "painted and dressed the hair" of all the count's serf actresses. He wasn't the ordinary, everyday hairdresser with a comb behind his ear and a bit of rouge mixed with lard on a tin plate but *a man with ideas*, in other words, an *artist*.

In the words of Lyubov Onisimovna there was nobody who could "give a better expression to a face" than he.

I cannot say with any degree of certainty under which of the Counts Kamensky these two artistic spirits flourished. Of the Counts Kamensky three are remembered by the older inhabitants of Orel and all three had the reputation of being "unconscionable tyrants." Field Marshal Mikhail Fedotovich was killed by his serfs in 1809 for his cruelty; he left two sons, Nikolai, who died in 1811, and Sergei, who died in 1835.

In the forties, when I was still a child, I remember a huge, grey wooden building with false windows painted on it in soot and ochre and enclosed by an extraordinarily long, half-ruined fence. This was the ill-famed estate of Count Kamensky and the theatre was located there. It was so situated that it could be seen splendidly from the cemetery of the Church of the Holy Trinity and for that reason whenever Lyubov Onisimovna wanted to tell me some tale she almost always began with the words:

"Look at that, my dear.... Isn't it awful?"

"Yes, nurse," I'd say, "it's awful."

"Well, what I'm going to tell you is even more awful."

Here is one of her stories about the hairdresser Arkady, a brave and tender-hearted young man of whom she had been very fond.

CHAPTER THE FOURTH

Arkady "did the hair" for and "painted" only actresses. The actors had another hairdresser and if Arkady ever visited the men's rooms it was only because the count had ordered him to "paint somebody like a perfect gentleman." The main feature of the artist's make-up was the idea underlying it, which enabled him to give the faces of the actors and actresses the most varied and subtle expressions.

"They would send for him," said Lyubov Onisimovna, "and say, 'We want such and such an expression on the face,' and he would draw back, tell the actor or actress to stand or sit down before him while he would fold his arms and think. At that time he was the most handsome of them all. He was of medium height but was so slender and upright that I can't even describe it; he had a thin, proud nose and the kind eyes of an angel and a thick forelock that fell down over his eyes so that he seemed to be looking at you through a cloud."

In short, the make-up artist was a very handsome man and "*everybody*" liked him." The count himself also liked him, favoured him above all the others and had him excellently dressed, but was very strict with him. He did not want him to shave or cut the hair of any man but himself and *always* kept him near his dressing-room: Arkady was not allowed to go anywhere except the theatre. He could not even go to church and receive the Holy Sacrament because the count did not believe in God and could not stand priests. Once at Easter he had let loose a pack of hounds on the priests of the Church of Boris and Gleb.*

According to Lyubov Onisimovna the count was so ugly on account of his perpetual bad temper that he looked like all the wild beasts put together. But Arkady knew how to change, even if only for a short time, that beast-like expression on his face so that when he sat in his theatre box in the evening he looked more impressive than many of the others there.

* This incident was known to many Orel people. I heard about it from my grandmother Alferyeva and from the merchant Ivan Ivanovich Androsov, a very righteous man who *himself* "saw how the hounds tore the priests to pieces." Androsov got away with his life only by "committing a sin." When the count summoned him and asked him, "Are you sorry for them?" he replied, "No, Your Grace, they deserved it, they shouldn't hang around the place." For that answer Kamensky pardoned him.—*Author's Note.*

To his great chagrin it was just that impressiveness and "military bearing" that the count lacked.

To prevent anybody else making use of the services of such an incomparable artist as Arkady he was kept indoors all his life and had never had any money in his hands although at the time he was twenty-five and Lyubov Onisimovna had just turned eighteen. They knew each other, of course, and that which usually happens to young people of their age happened to them—they fell in love. They could never talk of their love except by veiled hints in the presence of the others whilst they were being made up. A rendezvous between them was impossible, quite out of the question, indeed.

"They guarded us actresses as strictly as wet-nurses are guarded in great houses," Lyubov Onisimovna told me. "We had elderly women with children to look after us and if, God forbid, anything had happened to us, all the children of those women would have been exposed to terrible treatment by the tyrant."

Their chastity could be broken only by the man who had imposed it on them.

CHAPTER THE FIFTH

Lyubov Onisimovna was not only at the height of her virginal beauty at that time but it was also the most important period in the development of her many talents: she sang pot-pourri in the chorus, danced the "first steps" in the *Chinese Garden Maid* and, feeling tragedy to be her vocation, "learned all the roles *by watching them.*"

I don't know what year all this happened but it was the year the emperor passed through Orel (I can't say whether it was Alexander Pavlovich* or Nikolai Pavlovich**) and spent a night in the town: he was expected

* Alexander I.
** Nikolai I.

to attend the evening performance at Count Kamensky's theatre.

The count invited all the gentlefolk to his theatre (seats were not sold for money) and the best play was put on. Lyubov Onisimovna had to sing in the pot-pourri and dance *The Chinese Garden Maid* but during dress rehearsal one of the sets collapsed and injured the leg of the actress who was playing the Duchess de Bourblianne.

Never have I heard of such a role anywhere but that was how Lyubov Onisimovna pronounced it.

The carpenters who had knocked over the set were sent to the stables to be flogged and the injured actress was taken to her room but there was no one to play the part of the Duchess de Bourblianne.

"I volunteered," said Lyubov Onisimovna, "because I liked the way the duchess asked forgiveness at her father's feet and then died with her hair unbound. I had such beautiful long, fair hair and the way Arkady dressed it made it simply gorgeous."

The count was very pleased with the girl's unexpected readiness to play the part and receiving the producer's assurance that "Lyuba won't spoil the role," replied:

"She'd better not or your back will answer for it. And now take her the aquamarine ear-rings from me."

The aquamarine ear-rings were a gift both flattering and odious. They were the first sign of special favour to one who was to be promoted to be one of the master's odalisques for a brief moment. Soon after, and occasionally at the same time, Arkady would be ordered to dress the condemned girl "in the innocent garb of St. Cecilia" and, all in white, with a wreath on her head and a lily in her hand to symbolize innocence, she would be taken to the count's rooms.

"You're too young to understand that," Lyubov Onisimovna told me, "but it was the worst thing that could happen to a girl, especially to me who was so set on Arkady. I burst into tears, threw the ear-rings on the table, and kept on crying and couldn't imagine how I was going to play my part that evening."

CHAPTER THE SIXTH

In those fateful hours something no less fateful and trying was also happening to Arkady.

That day the count's brother arrived from his village to be presented to the tsar; he was even more ugly than the count and had been living in his village for a long time where he never wore his uniform and never shaved, for "bumps had grown all over his face." On that special occasion, however, he, too, had to be dressed and cleaned up and given that "military bearing" that was demanded in those days.

And a lot of it was demanded.

"People today don't realize how strict everything was in those days," the nurse said, "everything had to be uniform. There were special rules on the way gentlemen had to comb their hair, a way that didn't suit many people; if a man wore his hair according to prescription, with a forelock sticking up straight over his head and with small side-whiskers, his face would look like a peasant's balalaika without strings. The great gentlemen were terribly afraid of this. So much depended on the skill with which they were barbered—the barber had to leave little paths between the side-whiskers and the moustache and had to know how to curl or comb out the hair, for the slightest turn of the comb gave a different expression to the face."

According to our nurse civilian gentlemen did not find it so bad because little attention was paid to them, and all that was required of their faces was a humble expression; much more was required of the military, who had to express meekness in the presence of their superiors and boundless audacity in the presence of everybody else.

Arkady, by his wonderful art, was able to give this required expression to the ugly and insignificant face of the count.

CHAPTER THE SEVENTH

The country brother was even uglier than the town brother and, moreover, he had neglected his appearance in the village and "allowed his face to grow coarse" so that he was even conscious of it himself; he had nobody to barber him for he was an awful miser and had let his hairdresser go to work in Moscow and pay him quitrent; the face of this other count was all covered with bumps so that it was quite impossible to shave him without cutting one of them.

On his arrival in Orel he summoned all the barbers in the town and said:

"Anybody who can make me look like my brother, Count Kamensky, will get two gold pieces but if anybody cuts me—I'm putting two pistols on the table. Do your work well and take the gold but if you cut but one single pimple or take a hair too many off my side-whiskers I'll kill you on the spot."

He was only trying to frighten them for his pistols were loaded with blank.

There were not many barbers in Orel in those days and these mostly hung around the bath-houses where they did cupping or applied leeches. None of them had any taste or imagination. They realized it themselves and refused to "transform" Kamensky. "Keep your gold," they said to themselves, "and leave us alone."

But aloud they said, "We can't do what you ask for we aren't worthy to touch so great a person and we haven't got the proper razors. Ours are just ordinary Russian

288

razors and nothing but an English razor will do for your face. The count's Arkady is the only man to do it."

The count ordered the barbers to be kicked out and they were glad enough to get off so easily. Then he went to his brother and said:

"I've a great request to make of you, brother; let me have your Arkady this afternoon so that he can tidy me up before evening. I haven't shaved for a long time and the local barbers don't know how to set about it."

"The local barbers, needless to say, are no good," said the count to his brother. "I didn't know we had any for even my dogs are clipped by my own people. As far as your request is concerned, what you ask is impossible for I've made a vow that Arkady won't barber anybody else but me as long as I live. What do you think—can I break my word before my slave?"

"Why not? You made the decision and you can cancel it."

The count said that reasoning of that kind seemed strange to him.

"If I begin to act like that what can I expect of my servants? Arkady has been informed of that order and everybody else knows about it and that's why he's paid more than anybody else but if he ever dares apply his art to anybody except me I'll flog him to death and send him into the army."

"It's one thing or the other," said his brother. "You can either flog him to death or send him into the army. You can't have it both ways."

"All right," said the count, "as you will. I won't flog him to death but only half-way and then send him into the army."

"Is that your last word, brother?"

"Yes, my very last."

"And that's all there is to it?"

"That's all."

"Well, in that case, everything is all right," said the count's brother, "but I thought that your own brother was of less account to you than a serf. Don't break your vow, just send Arkady to me to *clip my poodle*. What he does there is my business."

The count couldn't reasonably refuse him that.

"All right," he said, "I'll send him to clip your poodle."

"That's all I need," said the brother and he shook hands with the count and left.

CHAPTER THE EIGHTH

It was winter. Evening was drawing nigh and dusk had fallen—the time when lamps are lit. The count summoned Arkady to him and said:

"Go to my brother's house and clip his poodle."

"Is that all I am to do?" asked Arkady.

"Nothing else," said the count, "but hurry back to make up the actresses. Lyuba has to be made up for three different parts and after the show bring her to me as St. Cecilia."

Arkady staggered.

"What's the matter?" asked the count.

"I beg your pardon, I tripped over the carpet," said Arkady.

"Look out, that's a bad sign, isn't it?"

Arkady was so depressed he didn't care whether it was a good omen or a bad one.

When he was told that I was to be dressed up as St. Cecilia he picked up his leather case of instruments, and went away as though he were blind and deaf.

CHAPTER THE NINTH

Arkady came to the count's brother and the latter had candles lit in front of a mirror and two pistols lying beside it, and next to them not two, but ten gold pieces;

this time the pistols were not loaded with blank but with Circassian bullets.

"I have no poodle," the count's brother said, "but what I want is this: do my toilet so that I look important and you can take the ten pieces of gold but if you cut me I shall kill you."

Arkady stared and stared and then suddenly—the Lord alone knows what made him do it—started to shave the count's brother and dress his hair. In a minute he did everything and did it well, put the gold in his pocket and said:

"Good-bye."

And the count's brother said:

"You can go, only I want to know what made you do such a desperate thing?"

"What made me do it is something my bosom alone knows," answered Arkady.

"Perhaps you've been charmed against bullets and that's why you're not afraid of pistols."

"Pistols are only toys, I didn't even think of them," answered Arkady.

"How so? Did you really dare think that my word isn't as good as your count's and that I wouldn't shoot you if you cut me? If you're not charmed you'd have lost your life."

At the mention of the count, Arkady shuddered and answered as though in a daze:

"I've never been charmed against bullets, but I've got the little amount of sense God gave me: while you were raising the pistol to shoot me I'd have cut your throat with the razor."

With that he rushed out and arrived at the theatre just in time to make up the actresses although he was trembling all over as he did so. As he waved each curl and stooped down to blow on it he would whisper in my ear:

"Don't be afraid, I'll take you away!"

CHAPTER THE TENTH

"The performance was going well for we were, all of us, like stone images; we had been trained to fear and to suffer; whatever our feelings were we acted in such a way that nobody ever noticed them.

"From the stage we could see the count and his brother and they both looked alike. Later, when they came behind the scenes, it was hard to tell which was which. Only our master looked very gentle, as though he had grown suddenly kind. He was always like that before his most savage acts of cruelty.

"We were all terrified and kept crossing ourselves.

" 'The Lord have mercy on us—who'll be the next victim?'

"At that time we still didn't know the desperate thing Arkady had done, although Arkady himself knew that he could expect no mercy and he turned pale when the count's brother glanced at him and then whispered something to the count. I was very sharp of hearing and heard what he said:

" 'Listen, I warn you as a brother: watch him when he's shaving you!'

"Our count just laughed softly.

"I imagine Arkady heard that whisper, too, for when he began making me up for the duchess in the last scene he did something he'd never done before: he put so much powder on my face that our French wardrobe-master had to brush it off.

" '*Trop beaucoup, trop beaucoup!*' he said as he cleaned me with a brush."

CHAPTER THE ELEVENTH

"When the play was over they took off the dress of the Duchess de Bourblianne and dressed me as St. Cecilia in a single white garment without sleeves and just tied up on the shoulders—we couldn't stand that dress. Arkady came in to do my hair in chaste fashion like that of St. Cecilia in the pictures and fix a thin band on my head; as he came in he noticed six men standing near the door of my room. That meant that as soon as he had finished me and went out he would be seized and dragged off somewhere for torture.

"Such tortures were inflicted on our people that it was a hundred times better to be sentenced to death than to torture. We had the rack and another machine to stretch the body like a violin string, and a thing to twist your head—yes, we had all of them. Punishment by the legal authorities was nothing to it. Under the whole house there were secret cellars where people were kept on chains, like bears. When you passed near you could hear the chains rattling and the shackled prisoners moaning. It seemed they wanted to make their fate known to the authorities, but the authorities didn't even dream that they might dare interfere. People were tormented in those dungeons for long periods, some even for life. One who had been kept there a long time composed a verse about it.

And the serpents come crawling your eyes to suck
out,
And the scorpions with poison will fill up your
mouth...

"Sometimes you'd repeat those lines to yourself and be overcome with terror.

"There were even men chained up together with bears so that the bear's claws came within an inch of their flesh.

"But they had no chance to do anything like that to Arkady because as soon as he came into my room he seized the little table, knocked the glass out of the window ... and that's all I remember.

"I began to come round because my legs were ex-

293

tremely cold. I tried to pull my feet up but found that I was wrapped in a bearskin or a wolfskin and everything all round was pitch black and three lusty horses were racing along, I knew not where. Two men sat huddled beside me in the wide sledge; one of them was holding me—that was Arkady—and the other was whipping up the horses for all he was worth. Clots of snow flew from the horses' hoofs, the sledge pitched violently from side to side and if we had not been sitting in the middle, on the floor, and holding on tightly with our hands not one of us would have survived.

"I could hear that Arkady and the driver were talking and that they were excited as people always are in moments of great suspense but all I could make out was: 'They're chasing us ... faster ... faster....' and nothing else.

"When Arkady saw that I was conscious he bent over me and said:

" 'Lyuba darling, they're chasing us.... Are you prepared to die if we don't escape?'

"I told him that I would gladly consent to death.

"He hoped to get to Khrushchuk* on Turkish territory where there were many people who had escaped from Kamensky.

"We flew across the ice of a small stream and in front of us could see the grey outline of a village where dogs were barking. The driver whipped up his horses still more and then leant heavily on one side of the sledge so that it tipped over and Arkady and I were thrown out on the snow.

" 'Don't be frightened,' said Arkady, 'it was arranged this way for I don't know the driver and he doesn't know me. I gave him three gold pieces to carry you off and now he can look after himself. Whatever happens

---

* The town and fortress of Rushchuk on the Danube.

now is the will of God. This is the village of Sukhaya Orlitsa where there is a fearless priest who marries runaway couples and who has helped a lot of people to escape. We'll give him money and he'll hide us till evening and then marry us. Our driver will return in the night and we'll escape.'"

"We knocked at the door and went into the anteroom. The priest himself opened the door to us—he was an old man, rather thickset and one of his front teeth was missing; his wife was an old, old woman and she blew up the fire for us. We just fell at their feet and begged them:

" 'Save us, let us warm ourselves and hide till evening.'

" 'Who are you, good people?' the priest asked. 'Have you stolen something or are you just runaway serfs?'

" 'We haven't stolen anything from anybody,' said Arkady, 'but we've run away from the brutality of Count Kamensky and we want to get to Turkish Khrushchuk where many of our people are already living. They won't find us and we've got money of our own; we'll give you a gold ten-ruble piece to let us stay the night and three more for marrying us, if you agree to marry us, that is, and if not we'll get tied up in Khrushchuk.'

" 'Why can't I marry you?' said the priest. 'I'll tie you up all right, why wait till you get across the frontier. Give me five ten-ruble pieces for everything and I'll tie you up here.'

"Arkady gave him the five gold coins and I took off my ear-rings and gave them to his wife.

"The priest took the money and said:

" 'My children, everything would have been easy enough, I've tied up harder jobs in my time, but the trouble is you belong to the count. Although I'm a priest I'm afraid of his brutality. But I'll take a chance and it must be as God wills; throw in another gold coin, even a chipped one, and then you can hide yourselves.'

"Arkady gave it to him and it wasn't chipped and the priest said to his wife:

" 'What are you standing there like that for, old woman? Give the girl a skirt or a coat or something: I'm ashamed to see her like that, she's almost naked.'

"He wanted to take us to the church and hide us in the vestry in a box where he kept his robes, but no sooner had his wife begun dressing me behind a partition than we heard someone rattling the door-latch."

CHAPTER THE THIRTEENTH

"Our hearts sank but the priest whispered to Arkady:

" 'You won't have time to hide amongst my robes so get under that feather bed, quickly!' Turning to me he said, 'And you go in there, my child.'

"He pushed me into the case of a tall clock which he locked and put the key in his pocket; he went to open the door and there were a lot of people outside, some at the door and two of them looking in at the window.

"Seven men came in, the count's huntsmen, armed with iron clubs and whips and with coils of rope in their belts; behind them was an eighth, the count's butler, in a long wolfskin coat with a high collar.

"The clockcase in which I was hidden had a fretwork front covered with thin muslin through which I could see.

"The old priest was shaking with fear as he stood before the butler for he must have realized that he was in for trouble. He crossed himself continuously and intoned in a loud voice:

" 'Oh, my good people, oh my dear people, I know, I know what you seek, but I'm quite innocent before His Grace the Count, quite innocent, quite innocent!'

"As he made the sign of the cross he pointed over his shoulder at the clock in which I was hidden.

"I'm done for, I thought, as I saw him performing that trick.

"The butler noticed it, too, and said:

" 'We know everything. Give me the key to that clock!'

"The priest began crossing himself again.

" 'Oh, good people, forgive me, don't do anything to me, I've forgotten where I put the key, I've forgotten, I've forgotten.'

"As he said it he stroked his pocket with his other hand.

"That trick the butler also noticed, got the key out of the priest's pocket and opened the clock-case.

" 'Come out, girlie,' he said, 'and your lover will come out himself now.'

"But Arkady had already shown himself—he threw the priest's feather bed to the floor and stood up.

" 'It seems there's nothing to be done—you win! Take me back to torture but she's innocent, I carried her off by force.'

"Then he turned to the priest and all he did was just spit in his face.

" 'Good people,' said the priest, 'you see how he insults my office and my loyalty? Report it to His Grace the count.'

" 'Don't you worry,' answered the butler, 'that'll be added to the account,' and he ordered his men to take Arkady and me out.

"We were placed in three sledges: Arkady, tied up, with the huntsmen were on the first, I was on the third under a similar guard while all the other people went in the middle sledge.

"Any people we met on the road made way for us, probably thinking it was a wedding."

CHAPTER THE FOURTEENTH

"We travelled back very fast and when we entered the count's courtyard I didn't see the sledge on which Arkady had been travelling but I was taken to my own room and questioned again and again—how long had I been alone with Arkady?

"To all of them I said:

" 'Not for a moment!'

"It seems that I was fated to belong to the man I hated and not to the one I loved and I did not escape my fate; when I returned to my room I buried my face in my pillow to weep over my misfortune when I suddenly heard terrible moans coming from under the floor.

"In that wooden building we, the girls, lived upstairs and down below there was a big, high room where we learned singing and dancing and from upstairs we could hear everything down there. Satan, the King of Hell, taught those cruel beasts to torment Arkady right under my room.

"When I realized that it was him they were torturing I rushed to the door and pushed against it . . . to get to him . . . it was locked. . . . I don't know what I wanted to do . . . I fell down . . . on the floor the noises were louder. . . . Not a knife . . . not a nail . . . nothing to put an end to it all. . . . I took my long plait of hair and wound it round my neck twisting it more and more tightly until all I could hear was a noise in my ears and there were black circles in front of my eyes and I fainted. . . . When I came to I found myself in an unfamiliar place, a large log building, full of sunshine, and there were calves there, lots of calves, more than a dozen, lovely little calves so gentle and sweet and they licked my hand with their cold lips thinking they were sucking their mother. It was the calves that had brought me round for their lips tickled me. I cast my eyes over the

298

room wondering where I was. As I looked, a woman came in, a tall, elderly woman in a blue striped dress and a clean kerchief of the same material on her head; she had a kindly face.

"The woman noticed that I had recovered consciousness and treated me with kindness; she told me I was in the calfhouse on the count's estate...."

"It used to be there," explained Lyubov Onisimovna, pointing to the most distant corner of the half-ruined grey buildings.

CHAPTER THE FIFTEENTH

The girl had been sent to the dairy farm because she was suspected of madness. Those who had lost their reason were tried out in the cattle yard because the people there were all sedate and elderly and it was thought that they would be able to "observe" mental cases.

The woman in the striped dress in whose shed Lyubov Onisimovna came to herself was a kind-hearted old woman by the name of Drosida.

"As soon as she finished work in the evening," the nurse continued, "she made me a bed of fresh oat straw and spread it so well that it was as soft as a feather bed. Then she said, 'I'll tell you everything, my girl. If you tell on me what is to be will be but I'm another such as you and I haven't always worn homespun dresses, but I, too, knew a different life, only God forbid that I should recall it, but I'll tell you what—don't worry about being banished to the dairy farm. It's better to be banished only beware of the terrible phial....'

"She took a little white bottle out of her neckcloth and showed it to me.

" 'What is it?' I asked.

" 'This is that terrible phial, it has the poison of forgetfulness in it,' she said.

299

" 'Give me the poison of forgetfulness, I want to forget everything.'

"She said:

" 'Don't drink it: it's vodka. I couldn't restrain myself on one occasion and drank it down ... some good people gave it to me.... Now I can't manage without it, I need it, but don't you drink while you can do without it and don't think badly of me if I suck at the bottle, I'm in awful pain. You have some comfort in the world—the Lord has delivered *him* from tyranny!'

"I screamed out, 'Dead!' and clutched my hair, and I saw that it wasn't my hair, it was white! What was it?

"But she said to me:

" 'Don't be afraid, don't be afraid, your hair went white over there when they unwound your plait but he's alive and delivered of all tyranny: the count has shown him mercy such as he never before showed anybody.... I'll tell you tonight.... But now I must suck my bottle.... I must have a good suck ... my heart's burning up....'

"And she sucked and sucked at her bottle until she fell asleep.

"In the night, when everybody was asleep, Auntie Drosida got up quietly, went to the window without lighting a lamp and I could see her standing there sucking at her bottle and then she hid it again and asked me softly:

" 'Is sorrow asleep or not?'

"And I answered:

" 'Sorrow never sleeps!'

"She came over to my bed and told me that the count had sent for Arkady after his punishment and said to him:

" 'You had to go through the punishment I ordered but as you were my favourite I'll show you mercy: I'm sending you into the army tomorrow as a volunteer but since you didn't show any fear of my brother, a noble-man armed with pistols, I'm opening the road to honour for you for I don't want you to be lower than the noble spirit you have proved you possess. I'm sending a letter tomorrow asking for you to be sent straight to the war and you won't serve as a private soldier but as a reg-imental sergeant where you can show your bravery. From now on you will obey the tsar's will, not mine.'

" 'It's easier for him now,' said Drosida, 'and he has nothing to fear any more; the chance of death in battle is the only power over him and he doesn't know the tyranny of a master.'

"I believed her and for three years the only thing I ever saw in my dreams was Arkady in battle.

"Three years passed and all the time the Lord was merciful to me and I wasn't taken back to the theatre but stayed in the calfhouse at the dairy farm as Auntie Drosida's helper. I was happy there and sorry for the old woman and at night, when she wasn't too drunk, I loved to listen to her. She could remember how our peo-ple had killed the old count—his personal valet helped them—because they couldn't bear his hellish cruelty any more. I didn't drink myself and was happy to do all I could for Auntie Drosida; the calves were like children to me and I was so used to them that when one was fattened and taken away to be slaughtered for the table I'd make the sign of the cross over it and cry for three days. I wasn't any good for the theatre because my legs had become unsteady and I didn't walk properly. I had formerly had a very light carriage but after Arkady carried me off unconscious in the cold night, I must have got a chill in my legs and my feet weren't strong enough to dance. I wore the same striped clothes as Drosida and Lord knows how long I'd have lived in that state of despondency when something suddenly happened as I was sitting in our hut one evening: the sun was setting and I was sitting by the window unwinding a skein of flax when a small stone wrapped in a piece of paper came suddenly flying to me through the window."

CHAPTER THE SIXTEENTH

"I looked out of the window, looked this way and that, but not a soul was to be seen.

"Somebody must have thrown it over the fence from outside, I thought, but it didn't fall where he wanted, it came to the old lady and me.

"I wondered whether or not to take the paper off. It seemed better to take it off because there would certainly be something written on it. It might be something somebody needed and I could find out and keep it secret and wrap the stone up again and throw it in the same way to the one it was meant for.

"So I unwrapped the paper and began to read.... I could scarcely believe my eyes!..."

CHAPTER THE SEVENTEENTH

"On it was written:
" 'My faithful Lyuba,
" 'I have fought and served the tsar and been wounded many times and they have made me an officer and a gentleman. Now I am home on leave a free man to recover from my wounds; I am staying at Pushkarskaya with the porter of an inn and tomorrow I shall put on all my medals and crosses and go to the count, and I'll take the money I have to pay for medical treatment, five hundred rubles, and ask him to take it to buy your freedom in the hope of our being married before the throne of the Almighty, our Creator....' "

"He also wrote," Lyubov Onisimovna continued with an effort to suppress her feelings, "that whatever troubles

I had undergone and whatever I'd been forced to do, he'd not think it was through sin or weakness, but that it was my cross and leave it to God while he himself felt nothing but the greatest respect for me. The letter was signed 'Arkady Ilyin.'"

Lyubov Onisimovna immediately burnt the letter in the grate and said nothing about it to anybody, not even the old dairymaid; but she prayed the whole night through, not for herself, but for him, "For," she said, "although he wrote that he was an officer with medals and wounds I could not imagine the count treating him differently from what he had done before."

In other words, she was afraid they would flog him.

CHAPTER THE EIGHTEENTH

Early next morning Lyubov Onisimovna had driven the calves out into the sunshine and was feeding them milk with a bark ladle from the trough when suddenly from the other side of the fence, from "freedom," she could hear people running somewhere in a great hurry and talking excitedly to each other.

"I couldn't make out what they were talking about," she told me, "but I felt a sudden pain as though somebody had pierced my heart with a knife. As one of the peasants, Fillip, the manure boy, had just driven in, I asked him:

"'Fillip, have you heard what the people are talking about so excitedly?'

"'They're running to Pushkarskaya,' he said, 'where the inn porter has murdered an officer in his sleep. Cut his throat and robbed him of five hundred rubles. They caught him all blood-stained with the money on him.'

"When he said that I fell down in a dead faint.

"It was true: the porter had murdered Arkady ... and they buried him right here, in the grave we're sitting

303

on.... He's under us now, lying under this earth....
You were wondering why I always brought you here for
your walks, weren't you? Well, I don't come to look over
there (she pointed to the gloomy grey ruins) but to sit
beside him and take a drop in memory of his soul...."

CHAPTER THE NINETEENTH

Lyubov Onisimovna stopped talking for she thought
she had finished her story; she took a little bottle out of
her pocket and "took a drop in his memory" or "had a
suck at the bottle" but I asked her:
"Who buried the famous make-up artist?"
"The governor himself, the governor was present at
the funeral. Naturally! He was an officer, remember. The
priest and the deacon called him the 'nobleman Arkady'
in the prayers and when they lowered his coffin into the
grave soldiers fired a salute over it. A year later the
public hangman flogged the porter on the market-square
on Elijah's Day. They gave him forty-three strokes for
Arkady and he survived it and was sent branded to
penal servitude in Siberia. Some of our men who could
get away went to see him flogged, and the old men, who
remembered how the murderers of the cruel old count
had been punished, said that forty-three strokes was too
little; that, they said, was because Arkady was not an
aristocrat, for the count's murderers got a hundred and
one strokes. It is against the law to give an even number
of strokes, the number must be odd. An executioner was
brought from Tula specially to flog the old count's murderer and he was given three glasses of rum before he
began. He flogged him so that the first hundred strokes
only caused pain but didn't kill and the hundred and
first he gave with such force that he broke the man's
back and gutted him. He was dying when they lifted him
down.... They covered him with a bast mat and carried

him back to prison but he died on the way. And they say that the executioner kept shouting, 'Give me another one, I'll kill every man in Orel!'"

"Did you go to Arkady's funeral?"

"I did. I went with the rest. The count ordered all the people from the theatre to go so that they could see how one of our men had made a name for himself."

"Did you take leave of him?"

"Of course I did. Everybody went up to take leave of him and I did too.... He was so changed I hardly recognized him. He was thin and pale.... They said all the blood had run out because his throat had been cut on the stroke of midnight.... And he had shed a lot of blood in the wars...."

She paused and fell into a reverie.

"How did you bear up afterwards?" I asked.

She seemed to come out of a trance and passed her hand over her forehead.

"At first I couldn't remember how I got home from the funeral," she said. "I suppose I came back with the others.... Somebody must have led me.... But in the evening Drosida Petrovna said to me:

"'You can't go on like this. You don't sleep but you lie there like a stone. It won't do, you must cry so that your heart will overflow.'

"'I can't cry,' I said. 'My heart's burning like a live coal and I can't get the pain out of it.'

"'If that's so,' she said, 'it seems you can't do without the bottle.'

"She poured me out a glass of vodka and said:

"'I wouldn't let you drink it before, I always persuaded you not to, but now it can't be helped. Pour it on the live coal—suck!'

"'I don't want to,' I said.

"'Don't be a foolish girl,' she answered, 'who does want to, at first? It's a bitter drink but the poison of sorrow is more bitter and if you pour this poison on the live coal in your heart it will die down for a while. Hurry up, suck.'

"So I drank the whole bottle. I hated it but I couldn't sleep without it ... and I drank the next night again ... and even now I can't sleep without it, I've got my own phial and I buy vodka.... But you be a good boy and never tell your Mummy anything about it. Don't give poor people away: you must always take care of poor people for they are all great sufferers. We'll be going home soon and I'll knock at the window of the pub round the corner.... We shan't go in ourselves, I'll just hand them an empty bottle and they'll give me a full one."

I was deeply touched and promised faithfully that not for anything would I tell about her "phial."

"Thank you, dearie: don't tell anyone, I can't do without it."

Even now I can see and hear her: at night when everybody was asleep she'd get up very quietly from her bed so that not even her old bones creaked.... She'd listen and then get up and steal on her long, chilled legs to the window.... There she'd stand for a minute or so, looking and listening whether my mother was coming from her bedroom, then the neck of the "phial" would rattle against her teeth very quietly as she put it into her mouth and "took a suck." One gulp, two, three.... She would drink to Arkady's memory until the live coal was quenched and then she'd go back to her bed, dive under the covers and would soon begin to whistle very softly—whew, whew, whew.... She was asleep.

Never in all my life have I witnessed such a horrible and heart-rending commemoration of the dead.

1883

Genius has no age—it overcomes everything that halts the common mind.

La Rochefoucauld

THE OLD GENIUS

CHAPTER THE FIRST

A FEW YEARS ago there arrived in St. Petersburg a little old lady, a landowner, who, to use her own words, had a most "disgraceful case." The fact of the matter was that she, out of her kindness of heart and her great simplicity, merely because she was sorry for him, had got a smart young society man out of trouble by mortgaging the house which constituted the entire fortune of the old lady herself, her crippled, bed-ridden daughter and her grand-daughter. The house had been mortgaged for fifteen thousand, all of which the young man had taken, promising to return it in the shortest possible time.

The kindly old lady had believed him and, indeed, there was no reason not to, since her debtor belonged to one of the best families, had a brilliant career ahead of him and was in receipt of a good salary as well as a substantial income from his estate. The financial difficulties from which the old lady had extricated him were the result of some momentary infatuation or carelessness at cards in his aristocratic club and would, of course, easily be set right "once he arrived in St. Petersburg."

At one time the old lady had known that gentleman's mother and had helped him for the sake of the old friendship; he left for St. Petersburg in good order and then, needless to say, began that game of cat and mouse that is all too common in such cases. Settling day came and went, the old lady sent letters to remind him of her existence—at first gentle reminders, then a little harder and, at last, abusive, with hints at dishonesty—but the debtor knew his business; not one of her letters did he answer. But time was passing, the mortgage would soon lapse and the poor woman, who had hoped to live out her life in her own house, suddenly saw the awful prospect of cold and hunger unfolding before her, her crippled daughter and baby grandchild.

In despair the old lady scraped some money together, entrusted the invalid and the child to a kindly neighbour and hurried off to St. Petersburg to get justice.

CHAPTER THE SECOND

At first her efforts met with some success: the lawyer whom she saw was kindly and sympathetic, the court settled the matter quickly and in her favour, but when it came to the execution of the court order she came up against a snag, and such a snag that she was at her wits' end to know what to do. It wasn't that the police or any of the court bailiffs were well disposed towards the debtor, they had long since had enough of him, were terribly sorry for the old lady and would gladly have helped her but ... they dared not. He was related by blood or through marriage to somebody in so high a position that he could not be called to account like other delinquents.

I do not know anything about his connections and I do not think it matters. Whatever they may have been, fate dealt kindly with him.

Nor can I tell you exactly what should have been done with him; the only thing I know is that the debtor had to be served with a writ and a receipt obtained from him—something that nobody, no official and no office, could achieve. Whoever the old lady turned to, gave her the same advice.

"Why do you want to go to all that trouble, madame? Better give it up! What can we do when he never pays anybody? If it is any consolation to you I can tell you that you are not the first and will not be the last."

"What consolation is it to me, gentlemen, that I am not the only sufferer? I'd much prefer that things were better for me and for the others."

"Well," they would answer, "you must get rid of the

idea of things being all right for everybody—that's an idea the *specialists** invented, but it's impossible."

But she, in her simplicity, still persisted.

"Why is it impossible? His fortune comes to much more than he owes me and all the others. Let him pay his debts and he'll still have plenty left."

"Oh, madame, a man who has a lot never has enough, but the main thing is that he isn't used to paying and if you bother him too much he may make trouble for you."

"What sort of trouble?"

"All right, madame, don't ask so many questions: you had better take a quiet walk along Nevsky Prospect or you'll find yourself leaving town very suddenly."

"You'll excuse me," said the old lady, "but I don't believe you: he's squandered his money but still he's a good man."

"Oh, yes," they answered her, "of course he's a fine gentleman, only he's a bad payer; and when a man is that he's capable of doing everything that's bad."

"Then take measures against him."

"And there," they replied, "is where we come to a stop. We can't 'take measures' against everybody. What did you want to get mixed up with such a man for?"

"What difference does it make?"

At that point the man to whom she was applying would turn away or would suggest that she complain to higher authority.

CHAPTER THE THIRD

And so she went to higher authorities. They were harder to get to, talked less and their conversation was still more abstract.

"Where is he?" they would ask. "We have reports saying that he is not here."

* Distorted—*socialists.—Tr.*

"O Lord," the old lady would weep, "I see him every day in the street—he lives in his own house."

"It isn't his house. He has no house of his own, it's his wife's house."

"But that's the same thing—husband and wife are one."

"That's what you think, but the law thinks differently. His wife has also lodged complaints against him at court and so he never goes to her either. . . . To the devil with him, we are all fed up with him—and why did you lend him money? Whenever he is in St. Petersburg he registers in furnished apartments, but doesn't live there. If you think that we are defending him or that we are sorry for him you are very much mistaken; find him, catch him, that's your business, then the writ will be served on him."

No matter how high the old lady went with her complaints she got nothing more consoling than that, and, being suspicious in her provincial way, began to suggest that it was all because "hands need palm oil."

"Don't believe me if you don't want to," she said, "but I can see that the cart won't move unless you grease the wheels."

So she went forth to grease the cart-wheels and came back still more disappointed. She said that she had begun with a whole thousand, that is, she had promised a thousand from the money when recovered, but nobody would listen to her and when she very reasonably began to raise her price and went as high as three thousand, she was even requested to leave the premises.

"They won't take three thousand just to serve a paper!" she said. "Now what do you think of that?! Things were better in the old days."

"But you," I reminded her, "seem to have forgotten just how well things used to go in the old days: he was right who could pay most."

"In that," she replied, "you are absolutely right, or amongst the civil servants in those days there were som as smart as they make 'em. You could ask one of them, 'Can you do this?' and he would answer, 'In Russia nothing is impossible,' and there and then would fish out some plan and get on with it. Why even now one of them has come to light and keeps pestering me only I don't know whether to trust him or not. I see him every day at lunch in Vasily's Bunshop in Mariinsky Passage, because I'm economizing now and tremble over every kopek I spend—I haven't had a hot meal for a long time. I'm saving everything for my case, and he, too, I suppose, goes there because he's poor or drinks . . . but he says with conviction, 'Give me five hundred rubles and *I'll serve the writ*!' Now what do you think of that?"

"I assure you, my dear," I told her, "that I greatly sympathize with you in your trouble but I cannot manage my own affairs let alone advise you what to do. You should at least ask somebody about him: who is he and who can recommend him?"

"I did ask the bunshop man, but he doesn't know anything. 'I suppose,' he said, 'he's a merchant whose business has gone wrong or somebody with a title who has come down in the world.' "

"Well, then, ask him straight out."

"I did ask him who he is and what his rank is. 'In society,' he said, 'such questions are superfluous and are frowned upon; you may call me Ivan Ivanovich and I have all the fourteen ranks* so that I can use whichever I think fit.' "

"So there you are, you see he's a dubious sort of person altogether."

"Yes, dubious is right. . . . I know what all the fourteen

* In pre-revolutionary Russia civil servants were divided into fourteen classes, the fourteenth being the lowest.

..ks means, I was married to a civil servant myself. . means he's a clerk of the fourteenth class and as far as recommendations are concerned he says, 'I disdain them and have the ideas of a genius in my head and I know worthy people who are prepared to put any of my plans into operation for three hundred rubles.'"

"'But why, sir,' I asked, 'do you stipulate *three* hundred?'"

"'Because that is the rule we have and we never break it and never take more.'"

"'I don't understand a thing, sir.'"

"'You don't have to. Nowadays other people take thousands where we take hundreds. I want two hundred for the idea and the guidance and three hundred must go to the hero who does the job in consideration of the fact that he will spend three months in prison at a hundred rubles a month—and that will be all. Anybody who needs our help must believe me, because I only undertake impossible jobs. I can't do anything for people who have no faith,' but as far as I'm concerned," added the old lady, "you can just imagine how I'm tempted: somehow I believe him. . . ."

"I really can't understand," I said, "why you should believe him."

"Just imagine, I have a sort of intuition, I have dreams and everything tells me strongly that I ought to trust him."

"Couldn't you wait a little longer?"

"I'll wait as long as I can."

Soon, however, the time came when she could wait no longer.

CHAPTER THE FOURTH

The old lady came to see me in a state of the most touching and acute anxiety: firstly, it would soon be Christmas; secondly, she had received a letter from home telling her that the mortgage would be foreclosed in a few days and thirdly, she had met her debtor arm in arm with a lady, had run after him and, seizing him by the sleeve, called to passers-by to help, shouting through her tears, "My God! He owes me money!"

The only result of this action, however, was that she was led away from her debtor and summoned to court for disturbing the peace in a public thoroughfare. But still more disturbing than all these three circumstances was a fourth—the old lady's debtor had been granted leave of absence abroad and no later than the next day was leaving for a foreign country with the elegant lady of his heart, and there he would probably remain for a year or two, or perhaps would never come back at all "because she is very rich."

There could be no doubt at all that everything was exactly as the old lady said. She had learned to keep track of every movement made by her elusive debtor and knew all his secrets from servants in her pay.

The next day, therefore, would see the end of that long and tormenting comedy: next day he would slip away for a long time, perhaps for ever, since his companion would certainly not consent to compromise herself for a fleeting moment.

The old lady had discussed this in all its details with the gentleman of fourteen ranks who there and then, while at his evening meal in the bunshop in Mariinsky Passage, gave her the answer.

"Yes, time is short, but it can still be managed: slap five hundred rubles on the table and tomorrow the weight will be lifted from your heart: if you don't trust me you may consider your fifteen thousand lost."

"And I, my friend," the old lady told me, "have already decided to trust him. . . . What else can I do? Nobody else will undertake the job but he does, and says confidently, '*I'll serve the writ.*' Don't look at me like

315

that, please, I'm not the least bit mad. I don't know why but I've got a sort of mysterious faith in him because of my intuition, and I see such dreams that I decided immediately and took him away with me."

"Where to?"

"Well, you see, we only meet in the bunshop once a day, at dinner time. That will be too late, so I'm taking him home with me and won't let him go until tomorrow. At my age, of course, nobody will think anything wrong of it, and I have to look after him because I have to give him the whole five hundred rubles now, and without a receipt."

"And you're not afraid?"

"Of course, not. What else can I do? I've already given him a hundred in advance and he's waiting for me, drinking tea in a teashop, and I've got a request to make to you: I have another two hundred and fifty rubles but I'm a hundred and fifty short. Be kind enough to lend me that amount, I'll return it all right. Even if they sell the house there will be a hundred and fifty left over."

I knew her for a woman of the greatest integrity. I was touched by her great sorrow, and thought—what does it matter whether she returns it or not—God bless her, a hundred and fifty rubles would not make me the richer or the poorer and she would not be tormented by the thought that she had not tried all possible means to serve the writ that would save her house.

She took the money she wanted and sailed to the teashop to meet her desperate agent. With great curiosity I awaited her coming next morning to learn what new artifices the St. Petersburg confidence men had devised.

What I did learn, however, exceeded all my expectations: the genius of the Passage did not betray either the trust or the intuition of the kindly old lady.

CHAPTER THE FIFTH

On the third day of the Christmas holidays she came hurrying to see me, dressed for the road and with her travelling bag, and the first thing she did was lay the hundred and fifty rubles she had borrowed from me on the table and then show me a bank draft for fifteen thousand odd rubles.

"I can't believe my eyes, what does this mean?"

"Nothing, except that I got my money back with interest."

"But how? Do you mean to say your Ivan Ivanich of the fourteen classes did the trick?"

"He did. Incidentally, there was another, the one he paid the three hundred rubles to, because it couldn't have been done without his help."

"And who's this other agent? Tell me all about it, how did they manage it?"

"They helped me quite honestly. As soon as I got to the teashop and gave Ivan Ivanich the money he counted it, put it in his pocket and said, 'Now, madame, we can go. I,' he said, 'am a genius of the mind, but I need somebody to carry out my plan because I am the mysterious stranger who cannot perform legal acts in his own name.' We went around many low-down places and bath-houses—we were looking for some Serbian Fighter,* but, for a long time, could not find him. At last we found him. That Fighter came out of some sort of a hole, he was in a tattered Serbian army uniform and had a tobacco pipe made of twisted newspaper between his teeth. 'I can do anything that anybody wants done,' he said, 'but first I must have a drink.'

* In 1876 the Balkan Slavs fought a war of liberation against the Turks. A large number of Russians went to Serbia to fight as volunteers. On returning home some of them found themselves unemployed and destitute.

We sat down, all three of us, in a tavern and began to argue over the terms: the Serbian Fighter demanded 'one hundred rubles a month for three months.' We agreed to this. I could not understand what was going on but saw Ivan Ivanich give him money so, apparently, he trusted him which made me feel easier. Then I took Ivan Ivanich with me to stay in my apartment and the Serbian Fighter went to spend the night in a bath-house on the condition that he came to us next morning. In the morning he came and said, 'I'm ready.' Ivan Ivanich whispered to me, 'Send for some vodka for him, he needs courage. I won't let him drink a lot but he needs a little to buck him up—the most important thing before us is his performance.'"

The Serbian Fighter drank up his vodka and they went to the station from which the debtor and his lady were to leave by train. The old lady could not make out what was happening, what exactly they had in mind and how they would carry out their plan, but the Serbian Fighter calmed her and said, "Everything will be fair and aboveboard." People began to arrive at the station, amongst them the debtor and his lady; a servant bought tickets for them and he sat there with the lady, drinking tea and glancing round the station with a worried look in his face. The old lady hid behind Ivan Ivanich, pointed to the debtor and said, "That's him."

The Serbian Fighter saw him, said, "Good," immediately got up and walked past the young dandy, then passed him a second time and on the third occasion stopped right in front of him and said:

"What are you staring at me for?"

The other answered:

"I'm not looking at you at all, I'm drinking tea."

"Aha!" said the Fighter. "You're not looking at me, you're drinking tea? Then I'll make you look, and here's lemon for your tea, and sugar, and a piece of chocolate!...." And with that he struck him three times across the face—slap—slap—slap!

The lady ran off and the gentleman wanted to run after her, and said he would not lodge a complaint, but the police came up and stopped him. "You can't let it go, it was in a public place," said the policeman and thereupon arrested the Serbian Fighter and the man he had struck. The latter was in a terrible dilemma, he did not know whether to run after his lady or answer the police summons. In the meantime the policeman had made out a report and the train was leaving.... The lady had gone and he was left ... and no sooner did he give his name and rank than the policeman said, "And, by the way, I have a writ in my bag to serve on you." There was nothing the debtor could do, he accepted the writ in the presence of witnesses and, in order to avoid giving an undertaking not to leave the city, immediately gave the old lady a bank draft for the full amount of the debt with interest.

In this way insurmountable difficulties were overcome, justice triumphed, peace was restored to a poor but honest home, and Christmas became a bright and merry feast.

The man who found a way to arrange such a difficult matter had every right to consider himself a genius.

1884

THE SENTRY

CHAPTER THE FIRST

THE EVENTS related in the following story are so touching, so horrible insofar as they affect the hero of the drama and with a denouement so unusual that it could only have happened in Russia.

It is a brief story belonging partly to the Imperial Court and in part finding its place in history; it very aptly typifies the manners and morals of a little-known but highly interesting period—the thirties of this present nineteenth century.

There is not one iota of invention in this story.

CHAPTER THE SECOND

Round about Epiphany, 1839, there was a great thaw in St. Petersburg. The weather was so warm that it seemed that spring was coming: the snow melted, water dripped from the eaves during the day, the ice on the river turned blue and was covered with a layer of water. The ice on the Neva was at its thinnest directly opposite the Winter Palace. The westerly wind was warm but very strong, driving water upstream from the sea, so that warning guns had to be fired.

The palace guard was provided by a company of the Izmailov Regiment commanded by Nikolai Ivanovich Miller, a young officer of high educational attainments and well placed in society (he later became a full general and director of the Lycée). He was a man of the so-called "humane" school, as the higher authorities had long since remarked, which, of course, was somewhat damaging to his career in the service.

Actually Miller was a competent and reliable officer and in those days the palace guard was not fraught with any particular danger. It was the calmest and most peaceful of times. Nothing was required of the palace guard but the accurate maintenance of the sentry posts, but it just happened that during Captain Miller's tour of guard duty there was a most unusual and alarming occurrence which is now just barely remembered by those contemporaries of the incident whose days are drawing to a close.

CHAPTER THE THIRD

At first all went well with the guard: the posts were allotted, the sentries posted and everything was just as it should be. Tsar Nikolai Pavlovich was in good health, had been for a drive in the evening, returned home and gone to bed. The palace had gone to sleep. The calmest of nights set in. There was silence in the guard-room. Captain Miller pinned his white handkerchief to the traditionally greasy high back of the officer's leather-covered armchair and settled down to pass the time with a book.

Captain Miller was a voracious reader and was, therefore, not bored, he kept on steadily reading and did not notice the time pass until suddenly, just before 2 o'clock, he was alarmed by a terrible disturbance; the sergeant of the guard, pale as a ghost and showing great fear, appeared before him and babbled in rapid tones:

"Trouble, sir, trouble...."

"What's the matter?"

"A terrible misfortune, sir."

Miller jumped up from his seat in alarm and with the greatest difficulty managed to discover what the "trouble" and "misfortune" was.

CHAPTER THE FOURTH

The facts were as follows: a sentry, Private Postnikov of the Izmailov Regiment, on duty outside what is now the Jordan Gate, heard a man fall through the thin ice that covered the Neva at that point and heard his desperate cries for help.

Private Postnikov, a serf and household servant of some nobleman, was a nervous and highly sensitive man. For a long time he listened to the distant cries and groans of the drowning man, which made him freeze with horror. He looked in dismay right and left but there was not a living being to be seen on the part of the embankment within view or on the river itself.

There was nobody to help the man in the water and he would most certainly drown....

In the meantime the man in the water was engaged in a terribly long and stubborn struggle.

It seemed that it would have been better for him to sink to the bottom without wasting his strength, but nothing of the sort! His groans and shouts for help became more feeble and died away only to begin again anew and each time they came nearer and nearer to the palace embankment. The man had obviously not lost his presence of mind and was struggling in the right direction, straight for the street-lamps although he would not, of course, get there because the Jordan Ice-Hole* was directly in his way. There he would be drawn under the ice and that would be the end of him.... Again silence but a minute later he started splashing and shouting, "Help, help...." The sounds were so near now that Postnikov could hear the splashing of the water as he struggled.

It crossed Postnikov's mind that it would be the easiest thing in the world to save the man at that moment. If he were to run out on to the ice the man would be

---

* In St. Petersburg, during the Festival of Epiphany a big hole was cut in the ice at which solemn mass was said and the water consecrated.

right there. He had only to throw him a rope or hold out a pole or his rifle and the man would be saved. He was so close that he could seize it and would be able to jump out. But Private Postnikov remembered his duty and his oath of allegiance: he knew that he was on sentry-go and a sentry dare not leave his box under any excuse whatsoever.

On the other hand Postnikov's heart was sorely troubled; it ached so, and would hammer so, and then stand still.... He could have torn his heart out of his body and thrown it under his feet, so troubled was he by those groans and calls. It is terrible to listen to a man perishing and not to offer help when it would, as a matter of course, be quite possible, because the sentry box could not budge from its place nor could anything else harmful happen. "Should I run there, eh? I won't be seen.... Oh, Lord, if it would only end! He's groaning again!"

For half an hour, while the noises continued, Private Postnikov's heart was torn to shreds and he began to feel that he "doubted his reason." But he was a smart and clever soldier, with a clear mind, who realized that for a sentry to leave his post was a crime that led to a court-martial and then to running the gauntlet through two lines of soldiers armed with withies and after that hard labour or, perhaps, "death by shooting"; but from the direction of the swollen river the shouts came again and again, nearer and nearer, until he could hear the gurgling of the water and the man's despairing struggles.

"Help, help, I'm drowning!"

It came from the direction of the Jordan Ice-Hole.... It was all over....

Postnikov looked up and down a couple of times. Not a soul in sight, nothing but the street-lamps swaying and flickering in the wind and the cries that came with each gust of wind and then broke off... perhaps that was the last cry?

Then another splash, a monosyllabic howl and the sounds of someone struggling in the water.

The sentry could stand it no longer—he left his post.

CHAPTER THE FIFTH

Postnikov rushed to the slipway and with furiously beating heart ran out on to the ice and into the water that flowed over the ice; looking for the drowning man he stretched out the butt of his musket to him.

The man grasped the butt and Postnikov pulled on the bayonet and dragged him to the bank.

Rescuer and rescued were both wet through and as the rescued man was dead tired and shivering and had collapsed on the ice, Private Postnikov could not make up his mind to leave him there but dragged him on to the quay and began looking round for somebody to hand the man over to. While all this was going on a sleigh appeared on the embankment and in it an officer of the Palace Invalid Company that in those days still existed (it was later abolished).

It seems that this gentleman, whose hurried approach was very untimely as far as Postnikov was concerned, was a man thoughtless by nature, not very intelligent and a regular scoundrel. He jumped out of the sleigh and began asking questions.

"Who's that man? Who are you?"

"Drowning, in the water...." Postnikov began.

"What? Drowning? Who's drowning? You? And why in this place?"

While the man was still gasping for breath Postnikov slipped away: with his musket on his shoulder he was back in the sentry box.

We don't know whether the officer realized what had

happened or not, but he did not waste time trying to find out; he immediately pulled the rescued man into his sleigh and drove him to the police station at the Admiralty on Morskaya Street.

Here the officer made a report to the police that the man in wet clothes whom he had brought with him was drowning in the ice-hole opposite the palace and had been saved by him, the officer, at the risk of his life.

The rescued man was still soaking wet, shivering and thoroughly exhausted. The shock and the tremendous effort he had made left him in a fainting fit and he was quite indifferent as to who had rescued him.

A sleepy doctor's assistant took him in hand while in the office a report was drawn up from the verbal statement of the Invalid officer, but with that suspiciousness that is typical of the police they could not understand how he had been in the water and had come out again without wetting his clothes. The officer, who was anxious to acquire the Life-Saving Medal, explained it by a fortunate coincidence, but he explained it clumsily and improbably. The policeman went to wake the captain and people were sent to make inquiries.

In the meantime things were taking a different and more rapid course at the palace.

CHAPTER THE SIXTH

The change in the situation that occurred after the officer had taken the drowning man into his sleigh was not known in the palace guard-room. The Izmailov soldiers and their officer knew only one thing—one of their privates, Postnikov, had left the sentry box and gone to rescue a man and as this was a terrible breach of army regulations Private Postnikov would certainly be court-martialled, would be made to run the gauntlet

328

and all the officers, from the company commander to the regimental commander, would suffer the greatest unpleasantness and would not be able to raise any objection since the afore-said action could not be justified.

Private Postnikov, wet and shivering, was, needless to say, immediately relieved of his post and when he was brought into the guard-room honestly related to Captain Miller all that he knew, giving all the details, right up to the point when the Invalid officer sat the rescued man in his sleigh and ordered his coachman to drive to the Admiralty police station.

The danger was ever greater and more certain. It went without saying that the Invalid officer would tell the police captain everything, the latter would immediately report it to Chief of Police Kokoshkin who in turn would report it to the tsar next morning and then the fun would begin.

There was no time to think things over; the senior officers had to be warned at once.

Nikolai Ivanovich Miller immediately sent an alarming note to his battalion commander, Lieutenant Colonel Svinyin, in which he asked him to come to the palace guard-room as quickly as possible and do everything in his power to help them out of their terrible predicament.

That was at about 3 a.m., and Kokoshkin would make his report to the tsar very early in the morning so that very little time was left to devise a plan and act on it.

CHAPTER THE SEVENTH

Lieutenant Colonel Svinyin was not possessed of that kind-heartedness and humanity that had always distinguished Nikolai Ivanovich Miller: not that Svinyin was heartless; he was firstly and mostly a "service man" (a type that has now disappeared but is regretted by some). Svinyin was known as a martinet and even loved to make a show of exacting discipline. He had no inclination to malice and never sought to cause anybody unnecessary suffering but if a man had failed to do the duties required by the service, Svinyin was implacable. He considered it out of place to enter into a discussion on the motives that had led the guilty one to commit his fault, and maintained the principle that where service is concerned every fault is a fault. The company on guard duty all knew, therefore, that Private Postnikov would suffer what was coming to him for having left his post and Svinyin would not be a bit sorry for him.

Such was the reputation this field officer had earned amongst his superiors and his fellow-officers, and amongst the latter there were those who were not in sympathy with Svinyin for at that time "humanism" and similar heresies had not yet been eradicated. It was a matter of complete indifference to Svinyin whether the "humanists" approved or disapproved his actions. It was quite useless to beg or pray Svinyin or even attempt to arouse his pity. He was inured to all this with the heavy armour of the careerists of those times but, like Achilles, he had a weak point.

Svinyin had also begun his military career well, and he cherished and nurtured it to keep it like a fulldress uniform, without the slightest blemish on it; nevertheless the unfortunate action of a man from the battalion under his command must undoubtedly throw an evil shadow on the discipline of the whole unit. Whether the battalion commander was guilty of what one of his soldiers had done when carried away by feelings of the most noble pity was something that would not be inquired into by those on whom Svinyin's well-commenced and carefully maintained career. depended; there were, indeed, many who would be glad to put a spoke in his wheel in order to make way for somebody of their own or for a young man with strong patronage, in the case, that is, if the tsar should say to the regimental commander that he had "weak officers" and that his "men were slovenly." And who had allowed such things?... Svinyin, of course. And so the word would be repeated, "Svinyin's weak" and, perhaps, the reproach of weakness would remain an indelible blemish on his, Svinyin's, reputation. Under those circumstances there would be nothing to make him outstanding amongst his contemporaries nor would he leave his portrait in the gallery of historical persons of the Russian state.

There were few who studied history in those days but they believed in it and were always very willing to take part in making it.

CHAPTER THE EIGHTH

Immediately Svinyin received the alarming note from Captain Miller at three o'clock in the morning, he jumped out of bed, donned his uniform and arrived at the Winter Palace guard-room still under the impression of fear and wrath. He immediately interrogated Private Postnikov and was convinced that the unlikely event had really taken place. Private Postnikov once more honestly related to his battalion commander everything that had happened when he had been on sentry-go and which he had previously told his company commander, Captain Miller. The soldier said that he "was guilty before God and his duty without hope of mercy," that he had stood at his post and had suffered for a long time, hearing the groans of a drowning man, that there had been a long struggle between duty and pity until at last he had been tempted, he could not hold out in the struggle, had abandoned his post, jumped down on to the ice, and brought the drowning man ashore and there by mischance he had run into an officer of the Palace Invalid Company who was passing by.

Lieutenant Colonel Svinyin was in despair: he gave himself the only satisfaction he could—he let loose his wrath on Postnikov who was immediately sent to the cells under arrest; he then said a few biting things to Miller, accusing him of "mildness" such as was not fitting in the service; all this, however, was not enough to set matters right. It was impossible to find any excuse, let alone justification, for a sentry leaving his post and there was only one way out left to him—to keep the occurrence hidden from the tsar.

Could, however, such an occurrence be hidden?

Apparently there was no possibility of any such thing, for not only did the entire guard know of the rescue of the drowning man, but that hateful Invalid officer also knew and had by then, no doubt, already reported the whole affair to General Kokoshkin.

Where could he rush off to? To whom should he apply? From whom should he seek help and protection?

Svinyin thought of hurrying to the Grand Duke Mikhail Pavlovich* and telling him the whole story forthright. Such manoeuvres were in vogue at the time. The Grand Duke was of a fiery nature and would grow angry and scream at him, but his manner and habit were such that the more severe he was in the beginning—and he could even be insulting—the quicker he cooled off and would then take the officer's part. There had been many such cases and sometimes they were even sought. "Hard names don't hurt" and Svinyin would very much have liked to take advantage of this favourable situation but

* A younger brother of Tsar Nikolai I.

how could he enter the palace in the middle of the night and disturb the Grand Duke? To wait for morning and visit the Grand Duke after Kokoshkin had already made his report to the tsar would be too late. While Svinyin's head was in a whirl from all these difficulties he suddenly saw light and became aware of another way out that had hitherto been hidden in a mist.

CHAPTER THE NINTH

Amongst other well-known military artifices there is one that is employed when danger threatens from the walls of a besieged fortress—don't withdraw from the walls but get right up under them. Svinyin decided that he would not do any of the things that had occurred to him at first but instead would go immediately to Kokoshkin.

Many horrifying and foolish things were related in St. Petersburg about Chief of Police Kokoshkin but it was also said that he was a man of very great tact and that in the employment of that tact he "was not only able to make a mountain out of a molehill but could equally well make a molehill out of a mountain."

Kokoshkin really was a very severe and dreaded general who inspired fear in others although at times he was very kind to officers who got up to mischief and were cheerful merry-makers; indeed, there were many of them and quite a number found in him a powerful and energetic protector. In general he could and was able to do a lot when he wanted to. He was known as such by Svinyin and by Captain Miller. Miller also persuaded his battalion commander to take the risk of going immediately to Kokoshkin and trust in the kindness of his heart and his "all-round tact" which would, no doubt, tell the general how to twist this unfortunate occurrence in such a way that it would not arouse the wrath of the tsar, something that Kokoshkin, be it said to his credit, always did his best to avoid.

Svinyin put on his greatcoat, turned his eyes to the heavens, exclaimed, "O Lord, O Lord," several times and went to Kokoshkin.

It was then just after four in the morning.

CHAPTER THE TENTH

Chief of Police Kokoshkin was awakened and informed that Svinyin was awaiting him on a matter of such importance that it would brook no delay.

The general immediately got up and went out to Svinyin in a dressing jacket, yawning, rubbing his temples and flinching from the cold. Kokoshkin listened with great attention to everything Svinyin had to say and kept quite calm. During the whole of this explanation and request for clemency he had only one thing to say:

"The soldier left the sentry box and rescued a man?"

"Yes, sir," answered Svinyin.

"And the box?"

"Remained empty at that time."

"Yes, I suppose it would be empty. I'm glad it wasn't stolen."

From this Svinyin became even more convinced that Kokoshkin already knew all about it and had already decided how he would deal with the matter when he made his report to the tsar next morning and would not now make any changes in his decision. If such were not the case such an occurrence as a sentry leaving his post in the palace guard would undoubtedly have disturbed the energetic Chief of Police much more than it had done.

Kokoshkin, however, knew nothing at all. The police captain to whom the Invalid officer had brought the rescued man did not regard it as an event of any great importance. It was not, in his eyes, an occurrence that made it necessary to disturb the tired-out Chief of Police in the middle of the night and, moreover, the police captain regarded the whole business with suspicion for the Invalid officer was quite dry which obviously could not be the case if he had really rescued the man at the risk of his own life. The police captain merely regarded the Invalid officer as an ambitious liar who wanted another medal on his breast and while the police sergeant was making out the report the captain kept the officer in his room and tried to get at the truth by asking him for the minutest details.

The police captain was not pleased at having such a thing happen in his district and at having the drowning man rescued by a palace officer and not by a policeman.

Kokoshkin's calmness was to be explained, firstly, by the fatigue he was feeling at the time due to a very hard day and then participation in the extinguishing of two fires that had occurred that night and, secondly, by the fact that the action of the sentry Postnikov had nothing whatever to do with the Chief of Police.

Nevertheless Kokoshkin immediately gave the necessary instructions.

He sent for the police captain in charge of the Admiralty police station and ordered him to bring with him the Invalid officer and the rescued man; Svinyin he told to wait in the smaller anteroom to his office. Kokoshkin then went into his office, leaving the door open behind him, sat down at his desk and would have begun signing papers but for the fact that his head dropped on to his arms and he fell fast asleep at the desk.

CHAPTER THE ELEVENTH

At that time there were neither city telegraphs nor telephones and urgent instructions from the authorities were transmitted by the "forty thousand messengers" who galloped in all directions and who have been perpetuated in Gogol's comedy.

It goes without saying that this was not as quick as the telegraph or telephone but it lent the city a great liveliness and was evidence of the sleepless vigilance of the authorities.

By the time the police captain from the Admiralty station had arrived, panting, together with the rescuing officer and the rescued man, the nervous and energetic General Kokoshkin had finished his nap and felt refreshed. This was noticeable in the expression on his face and in his mental abilities.

Kokoshkin invited all of them into his study, Svinyin together with the others.

"Report?" Kokoshkin demanded of the police captain in sprightly tones.

The captain handed him a folded sheet of paper in silence and then whispered:

"I must ask Your Excellency to permit me a few words in private...."

"Very well."

Kokoshkin went to a window alcove, the captain following him.

"What is it?"

The indistinct whispering of the captain could be heard, followed by the distinct grunting of the general.

"Hm ... yes.... So what about it? He's the sort that would fall into the water and not get wet.... Nothing else?"

"That's all."

The general left the alcove, sat down at the desk and began to read. He read the report without displaying either dismay or doubt and then turned directly to the rescued man with a loud and firm question.

"How did you get into the ice-hole opposite the palace, my man?"

"I'm sorry," answered the man.

"So, you were drunk, I suppose."

"Not drunk, but I'd had a drink."

"Why did you go into the water?

"I wanted to go the shortest way across, on the ice, lost my way and fell into the water."

"Everything went dark before your eyes?"

"It was dark, it was dark all round, Your Excellency!"

"And you couldn't see who it was pulled you out?"

"Excuse me, but I didn't see anything. I think it was that gentleman." He pointed to the officer and added, "I couldn't see anything, I was so scared."

"That's how you go on, you hang around the streets when you ought to be asleep! Take a good look now and remember for ever who your rescuer is. A noble gentleman risked his life for you!"

"I'll remember him all my life."

"What is your name, sir?"

The officer named himself.

"Do you hear?"

"Yes, Your Excellency."

"Are you a Christian?"

"Yes, Your Excellency."

"Remember that name so that you may have masses said for him."

"I will, Your Excellency."

"Pray for him and get out of here: I don't need you any more."

The man doubled up in a bow and rushed away only too glad that they had let him go.

Svinyin stood there in great perplexity: what a turn things had taken, by the grace of God!

Kokoshkin turned to the Invalid officer.

"You saved that man at the risk of your own life?"

"Yes, Your Excellency."

"And there were no witnesses, there could not be any witnesses on account of the late hour, is that it?"

"Yes, Your Excellency, it was dark and there was nobody on the embankment except the sentries."

"You needn't mention the sentries: a sentry remains at his post and must not have his attention diverted by anything extraneous. I believe what is written in the report. It was written down from your words, wasn't it?"

Kokoshkin pronounced those words with special stress as though he were either making an accusation or threatening.

The officer was not abashed, his eyes bulged and he stuck out his chest.

"My own words and perfectly true, Your Excellency."

"Your deed is worthy of an award."

The officer immediately bowed in gratitude.

"There is nothing to thank me for," continued Kokoshkin. "I will report your selfless deed to His Majesty the Emperor, and, perhaps even today your breast will be adorned with a medal; you may now go home, take a warm drink but don't go out; you may be needed."

The Invalid officer beamed, bowed his farewell and left.

Kokoshkin followed him with his eyes and said:

"It is quite possible that His Majesty will want to see him himself."

"Very well," said the police captain, understandingly. "I don't need you any more."

The police captain left, closed the door behind him and, as was his pious habit, there and then crossed himself.

The Invalid officer was waiting for the captain at the bottom of the stairs and they left together much more friendly than they had been when they arrived.

Svinyin remained alone in the office of the Chief of Police: Kokoshkin first looked at him with a long, searching glance, and then asked:

"You haven't been to the Grand Duke, have you?"

At that time, whenever anybody spoke of the Grand Duke, it was understood to refer to Grand Duke Mikhail Pavlovich.

"I came straight to you," answered Svinyin.

"Who is the officer of the guard?"

"Captain Miller."

Kokoshkin again glanced at Svinyin and said:

"It seems you were saying something quite different before this."

Svinyin didn't understand what he was referring to so he did not answer and Kokoshkin added:

"Well, it doesn't matter. Good night."

The audience was over.

CHAPTER THE THIRTEENTH

At one o'clock in the afternoon Kokoshkin really did send for the Invalid officer and told him in gentle tones that His Majesty was very pleased that there were such vigilant and selfless people in the Invalid Company of his palace and had awarded him the Life-Saving Medal. Kokoshkin thereupon himself presented him with the medal and the hero went forth to show it off. It seemed that the affair could be considered closed but Lieutenant Colonel Svinyin thought that there was something unfinished about it and felt it incumbent upon him to put the *points sur les i.*

He was so greatly troubled that he was ill for three days but on the fourth he got up from his bed, journeyed to the House of Peter, offered prayers of gratitude before the Icon of the Redeemer, and, returning home with his soul at peace, sent for Captain Miller.

"Thank God, Nikolai Ivanovich," he said to Miller, "the cloud that hung over our heads has passed. That unfortunate affair with the sentry has been set right. I believe that we can now breathe freely. For this we are indebted, firstly to God's mercy and secondly to General Kokoshkin. Let them say that he is harsh and heartless but I am filled with gratitude for his kindness and respect for his resourcefulness and tact. He was surprisingly clever in the way he made use of that Invalid officer's boasting, a man who, if the truth be told, should not have got a medal for his insolence but should have had a good horse-whipping in the stables. There was nothing else to be done about it: he had to be used to save many people and Kokoshkin fixed things so cleverly that nobody had to suffer the slightest inconvenience, on the contrary, everybody is pleased and satisfied. Between you and me, I have been informed by a trustworthy person that Kokoshkin is *very pleased* with me. He was flattered that I didn't go anywhere else but went straight to him and did not argue with that scoundrel that got the medal. In a word, nobody had to suffer and everything was done with such great tact that there is nothing to be afraid of in the future, but we have been lax in one respect. We must also follow Kokoshkin's example tactfully and finish off the business at our end in order to make sure there will be no consequences for us. There remains one person whose position is still undefined. I have in mind Private Postnikov. He is still in the cells under arrest and is no doubt in great trepidation wondering what is going to happen to him. We must put an end to that tormenting uncertainty."

"Yes, it's time we did," added Miller in pleased tones.

"And, of course, nobody could do it better than you; please go at once to the barracks, muster your company, bring Postnikov out of the cells and punish him with two hundred strokes of the birch before the assembled company."

Miller was astounded and made an attempt to persuade Svinyin, in view of the general gratification, to show mercy towards Postnikov and forgive him as he had already undergone great suffering in the cells, wondering what was going to happen to him; Svinyin, however, flashed up in a rage and did not even let Miller finish what he was saying.

"No," he interrupted him, "drop that: I have only just been speaking to you about tact and you immediately show your tactlessness. Drop it!"

Svinyin changed his tone to one that was dry and official and added with great firmness:

"And since you, yourself, are not without blame, and are, in fact, even guilty because you display a mildness that does not become an army man and that trait is reflected in the behaviour of your subordinates, I order you to attend the punishment in person and to insist that it be carried out properly, as strictly as possible. And please be good enough to order the flogging to be administered by young soldiers recently sent to us from the army as the old hands are all infected by the liberalism of the guards: they do not flog their comrades but only flick the fleas off their backs. I will ride over myself and see how the guilty man is handled."

There could not be, of course, any evasion of direct orders issued by a superior officer, and kind-hearted

Miller had to carry out with precision the order given him by his battalion commander.

The company was assembled on the square at the Izmailovo barracks and issued with birch rods. Postnikov was brought out of his cell and "handled" with the willing assistance of younger soldiers recently transferred from the army. These men, unspoiled by guards' liberalism, put all the *points sur les i* with the absolute perfection laid down by the battalion commander. Postnikov was immediately carried from the execution ground to the hospital on the greatcoat on which they had flogged him.

CHAPTER THE FIFTEENTH

Battalion Commander Svinyin, on receipt of the report that the punishment had been administered, himself paid a paternal visit to Postnikov in hospital and to his great satisfaction had ample evidence that his orders had been scrupulously fulfilled. The compassionate and nervous Postnikov had been "handled" thoroughly. Svinyin was pleased and ordered the punished man to be given a pound of sugar and a quarter of pound of tea at his expense to help towards his recovery. Postnikov, lying on his cot, heard the order about the tea and answered:

"I'm very pleased, sir, and thank you for your fatherly kindness."

And he really was "very pleased" for during the three days he had spent in the cells he had been expecting something much worse. Two hundred strokes in those brutal times was nothing compared with the punishments inflicted on men by order of the courts-martial; some such punishment would also have been the fate of Postnikov if the above-mentioned bold and tactful evolutions had not been performed.

This, however, is still not the last of those pleased with the outcome of the event we have related.

CHAPTER THE SIXTEENTH

The story of Postnikov's brave deed made the rounds of Petersburg circles by all sorts of underground channels, for in those days when news was scarce the capital lived in an atmosphere of constant gossip. Transmitted by word of mouth the name of the real hero, Private Postnikov, was lost, but the episode itself grew in size and acquired a most romantic character.

It was said that some very unusual swimmer had come swimming across the river towards the palace from the direction of the Peter and Paul Fortress and that one of the palace sentries had fired and wounded the swimmer and that a passing Invalid officer had jumped into the water and rescued the wounded man for which one of them received the reward and the other the punishment he merited. This silly rumour even reached the episcopal palace where at that time there lived a Metropolitan of the Church, a cautious man not absolutely indifferent to "worldly events," and who showed Christian good will towards the pious Moscow family of the Svinyins.

The story of the shooting did not seem plausible to the perspicacious priest. And who was the swimmer of the night? If he was an escaped convict then why was the sentry punished for shooting him as he swam across the Neva from the fortress? If it was not a convict but some other mysterious man who had to be rescued from the Neva, then how did the sentry know about him? It was impossible for things to have occurred in the way the idle talk of the town depicted them. Worldly people have a very thoughtless attitude to many things and are fond of "idle chatter," but those who inhabit the cloisters and the episcopal palace have a much more serious attitude and know the real truth concerning all affairs of the world.

On one occasion when Svinyin visited the Metropolitan to receive his blessing, his right reverend host spoke "incidentally, about the shooting." Svinyin told him the whole truth which, as we know, bore no relation to that which was said elsewhere "incidentally, about the shooting."

The Metropolitan listened to the real story in silence, counting over his white beads and never once taking his eyes off Svinyin. When the latter had finished the Metropolitan asked in his softly murmuring tones:

"It is to be assumed from what you have said that this story has not been told everywhere in conformity with the whole truth?"

Svinyin hesitated and then evaded the question by saying that General Kokoshkin and not he had made the report.

The Metropolitan ran the beads through his waxlike fingers several times and then murmured:

"A distinction must be made between a lie and an incomplete truth."

Again the beads moved, again there was silence and at last came the softly murmuring speech:

"An incomplete truth is not a lie. But least of all does that matter."

"That is so," said Svinyin, encouraged. "I, of course, am most of all worried at having had to punish that soldier who, although he neglected his duty...."

The beads and again the murmuring speech by way of interruption:

"Duty must never be neglected."

"True, but it was done out of the goodness of his heart, out of pity, and also in a magnificent struggle against danger: he realized that in saving the life of another man he was ruining himself.... This was a lofty and sacred feeling!"

"That which is sacred is known to the Lord. Corporal punishment inflicted on the common folk is not fatal and does not stand in contradiction either to the customs of the nations or to the spirit of Holy Scripture. It is easier to bear the blows of a stick on a rude body than refined suffering of the spirit. In this respect justice did not suffer at your hands."

"But he has been deprived of his reward for saving life."

"Saving life is not a merit but rather a duty. He who could save somebody and did not is punished by the law; he who has saved has done his duty."

A pause, the beads and then the murmuring speech again.

"It may be better for a soldier to suffer indignity and hurt for his brave deeds than to be rewarded with a medal. That, however, which is of the greatest importance in this matter, is to preserve the necessary caution and never again to mention what has been said to anybody concerning this matter."

Apparently the Metropolitan was also pleased.

CHAPTER THE EIGHTEENTH

If I were possessed of the audacity of Heaven's chosen few, who, because of their great faith, have been granted the power to penetrate into the mysteries of God's will, I should probably dare to permit myself the assumption that most likely the Lord himself was pleased with the behaviour of the humble spirit of his creature Postnikov. My faith, however, is insufficient; it does not permit my mind to penetrate such lofty spheres: I confine myself to things of this earth. I have in mind those mortals who love goodness for its own sake and do not expect any reward now or hereafter for their goodness. These straightforward and honest people should, I believe, find pleasure in the sacred outburst of love and the no less sacred patience of the humble hero of my truthful and artless story.

1887

To the Reader

The Foreign Languages Publishing House would be glad to have your opinion of the translation and the design of this book.

Please send all suggestions to 21, Zubovsky Boulevard, Moscow, U.S.S.R.

517

Printed in the Union of Soviet Socialist Republics